A Fate Worse than Death

HETTIE ASHWIN

Published by Slipperygrip

A Fate Worse than Death 2022
Copyright
© Hettie Ashwin

Paperback
ISBN: 9782491490256
Pocket Edition
ISBN: 9782491490218

Books by Hettie Ashwin

<u>Humour</u>
<u>(10 terrific laugh-out-loud series)</u>
Literary Licence
The Reluctant Messiah
Mr Tripp Buys a Lifestyle
Barney's Test
The Truffle War
Fat Bits
Murder! Mayhem! and Lesser Cuts of Meat.
I'd Rather Glue me Nut Sack to a Bullet Train
Nowhere Near Anywhere

<u>Humorous Memoir</u>
Boat to Baguette
Living it up in France

<u>Thriller</u>
The Crowing of the Beast

<u>Speculative fiction</u>
The Mask of Deceit
Pi - Trilogy

<u>Short Stories</u>
After the Rains & Other Stories
A Shilling on the Bar

<u>Novella series.</u>
A Strange Kind of Paradise. 1-5

<u>Non fiction</u>
Productive Procrastination

Fame is a fickle food
upon a shifting plate.

Emily Dickinson

One

'I'm sorry, Mr. Stitt, Miss Avella is in a meeting. Would you…'

'Blast and double damn.' Crispin threw his phone into the rubbish bin at the side of his writing desk, sulked his way to the two-seater settee and plomped into the cushions with as much plomp as he could muster,

He lay in this abject state for some time, almost as if waiting for a second curtain call, or applause. When none was forthcoming he rolled over and looked at his desk.

The desk fitted the bill of a writer's desk. Typewriter, papers, pens, pencils and a pile of books that one might assume the owner well read. Yet it lacked a certain something. It lacked a writer.

The last line of Crispin Stitt's novel, *Il Est Mort* (*He Is Dead*) stared from the paper at the empty chair. After a prolonged dry spell and a hideous bout of writer's block that had lasted from 1948 (*A new voice in literature)* to 1950 (*Stitt? Stitt who?)* which had the effect of making Crispin's arse gain weight and spread itself copiously on his chair while his face grew a scrappy beard, Crispin felt a bit mort himself. He dragged his sorry carcass over to his chair and once more plomped.

Il Est Mort stared at him.

He liked to use French in his novels. Not that he was French, or spoke it for that matter, but he just thought it showed a level of intelligence, and Crispin needed all the help he could get in that department. He roused himself from his torpor and looked at the paper threading its way around the typewriter roller. He added an exclamation mark after mort. There was a temptation to add 'fin' justified in the middle of the manuscript, but he resisted the urge. In his experience, his agent, his editor, his proof reader and his wife would all have something to say about his latest manuscript—and it would be foolhardy to say it was finished. All the women who held the above positions were only there, it seemed to Crispin, to make Crispin Stitt's life one of misery, servitude and anguish.

'They'll love it,' he said to the manuscript piled neatly on the side of his desk. He patted the paper tower in reassurance. That his agent wasn't answering his calls, his editor was always in a meeting, his beta reader conveniently contracted conjunctivitis and his wife wasn't speaking to him at the moment didn't help. He thought on Amanda's last word. *'Narcissist' was such an ugly word.* As a wife, she should be the staff his creativity could lean upon. She didn't understand his artistic torment, his particular needs.

They had to love it, or he was a dead man. He should have been happy. He had beaten his writers block. Amanda had scoffed at his inability to write another best seller. She had actually said it was just like constipation. All he needed was some fibre. Whether she was speaking metaphorically or literally, he didn't know, but the jibe wounded just the same. Although if one were to analyse his angst, it might be brought down to the fact that he hadn't thought of that quite smart, yet cutting remark himself. He was the famous writer, after all, with a stunning vocabulary, or so the *Evening Chronicle* said in their shining review.

The 90,000ish words in front of him meant he had finally fulfilled his contractual obligation to his publisher and could finally sit back and relax.

But he couldn't relax. He hated the manuscript from the first line to the last. It was rotten. It could never live up to his meteoric rise to fame from his first novel *He Lives*. It would never pay the mortgage. It would never clear the overdraft his wife thought was unlimited. It was absolutely, excruciatingly dreadful. And to top it off he had spent the advance. On what he couldn't remember. It was so long ago, or felt like it anyway.

'I might as well kill myself now.' Crispin's head thumped down on the desk and he closed his eyes. For a man who talked to himself constantly, he didn't have much to say.

A lawn mower kerruppfft into life and broke into Crispin's contemplation at burning the one and only copy. *Now there is a happy man*, he thought.

The happy man in question was Crispin's next-door neighbour Jim Broker, who was at that moment swearing blue murder at his lawn mower which had decided today was not the day for getting to work and spluttered once then threw in the towel.

Crispin sighed—one of those depths of despair type of sighs—and ripped the last sheet from his typewriter and placed it on the pile.

Crispin Stitt's light once shone brightly.
He was,

Fresh.
Capricornian bestseller list

New and exciting. One to watch.
The Sydney Oracle

A marvel
The Equatorial Post

And his all-time favourite,

The most exciting voice from a writer we have
seen in a long time.
The Melba Review.

He knew all the accolades by heart, never mind
he had them framed on his study wall.

Now, just two short years later he was off the
radar. He was never invited to anything and if you
asked the man in the street had they heard of Crispin
Stitt, the answer might be,

'Didn't he invent that kitchen gadget thingy?'

In fact, Mr Stitt might as well be dead for all the
once adoring public knew.

Two

There was a well-worn track from Crispin's desk to the refrigerator. He slopped his way to the kitchen and opened the top-of-the-line Kelvinator to look for comfort and solace. It didn't immediately jump out and hit him in the face, so he let the door shut and sat down at the new green Formica table with matching chairs. Amanda had insisted they get the matching chairs. The vinyl stuck to his back and gave a squeak of agony as Crispin shoe- horned his overweight arse into the bucket seat. The house was spotless, but lifeless. Everything was in its place, and there was a place for everything. He ran his accusing eye over the things he had provided to make a house a home. New mix-master, new coffee percolator, stove, fridge and the green kitchen table. It was all paid for from his writings. His artistic genius had provided his wife with all that she desired. Crispin wished she would desire him as much. He picked up the *The Mercury Daily* and scanned the headlines. A politician kissing a baby. A train late. A bumper crop of tomatoes and those hideous advertisements extolling the hoi polloi to buy household items by the bucket load.

Recliners, straight from America...
LAZY BOYS
TIME PAYMENT PLANS AVAILABLE!

It was all too hideously mundane, he thought. How could his life have come to this? How?

'You're living in a backwater Crispin, that's why. The back of beyond.' He looked for the arts section of the paper and found a knitting pattern.

'Grrrh. Philistines.' He threw the paper down in disgust, retraced his steps to his desk, and looked at his manuscript. Crispin closed his eyes and wished it would just disappear. Opening them again, it was still there. What he needed was a stiff drink.

'Things always look better with something under your belt,' he said. Not that he was wearing a belt, more like under a pyjama cord.

'What the heck, who cares if it's only 10am on a Sunday.' Six half empty bottles stared back at him without a murmur of disapproval. He made a whisky soda and consoled himself that all good authors drank. It was de rigueur to have something that could be considered socially antisocial. All he had ever done was belch in public and then only the once. He wasn't even a decent alcoholic. In America, they had decent alcoholics. Hemingway, apparently, was in a league of his own.

'In America you can really get stuck into being antisocial. They loved the artistic temperament,' he mused. Crispin just about loved everything American. He wondered if he only married Amanda because she was American. 'Selfish, I know, but sometimes one wonders just the same,' he said to the now empty glass. She was exotic, intelligent and she could give him access to the American market, if only they were living there. It was an irresistible lure. Over there they appreciated talent and he wouldn't be competing with Mr Shute and his prolific 19 novels. All the papers could ever talk about was Mr Neville Shute and his 'wonderfully prolific' 19 novels.

Amanda Stitt was the love of Crispin's life, and yet he didn't like her. If he tried to think clearly he'd say she loved him. Well, he thought, she loved his bank balance and that was a start. She was, in Crispin's estimation, a stunner. Other men thought the same, and the way she collected them at functions it was as if she was coated in honey. It was a pity she wasn't talking to him at the moment, but the minute she started to talk to him again he'd tell her how much he loved her.

'It's just a matter of waiting for the right moment,' he slugged back his second whisky soda and with glass in hand made his way once again to the kitchen for icecream, chocolate topping and homemade cake.

The cake was particularly moist and delicious, but it stuck in his throat like cotton wool.

'Oh, it would be perfect, wouldn't it, Mrs Perfect.' Mrs Amanda Stitt was an excellent cook, an exemplary housekeeper, the perfect hostess, and dressed immaculately.

'And you can't write one lousy book.' Crispin looked at his refection in the high polish of the buttercup yellow cupboard doors.

His features were once called chiselled, now they were rounded on the edges like a river pebble. His hair was wavy brown and parted on the left, but the tide was on the way out, leaving a freckled beach behind and this accentuated his small button brown eyes.

'Beady,' he reiterated Amanda's estimation.

He struck a pose and thought on the prospect of playing the lead, if they ever called him to make a movie of his bestseller.

'Everyone else has a movie from their book. What's the matter with you Stitt?' He tried to look rakish, debonair and movie star potential. It wasn't working. He grabbed his burgeoning layer of fat, which sat quite comfortably over the top of his pyjama pants, and gave it a good wriggle. It set up a small wave that ended at his buttocks.

'You don't even get dressed anymore,' Crispin mimicked his wife and her American accent, 'You're not Noel Coward you know.' And didn't he know it!

Hemingway, Coward, Vidal, Waugh, Steinbeck and his nemesis Nevil Shute, they all had that one word attached to their work that Stitt didn't.

'Prolific.'

His life reflected a B-grade movie, a bad one, he thought. He took his icecream to the study and looked at his bookshelf. The hardcover, the paperback, the translations, the proof copy. 1950 was a whirlwind of adoration.

'They loved me.'

He looked over at the photographs on his wall. Amanda stared back, hanging off his arm when they were at the award night. Gorgeous as always in *that* dress, which she only wore the once. He had bought a tuxedo for the occasion from Messer's Meyer and Goldstein. It fitted like a dream and made him feel a million dollars, which wasn't far from the truth if you converted it to pounds, shillings, and pence. His publisher smiled at him in the photo, a rare occurrence for Plethora (it's Ple-thor-a). Mrs Carmichael hadn't been known to smile since 1942, when she divorced her third husband. His agent was crying, Imogen Libevitz was one of those emotional types that cried all the time, at everything. He was surrounded by happy people. All because of his efforts.

'All because of my talent.'

It's not every day a new author scoops all the awards in one year. The Brinkley, the Schloss Award and the Arthur Crowther Medal for Writing Excellence. They were mighty accolades indeed, with enough prize money to see him through to a sequel. The royalties bought the Pontiac, the translations bought the mix-master and the foreign rights bought Amanda's happiness. She had bought him a Mont Blanc fountain pen. A really expensive fountain pen, because, she said, 'every successful writer has one.' She signed the card with kisses and love. He looked at his pen sitting on his desk. He thought fond thoughts of his wife.

But what he really hankered for—what Stitt really wanted—was the adoration of the reading public. The People's Choice Award was the one that had validation written all over it. It was the one that would make him a household name.

'Shute.' He spat the name, although he had all of Mr Nevil Shute's prodigious output on his book shelves and had read them all, more than once.

'Brinkley shminkley,' he said to the photo. Still…the literati thought he was worth it. Plethora

Carmichael thought he was worth it, to her bottom line anyway. The Schloss academy thought something of his novel to give him a trophy and 5000 to pay his writer's block overdraft. He was a success, and yet…Amanda thought his new effort *He is Dead,* stank.

'So, you read the whole thing, darling?'

'Mmmm.'

'And?'

'Well…'

It was the way she said it. The way she lingered over the 'e'.

'At least she could have lied to me. Isn't a wife supposed to be loyal?' He licked his fingers and went back to his desk and sat down. His stomach gave a grumble and settled on his lap.

'They will love it,' he said to the typewriter. He imagined the headlines.

'STITT DOES IT AGAIN.'

'A WINNER FROM THE PEN OF GENIUS.'

'MORE PLEASE, MR. STITT.'

They were all possible

'Who am I kidding? It stinks.'

Three

The lawnmower once again coughed into life and Jim Broker revved the engine sending up a cloud of smoke into the quiet suburb of Eden Grove. Crispin stood at his window and watched his neighbour.

'If only my life was as simple.' It was a mantra he often repeated.

Jim, at over six feet was a bear of a man, and to look at him you wouldn't hesitate to have him by your side in a dark alley, but in reality, he was a pushover. His six daughters knew this. His wife knew this and his mother knew this. The Broker household ran on Jim's goodwill and his unfailing even temper.

He spied Crispin looking at him from the upstairs window and waved. Crispin waved back.

'How's it going?'

'Fine,' Crispin said. His answer lacked conviction.

'Wanna come over for a beer?' Jim hoicked his thumb towards his shed.

'Alcohol,' Amanda Stitt always said, 'isn't going to solve your problems. You can't drown someone's ego that easily.' She always had a way of twisting the last bit of the knife in Crispin's back.

'I'll be right there.'

It only took a minute for Crispin to slip out of his PJs and into something that resembled a magazine cover for *Golf Weekly*. He looked in the mirror, adjusted his cravat, put a packet of cigarettes in the top pocket of his sweater with contrasting collar and ran his fingers through his wavy hair. He always thought he looked quite debonair, every inch the artist, intellectual with a bit of aristocracy thrown in for good measure. Someone had once said he had a regal bearing. He puffed up his chest and struck a pose in front of his Cheval mirror. Yes, there was definitely something quite regal about his jaw. (Crispin hadn't done well in history. The Habsburg jaw, a case in point.) He looked, to his way of thinking, every inch the man who wrote a bestseller.

'You look like you should be on the cover of a knitting pattern,' Amanda once said when he started wearing his cravats and his Fair Isle sweater with the leather patches on the elbows.

The sound of the shed door scraping open intruded on his thoughts and he rushed downstairs, out the back door, through the side gate, and into Jim Broker's sanctuary. Jim's shed was where men could be men without the interference of women. Crispin and Jim had spent many an afternoon in the shed, putting the world to right.

'I thought you weren't coming,' Jim had started to fiddle with his lawn edger.

'Just had to clean up a bit,' Crispin said, then changed the subject. 'Working hard I see.' Jim was one of those men who didn't give two hoots what he looked like, and to Crispin's eye, let his wife dress him.

'Not anymore.' Jim downed tools and walked to

his beer fridge, closely followed by Crispin.

'What's that thing?' Crispin pointed to a bit of pipe with what looked like an engine on one end.

'It's something that will revolutionise the way we do the garden. That's a prototype, but it's going to change things.'

'What does it do?'

'It's got a bit of wire on the end and whips about and snips things.'

'Like scissors?'

'Nope, like a blade.'

'A whipper snipper, eh?' Crispin offered.

'Sort of.'

'Another one of your inventions?'

'It's a beauty. I'm gonna call it the Whip Round.'

'Cheers to that.'

The men contemplated the future of gardening while sipping their beer.

'Take a seat.' Jim smiled and pointed to a comfortable looking chair. Crispin sat in an old armchair that Jim had converted into a reclining seat with a footstool.

'I still think you're on a winner with this one, Jim.' Crispin threw the footstool out with his weight and lay back.

'Yeah. I had an idea to call it the lazy days.'

'Really,' Crispin said as somewhere in the back of his mind he had the idea it had already been done.

Jim handed another beer to his neighbour and sat down on a bar stool and began to swivel around.

'Dad,' someone called from the yard.

'I think they want you.'

'Not here.' Jim took a long drink.

'What's up?'

'Well…' Jim downed his beer and cracked another bottle. 'Jeanie is going a bit… a bit… crazy over this wedding thing.'

'Wedding thing?'

'Yeah. She has the idea that Brenda wants the whole box and dice.'

'Box and dice.'

'Yeah.'

The men contemplated the box and dice in silence.

'Dad,' a voice called.

Jim put his finger to his lips and the men drank in silence.

'Brenda, do you really want those roses to be yellow?' Jeanie's voice cut through the stillness of the afternoon.

'Coming, Mum.'

Jim let out a breath and winked.

'Another?'

'Don't mind if I do.'

'Cigarette?' Crispin offered.

'Nope, Jeanie says it makes me stink.'

'Oh.' The word brought his thoughts back to his manuscript. Crispin struck a match and took a deep drag.

'Amanda and I stink together, so I guess it's ok.'

'Haven't seen you for a bit. You working on that thing?' Jim threw his head in the direction of Crispin's house.

'That thing, as you so eloquently put, is finished.'

'You don't say.'

'I do.'

'What's it about then?'

Oh, how Crispin hated that particular question.

Everyone always wanted to know 'what's it about then?' As if genius could be described on the back of a cereal packet. When he had been on the speaking circuit and invited to the best addresses in town, the first question anyone always asked was, 'What's it about then?'

'I'll let you decide that when you buy and read a copy.' That was his stock answer and usually sorted the wheat from the chaff. Amanda called him Mr Glib for about six months after the initial adulation had subsided.

'Well… it's a sort of awakening of man, and sort of about a man who has an awakening.'

'Oh. High-brow then?'

'Um, it's very readable.'

'Ah.' Jim offered an ashtray to Crispin's drooping ash.

'Jeanie says I don't even read a cereal packet when it says open this end. She says not everyone can write a good book, you know.'

Crispin winced. Amanda often said the same thing.

'So, tell me Jim, as the everyman, as the man in the street, what does success mean to you? What do you get out of life?'

'Success. It's simple. A good snapper.'

'What?'

'You know, a good dump.'

'Really?'

'Yep.'

'You mean…' Crispin tried to put his mind to what exactly a good dump might entail.

'Nothing like it Stitt. You just feel like your guts have fallen out.'

'Oh.' Now Crispin was in no doubt.

'What about the higher things of life?'

'Nah.'

If only my life were so simple, Crispin thought.

'But don't you want people to love you?'

'They do.' Jim nodded towards his house. His daughters adored him, his wife was in love with him and he loved his job in civil engineering.

'Yes, of course.' Running his fingers through his hair, Crispin tried to get to the nub of the issue. 'But I mean, don't you find that having acceptance from one's peers is important for your success?'

'Well Stitt, I don't think much about all that. All I know is Jeanie and the girls have a home, a father and a husband.'

'But is that all, Jim?'

'It's enough for me.' Jim opened another beer and handed it to Crispin. 'Jeanie says my blood's worth bottling.'

'Simple.' Crispin said and downed his beer in one.

There is only so much beer one man can consume before his liver begins to object. Crispin had reached the high-water mark when he finally staggered out of the shed and retraced his steps home.

The kitchen light was blazing and Amanda had left a note next to a beautifully executed dinner on a plate. Crispin looked at the symmetry of his dinner.

'At least she was thinking of me.' He dipped his finger in the congealed gravy and sucked it clean.

Then he made his way to his study and flicked

on the light. The phone was beeping in the bin. He replaced the receiver and lit a cigarette, contemplating his novel. His plot lines were littered over the floor, his notes scattered over his drinks cabinet, and his second and third drafts shoved under the desk. He once told a reporter that he lived his character's lives. It was like method acting. Now he wished he was dead like his character, although committing suicide was not his preferred method of shufflling off to Buffalo.

Nothing was going to save him from the scorn, the contempt and derision his new work would garner. He stubbed his cigarette out on a crumpled paper and went to bed. Even in the dark, he could see that Amanda wasn't there.

'Tomorrow it will all be better. Tomorrow the sun will shine and everyone will love me.'

Four

There was a constant ringing in Crispin's ear and he rolled over, trying to alleviate the pain. It was insistent and then somewhere in the haze his brain joined the real world and recognised it was the telephone. He rolled over and felt the bed. It was cold, but had evidence of Amanda.

'All I need is a good snap,' he said as he slowly opened his eyes to the day. The phone had stopped ringing and Crispin turned to see it was 9:30. Amanda should be getting his breakfast. Isn't that what wives do? Shouldn't she be the dutiful housewife at home? All the adverts extol the virtue of having a wife at home. Apron, cooking, a smile on their face.

'And a new mix-master,' he said to her pillow.

The phone rang again. If she was home, she'd answer it. It stopped.

'If it was important, they will ring back,' Crispin's logic erred on the side of inaction. He lay in bed looking at the ceiling, when his bladder made the final call to get up.

Some men do their best thinking on the toilet. Crispin was no exception. He sat down and thought on Jim's words.

'Is that all it takes? What about lofty ideals?' Taking the method acting approach, Crispin tried… and failed.

His wife was right. It's just like constipation.

'I can't even do that right.' It was a lament that did nothing to cheer his day.

The phone rang again.

'Amanda,' Crispin bleated from the bathroom.

'Amandaaaaa.' The house was silent.

He raced to the study, pulling up his pyjamas on the way and took the call.

'Hello?'

'Hello. Mr Stitt?'

'Yes.'

'*The Mercury Daily* here, Mr Stitt.'

'Yes.' Crispin's ego gave him a jump start.'

'We heard a rumour you have finished another novel. Is it true?'

'Well…yes.'

'And that—'

'Who told you?' Crispin's brain joined the rest of his body.

'And that it hasn't been accepted by your publisher.'

'Well. It's very new.'

'They are calling you a one hit wonder, Mr Stitt.'

'They?'

'Yes.'

Crispin hung up and put the phone in the bin.

'One hit wonder. Pffffhhht.'

It was while contemplating the thought of being a one hit wonder that he heard the front door open and immediately wanted to hide. A better idea presented itself and he struck a pose, typing away, sitting at his desk.

'Morning darling,' he shouted, hoping to lure her to his study to see him working.

Amanda appeared at the door immaculately dressed in a white skirt, yellow shirt and cardigan casually draped over her shoulders. He couldn't help but admire her figure in the clothes.

'Working?'

'Yes.' He shrugged. 'You know, when the muse strikes.'

'Didn't managed to get dressed?'

Of course, now she was talking to him she always had a way to get that one last dig.

'Hemingway writes in the nude, you know.'

'Does he? I guess that's why he's a great writer.' Crispin let the insult slip.

'Where have you been, anyway?'

'To the fish market. Best to get in early.'

'What did you get?'

'Oh, just something for dinner.' They were distracted by a car horn. 'There's my lift. Tennis. I'll be away all day.' And she was gone.

He sat and thought about his wife, then on the urging of his ego he slipped off his pyjamas and stood at his desk in the nude. At one time, he could have looked down and seen his genitals. Now his stomach spoilt the view.

Amanda began talking before she reached the door of his study 'Crispin, I've made your lunch, and just remember we're going to the Joneses for…' she popped her head into the study and began laughing. He had been caught in the nude, the nuance of the situation not lost for one moment.

'One hit wonder.' The words propelled him to the fridge, then to his desk, to the fridge again, and back to his study. He wanted to send the manuscript to his agent. Miss Imogen Lebovitz would love it. Imogen loved everything and her benchmark was so low her opinion didn't count. His publisher, on the other hand, had a benchmark that would give a nose bleed. The reporter's words niggled.

'What do *they* know?' Perhaps it was a ploy from another publisher. He dreamt of the prospect of a bidding war for *Il Est Mort*. The thought sustained him until lunch.

Amanda's lunch offering was a club sandwich with his favourite tomato relish. She had punctured the whole thing with a skewer topped by an olive. It looked like it was up for an award and got Crispin musing.

'How the heck does she do all this before 9:30?' He could only just manage to get out of bed and smoke a cigarette. 'Perhaps it's passive aggressive? Perhaps she's trying to make me feel inadequate. Well, it won't work, Amanda,' he said to the sandwich.

With lunch over, Crispin felt his moral fibre strong enough to ring his publisher. He rehearsed a few lines.

'I've written the definitive novel about man's struggle.' That didn't really hit the mark.

'I've done it!' He put the exclamation in his voice. It wasn't quite what he was aiming for in the way of breaking the news.

'You're a grown man Stitt. She's only a woman…an old one at that.' His fibre gave a burp and let him know it only had so much in the way of a backbone.

He flipped his teletext to C, and it popped open.

'Crispin Stitt for Mrs Carmichael,' he announced on the phone to Angel, Plethora's long-suffering secretary, and took deep breaths while he waited.

'Stitt? Stitt? Oh Stitt.' He could almost see her furrowed brow.

'Yes.'

'Back, are you?'

'I never left.'

'Oh, Stitt.' Plethora rolled her eyes. Now she remembered Stitt, and the memory sat like a grease spot on her two-piece wool Chanel. His contract required another book. He was overdue and the marketing machine of Raven & Square Publishing had passed him by. In fact his contract stipulated his association with that side of things at an end. The buck (literally) has to stop somewhere. She flicked through her Roladesk organiser to Stitt. One year overdue. Time to give the little twerp a dressing down.

'I've done it,' Crispin tried to jolly the woman along. Plethora wasn't the jollying type.

'What?'

'I've written it.'

'What?'

'The book.'

'Look Stitt. My time is finite on this earth. I can't play guessing games. You're overdue. By my reckoning, you are in breach, no matter what grocery list you've managed to write. It's payback time.' Plethora particularly liked this part of the game. Authors had the rarefied idea they were worth the money. She heard Crispin's sharp intake of breath and smiled. *The advance*, she thought, *had disappeared, probably onto his hips, long ago.*

'But I've written it, Mrs Carmichael, Plethora.' He added her name trying to get cosy with the woman who had his testicles in her hand at that very moment.

'Listen Stitt. George Bernard Shaw had finally shuffled off this mortal coil. He's as dead as they get. Fell out of the tree. I'm up to my neck in reprints. Now if you were dead…' Carmichael looked at the mountain of paperwork on her desk. 'Glad you rang Stitt. A cheque in the post or check out.' And she hung up.

'Check out.' The thought scared Stitt witless. To be cast out into the milieu of the hoi polloi without a publisher. To be a writer without an editor. To begin the submission process all over again. It was too awful to think about. It was a fate worse than death.

Three Scotch sodas later, his heart started beating again.

The fourth Scotch did the trick, and he began to see Mrs Plethora Carmichael as the wicked witch from the west. She didn't deserve his genius. She wasn't fit to publish a grocery list, never mind his masterpiece. She could just go and jump.

Number five, and every publisher on the planet would want *Il Est Mort*. There would be a bidding war, film rights, screen plays, theatre, Oscars and he'd get to keep his advance.

'PLE-THOR-A,' he shouted to the phone, 'go boil your head and stick it in aspic.' The genius had spoken.

'Carla will understand.' Crispin's editor, Mrs Carla Avella, looked like a sex goddess, but was hot headed. Everything was a crisis.

'Crispin Stitt for Mrs Avella.' He waited, listening to the clicks as the switchboard put him through.

'Crispin?' Avella asked.

'I rang before, but you were out.'

'Oh, yes, out,' Carla gave a small snort.

'Yes, well, it's me.' Crispin remembered the last time he spoke with Carla and the dressing down she gave him regarding his bestseller.

'It's been a long time between drinks,' Avella said.

Not so long, Crispin thought as he sipped his Scotch.

'So, what's going on?'

'I've done it.'

'Really. You've given up writing.'

'No,'

'Oh.'

'I've written another book.' He thought he detected a moan. She hadn't exactly loved *He Lives*. In fact, she said it was,

'The worst piece of detritus she had had the pleasure to edit.'

'And I suppose you want me to edit it?'

'Well, shall I just read you a little, you know, to get a feel?' Crispin picked up his papers and read a small passage with as much feeling as he could muster.

'Well?'

'Look Stitt. You murdered the English language once. This time you need to do a better job and put us out of our misery once and for all.' And she hung up.

'PHILISTINE.'

When you are on a roll, it's easy to keep going. It's a momentum thing. Crispin was rollin' and so he rang his agent to tell her the good news—for he had massaged his ego sufficiently to know when he was sitting on literary gold.

'Imogen,' he began, 'Nice of you to ring.'

'Crispin?'

'Yes.'

'Are you drunk?' She said it with such distaste. What would a twenty-nine-year-old year old know about the artistic temperament?

'Me?'

'Yes.'

'No, no. What gave you that idea?'

'Oh, well, I just thought that, well, it was silly of me. What's happening?' Imogen was the most unsuited person to be in the cut and thrust of publishing. She was one of life's innocents. You could tell her they put a man on the moon and she'd believe it.

Crispin smiled and patted his manuscript.

'Well, my little darling, I've done it.'

'What?'

'I've written it.'

'What?' This was beginning to sound familiar. Why was everyone so ignorant of his artistic endeavours?

'The book darling.'

'Oh, *the* book. How marvellous. Wonderful Crispin.'

'How bloody marvellous. Wonderful Crispin.' He mimicked Imogen's generosity.

Number six scotch had turned the genius into a nasty drunk.

'But it is wonderful Crispin. I know how hard you've worked. Does Mrs Carmichael know?'

'HA!'

'Pardon?'

'HA I say to Mrs Carmichael.'

Number seven had Crispin blabbering like a baby.

'You love my work don't you, Immy?'

'Of course.'

'You think I've got talent, don't you?'

'Yes Crispin. I think you're terrific.'

'You love me, don't you?'

'Well, I think your wife loves you. I'm sure she does.'

'But you love me too, Immy?'

'I guess I do…in an agent-author type of way.'

'I love you too, Immy.' Crispin blew his nose on the last line of the book and crumpled it in the bin.

'I'm dying to read it. I'll be in touch.'

'Are you?'

'Yes. Of course.'

Crispin looked down at the manuscript and couldn't quite figure out why it wasn't finished. He was sure he'd put it to bed with his killer last line.

'I'm going to end it, you know. It's gotta happen Immy, or I might as well be dead.'

'Look Crispin. I've got to go. We'll talk soon.' And she hung up. Stitt looked at the receiver in his hand and then laid it on his desk.

'One for the road,' he said to his typewriter.

Number eight slid down his neck just before he slid to the floor.

He woke up with a crick and a dribble mark on the carpet.

'Ammmaaaaannnnnnndddda,' he bleated.

Footsteps came to the door and from his position on the floor he recognised his wife's shoes.

'Amanddddddda.' He closed his eyes and hoped for some pity.

'Crispin. Why don't you do us all a favour and just drop dead?'

Five

They say alcohol takes over five minutes to go through the human body. After a good nudge at the Scotch, Crispin's body thought it might take a week or two. He had slept on the floor and when he tried to sit all the blood that wasn't 14% proof drained from his eyeballs and left him feeling less than adequate. He burped and lay down.

'What I need is the hair of the dog,' he said, although if a linguist were to be listening it might have sounded something like, 'TTvvvat I neeeeeebd ith the haith of tha dbbbloooog,' Such was the state of his tongue.

A man who crawls to the drinks cabinet first thing in the morning has a large drinking problem or has flat tyres on his wheelchair. Crispin hung onto the cabinet and in steady increments, hauled his sorry carcass to the upright position. The oxygen at that altitude made his head spin.

After he had latched onto the soda bottle like a baby and squirted, he sucked from the Scotch bottle and downed the concoction in one, then waited for the medicine to take effect.

He heard his neighbours shed door scrape, and the sound propelled him into action. He popped an olive into his mouth and chewed, then donned his smoking jacket, pulled on a pair of trousers he found on the floor, and made his way through the house, out the back door, through the garden gate, to wave at his neighbour.

'Hi Jim.'

'Hi Stitt.'

Crispin hung about, jiggling from one foot to the other.

'Looks like you could do with a Broker special.'

'Don't mind if I do.'

'You pull an all-nighter or something?' Jim looked over his neighbour.

'Something like that.'

Once in the privacy of the shed, Jim went to work making his Broker special. It's restorative powers were legendary to Crispin. Jim mixed the drink, then handed it over. He took to it like a dying Scotsman latches onto his purse. The men waited in anticipation as Crispin's stomach discussed the merits of keeping a raw egg, paprika, orange juice and a dollop of cream on the inside or the outside. One burp later Crispin felt he had enough energy to smile at the world once again.

'Magic, eh?'

'You betcha.'

There is a certain optimism that is had from beating a doozy of a hangover. Crispin felt he had conquered his demons and looked expectantly at Jim.

'It's your funeral.' Jim grabbed two beers from his bar fridge and plinked the lids.

'I'll see you on the other side.' The men clinked the bottles and suddenly, everything was right with the world as the cold liquid hit the spot. Crispin's blood corpuscles broke out the pretzels, thinking it was party time once again. His second beer went down like mother's milk and reinvigorated his liver to go on a holiday.

'Isn't life funny.' Crispin giggled as the alcohol collected in his head.

'Yeah,' Jim sighed, 'funny.'

'Wazup Jimbo?' Crispin's empathy was at an all-time high.

'Ah, just women I guess.'

'Women Jim?'

'Yeah. The wedding thing.'

'Wedding thing Jim?'

'Yeah, I'm a patient man, but all this wedding stuff is driving me crazy.'

'Crazy Jim?'

'You said it.'

The men drank in contemplation of going crazy. It required four more beers each before their study was complete.

'You know what?'

'What Jim?'

'We need to just go wild.'

'Wild?'

'Yeah, just, you know wild. Live it up type of wild.'

'Sounds like a plan Jim.'

'You betcha.'

Going wild requires some cognitive thought, no matter how hard it might be to cognize with an alcohol level that could make your breath pass as fuel for a Bunsen burner. The plan was to meet up in the afternoon and just get out of Dodge.

Crispin slopped home and began to pack.

He tried to envisage every eventuality. His tuxedo was a start. He added a bow tie or two, five dress shirts, several pairs of silk socks, underwear, PJs, loafers with and without golf tassels, casual slacks, waistcoats x two and then a few casual sweaters, his sports coat and a dinner suit… just in case. His fedora with the narrow brim and his summer version with the silk band completed the task. He dressed in his sports coat, wide leg slacks and loafers.

'Eat your heart out Cary Grant,' he said to the mirror. The one thing missing was some writing paraphernalia.

'Hemingway always travels with a typewriter.' He grabbed his little portable and a bundle of paper.

'Every inch the man about town. Knitting pattern, pffft.'

He closed his suitcase and hauled it downstairs.

'Better leave her a note.' It was a short moment when he wasn't thinking of himself. He raced to his study and scribbled,

I'm leaving all this to you.

His dry cleaning lay in a heap on the floor and he added an arrow to let Amanda know, then with one last look at his study, he closed the door.

'On second thoughts,' he raced back and grabbed his pipe, then hauled his bag to Jim's station wagon and put it in the back and waited.

Jim's packing was of an altogether different flavour. His first item was a rifle and then some ammo. Mosquito repellent was a must and tinned food plus a hunting knife.

He grabbed a couple of pairs of old corduroy

trousers and hunting shirts, donned his fishing hat, slipped on his old moccasins and whistled up his wife.

'Going now Jeanie.'

'Righto Jim. Honey, I put some liquid refreshments in the icebox for you.'

'Thanks sweetie.'

'Bring back a big fish.'

'You betcha.'

'All set?'

Crispin nodded and slipped into the passenger seat.

They hit the open road in just under twenty minutes. It was just long enough for Crispin to get stone cold sober after his monumental bender.

There is often, when sobriety rears its head, a sudden realisation that the world was turning in your absence and you missed it. Crispin had that sudden realisation that he had got it all wrong. It was more than packing the wrong colour tie. He was going to look an idiot.

'You know Jim,' Crispin gave a little hollow laugh, 'When you said go wild, well, I had the crazy idea—for a second—that you meant go to town.— You know—really rev it up—in town, sort of.'

'Oh.'

'Yeah, sort of go wild. Dancing girls, drinking, cocktails, night-clubs.' Crispin gave a gormless grin.

'Yeah.'

'We're not going to the Casino, are we?'

'Nope.'

'Thought so.'

As the suburbs gave way to the Australian bush, Crispin tried to form the words, but they stuck in his throat as he was already swallowing his pride.

'Er, Jim,'

'Yep.'

'Where *are* we going?'

'We are going to my small slice of heaven.'

'And it's this way, is it?'

'Yep.'

'Oh.' They sat in silence as the miles ticked by.

'You're gonna love it, mate.'

'Am I?'

'Yep.'

'And it's not far?'

'Far enough.' Jim began to whistle. Crispin thought that a week without dry-cleaning was far enough.

The road stretched endlessly ahead, the mirage of heat playing havoc with Crispin's eyes. Or it could have been his hangover, it was a debatable. He nodded off and was woken up with a savage neck snap.

'Where are we?' the car had just pulled into a small clearing in the bush.

'Wolluppy.' Jim took a deep breath and then coughed up a fly that had been sucked in at the last moment.

'Woll up a what?'

'Yep. Gloria called it Wolluppy when she was about six. Cute as a button, my Gloria. Well, it just kinda stuck.'

'Wolluppy.' Crispin tried the name again.

'I bought it for a song years ago. It's a beaut little shack right on the lake.'

'Lake?' Crispin couldn't see a lake.

'Down there.' Jim pointed to a well-worn path that trekked off into the scrub.

'So… um we need to walk.' Crispin looked at his clothes.

'Yep.' Jim began to assemble their supplies. 'But we don't need to carry any of this.' He spread his hands wide over the icebox, Crispin's suitcase, valise and other necessities.

'So… um.' Crispin stepped out of the car and looked at his Italian loafers standing in the Eucalyptus leaf litter. He felt them cringing in mortification at anything other than wool carpet or the parquetry in the clubhouse bar, overlooking the 18th tee.

'You're gonna love it.' Jim found a wire strapped to a tree and turned to his companion. 'Watch this.' He pulled, and somewhere in the distance Crispin heard the screech of metal. The men waited, and then in the distance they saw a wooden basket making its way through the trees. 'It's on a cantilever system, my own design.' The basket was attached to a wire running through the trees. It swung to a halt at the car.

'Load 'em up.' Jim started to hump the gear into the crate.

'I'll get that.' Crispin heaved his suitcase onto the platform, hoping Jim's contraption could take the weight. He'd packed hoping a bell boy would be the only one to lift it to his room.

'Jeez, what ya got in here ,Stitt?' Jim helped to hoik it.

'Oh, just some essentials.'

With everything packed, Jim pulled the wire trip and the load began its journey to the shack. The men followed.

'Er, Jim. There aren't any snakes are there?'

'Not many.' Crispin stuck close to Jim and looked around in terror at the native Australian bush. The closest he'd ever been to the wilds was his mother's shrubbery. A flock of galahs were frightened into flight and Crispin just about climbed onto Jim's back.

'Hey.'

'Sorry, slipped.' He climbed down.

'Here we are.'

The two men stood in front of a small wood and corrugated iron shack.

'I've made a few modifications over the years.' Jim stood proud and surveyed his kingdom. Their luggage ground to a halt next to the house and snagged on a tree, tipping its contents over the ground.

'Just a few modifications and she'll be as right as rain.' Crispin gathered up his bags as Jim opened the front door. A possum bolted out screaming and disappeared into the bush.

'What was that?' Crispin squealed.

'Bloody possum. They get in under the roof.'

'Will it come back?'

'You never can tell with possums. Anyway, come in Stitt,' Jim held the door. 'No women. No work…'

'No hot water,' Crispin said under his breath.

The shack had one room. There were two triple bunks, a double bed, a rudimentary kitchen, and a large table with eight chairs that dominated the room.

'We love it here.' Jim threw his clothes on the bed. Stitt tried to smile as he looked around.

'Er. Where's the bathroom Jim?'

'You gotta wash in the sink.'

'And the toilet facilities?' Crispin crossed his fingers.

'Out back.'

'Out back Jim?'

'Yep, I'll show you.' They walked out the door, down a small path and came to the dunny sitting proudly on its own, surrounded by the bush. Its corrugated walls were covered in creeper.

'She's a beauty. Made it myself.'

'Is it safe?' Crispin looked at the plank of wood over the black hole of Calcutta.

'What da ya mean?'

'Well, I mean, you know. Spiders, snakes, that sort of wild life.'

'Oh, nothin' to it. Look.' And Jim showed Crispin how to give the door a whack with a stick to frighten away anything that might poison, bite, sting, spit or scratch.

'Oh.'

'Dug it myself. Half way to China that hole.'

'Hole.'

'Yeah.' Jim had the look of a man who knows a decent hole when he sees one.

'You mean...'

'Yep.'

Crispin had heard of a long drop toilet, but as for the experience, it would be a new one. His childhood was safely cocooned in middle class suburbia with porcelain fittings.

'Sleep anywhere.' Jim pointed to the three-tiered bunks. Too high and the possum might just decide to rip his throat out in the night. Too low and snakes were the issue. He opted for the middle bunk and tried it out for size. It was a comfortable enough as long as he didn't want to sit up in bed. It felt like he was sleeping in a drawer.

'This is the life eh, Stitt?' Jim spread himself all over the bed and his possessions all over the room in about as much time as it takes to scrape possum poo off an Italian loafer with a silk handkerchief.

'How about we go down to the lake Stitt?'

'Alright.'

'Follow me.' Jim strode confidently along a track and at the last turn, a body of water came into view.

'I think the tide is out.' Crispin eyed the mud that was nothing like a beach and stretched for a good 100 yards before the water began.

'Nah. It's always like this. I have the patented Broker bridge.' Jim went to a small lean-to and pulled out what looked like a pile of wood.

'We just roll it out and "by Godfrey", we can walk to the water.'

'And then?' Crispin looked at the expanse of mud.

'We drag the canoe and go fishing.' He said it with such enthusiasm, Crispin couldn't help but get caught up in the possibilities. Not that he had ever dragged a canoe, or gone fishing, for that matter, but out in the wilderness where men are men and the flies outnumber oxygen molecules ten to one, anything was possible.

Crispin inhaled one of the suckers and then coughed it up again.

'Keep your mouth shut, Stitt.'

'Mmmm.' Crispin put his hand over his nose and squinted into the sun.

'Best fish I ever tasted was right here, Stitt.'

'Mmmm.'

'Say, how about we get a drink?'

'Mmm.' Crispin nodded. It sounded like a grand idea, because standing in the sun can give a man a powerful thirst.

There is something comforting about supping a cold beer after a hectic day. Jeanie had packed enough beer in ice it would last Jim until, as she always said with a laugh, 'they put a man on the moon.'

'She certainly thought you'd be thirsty.' Crispin sat at the large table and took a good look at his rustic surroundings. At the very least, he could put his time in the wilderness down to valuable experiences for his writing career.

'Yeah.' Jim smiled at the thought of his wife. 'She's the ant's pants. I love her to bits.'

'Do you?'

'You betcha.'

If only Crispin's life was so simple.

Six

When the beer is cold, the sun is setting, and there is that sweet moment before the mosquitoes take over from the day shift of flies, everything is right with the world. The men sat back contented as the light faded.

'Should we, you know, eat something?' Crispin's stomach gave a gurgle. As far as he could remember, all he'd had was an olive at about 10am.

'I dunno?' Jim shrugged. As far as Broker was concerned, beer was steak and chips in a bottle.

'Perhaps we could go out. You know, to a restaurant or something.'

'Nuthin' round here Stitt.' The men contemplated the thought of nuthin'. 'I know.' Jim began, 'how about beans an' eggs?'

'You mean out of a tin?'

'That's it.' Jim lay back on his bed. I like mine good an' hot Stitt.'

Crispin was accustomed to Amanda's excellent culinary skills. He tried to recall if he'd actually eaten beans from a tin. Nothing came to mind.

'I can do this,' Crispin said. The most he'd ever made in the kitchen was a mess.

'Do you have a can opener?' Stitt ran his fingers through his hair.

'You know Stitt. I always thought you were a bit of a sissy. Funny, eh?'

'Sissy.' Crispin cringed at the word. He'd had to wear that moniker for a good portion of his schooldays. He couldn't help it if he had wavy hair and a milk complexion, with an uncanny flair for colour co-ordination, as his mother often said.

'Me? Nope.' Crispin clattered around trying to find the stove.

'Er, Jim.'

'Yep.'

'Where's the stove?'

'It's the camping ring. I rigged it up to hook straight onto the gas bottle.' The contraption looked like a bomb. It ignited with a ferocity that could melt your polyester shirt at 50 paces.

'Jeanie cooks everything on it. She's just bonza at it.'

The beans and eggs were duly cooked while Jim prattled.

'You know Stitt, I don't know what I'd do without the missus.'

'No?'

'Nup. She's the full bottle on just about everything.'

'Full bottle?'

'Yeah. You know, the full quid.'

'Oh.'

'You know Stitt. I like you.'

'Thanks Jim. You're pretty fine yourself.' Crispin handed up beans and eggs that looked like something the cat had deposited on the front door mat after a hard night on the tiles. It wasn't a culinary vision, but it was hot. If only Amanda could see him now.

'Perfect Stitt.' Jim spooned the concoction onto

a piece of bread and it disappeared into his mouth. 'Beats eating flies.' Jim laughed and washed his meal down with another beer.

With enough beer in your system, little things like mosquitoes biting every exposed piece of skin are mere flesh wounds. Crispin didn't feel a thing as the neon sign lit up in the insect world, indicating the bar was open for business. Jim was one of those particularly annoying individuals who didn't attract attention.

'You know Stitt.'

'Yeah.'

'We must be the luckiest blokes alive.'

'How's that Jim?'

'Jeanie is just about the loveliest wife a man could have.' Jim wallowed in his sentimentality. 'And your wife too, Stitt.'

'Um. Yeah.' Crispin's voice cracked.

'She's a ripper girl.' Jim sat back and thought of his wife with a smile on his face. 'Don't ya just love 'em.'

'Yeah.' At this stage of the evening, Crispin loved just about everyone and everything.

'And what about…' Crispin's voice trailed off.

'Yeah.' Jim felt the well of human kindness in his bosom.

There is a time when imbibing alcoholic beverages, you reach your limit. What comes out of your mouth has nothing to do with rational, cognitive thought. Broker and Stitt had reached that limit.

'You know, Stitt if the politicians and the

scientists, could just give me five minutes, I'd have the place running like clockwork.'

'And the literary hobnobs.'

'Yeah, those literary hobnobs. We'd show 'em how things work around here.'

'You betcha.' Crispin patted Jim on the back.

And no matter how drunk a man might be, there is a moment in his drinking career that is universal, and that is the first time he needs to visit the toilet.

'Gotta go Jim.'

'Go where?'

'To the toilet Jim.'

'To bleed the lizard, eh?'

'What?'

'To slash.'

'Pardon?'

'To take a leak mate.'

'Gotta go, Jim.' Crispin stood up and sat down again.

'Back already, Stitt.'

'Gotta go.'

'Yeah.'

Jim was confident he was following the conversation for as anyone who has had a drink will tell you, you can hold onto your liquor for hours, but once you unplug, it's a given you'll need to go again and again from that moment onwards.

Crispin stood up and made his unsteady way to the door. The kerosene lantern cast a pool of light around the front step, but beyond was darkness.

'Won't be long.' Crispin stepped into the night. He knew the dunny was somewhere in the general direction of 'out there' and stumbled about for a bit, then decided to just go native.

Once back inside. it was obvious the night was over. Jim had fallen asleep. Crispin climbed up and slotted into his drawer bed and muttered, 'If only my life were as simple.'

The mosquitoes had decided to crack an all-nighter as the Stitt blood bank was a 2 for 1 special.

Seven

The birds in the bush might get up at the crack of dawn, but after a hard night of putting the world to right, Jim and Crispin slept on until the sun hit the tin roof and the room buzzed with flies.

Flies in the bush are pesky little creatures. What evolution was actually thinking when they hit the design table is a mystery, for they are only there, it seems, to annoy the hell out of you and get right up your nose. One particularly adroit member of the annoying brigade was doing that tricky manoeuvre as Crispin took a deep breath and stretched. He snorted and sat up, banging his head on the bunk above, which does nothing to help a hangover, but does get rid of the fly, albeit with a bump to take its place.

'Bloody hell.' The world came into focus and Crispin remembered where he was and why he was there.

'Huh?' Jim roused himself. 'Stitt?'

'Yes?'

'Is that you?' Jim hadn't quite got to the point of knowing the whys and wherefores.

'Yes.' Crispin slithered out of his bed and landed on the floor in an upright position. Always a handy trick when your head and body feel detached from one another and your alcohol level could pickle your grandmother.

'Gotta go Jim.'

People's personal habits are quite private. Crispin was of the opinion he didn't need to explain his every decision to his companion. He quietly walked outside into the blinding Australian sun, steadied himself, took a deep breath, slipped on his loafers, and asked,

'Er, Jim. Do you have toilet paper?

'Course I do. Better than a corncob.' The thought of a corncob as toilet paper left Crispin speechless. He scooted out to the dunny before Jim had any other alternatives to offer. Crispin really should have listened a little more closely to his history lessons—corncobs were a viable alternative from way back.

Crispin Stitt was one of those people in life who are regular as clockwork. No matter where he was or what had happened the night before, his bowels were the ones calling the shots. He looked at the dunny and felt there was no time like the present to get acquainted. The door squeaked open and then Crispin remembered the stick. He beat the door, watching for instant death to slither out, but all was quiet.

'Right. In you go Stitt.' He sat down on the wooden seat which was a plank with a hole in it and began to contemplate, meditate, and cogitate on things. It was while in this reflective mood he glanced up and came eyeball to eyeball with a big male possum.

It is a moot point who was more frightened of whom. The possum on hearing a scream jumped down and ran out the door. Crispin didn't wait for it to claw his eyes out and bolted out the door and didn't stop until he reached the front door of the shack, his trousers around half mast.

'Put the kettle on will ya, Stitt.' Jim stirred from his bed as Crispin fell into the room pulling up his trousers.

'I was nearly attacked.' The urgency in Crispin's voice did nothing to bring Jim to panic stations.

'Broker, I…' Crispin was about to launch into the whole situation when he realised it would sound like he was bleating for no apparent reason. His father always asked him if he was dead yet.

'You dead yet?' He could hear those words as clearly as if his father were in the room. His mother was of the opinion that everything was a crisis.

'You met Bob, did ya?'

'Bob?'

'Yeah. Big ol' Bob.'

'You mean…'

'Yeah.'

'Bob.' Crispin said it as if one meets a possum every day of the week and has a chat about the weather.

'Yeah.' Jim lay back on the bed and closed his eyes. 'Might need to go and see Bob myself. By Godfrey I think I will.'

With a man like Jim who takes life pretty easy, nothing is surprising. The exception was when he opened his eyes and looked at his neighbour.

'Holy cow Stitt. What happened to you?'

'What?' The panic began to rise.

'Have ya seen ya mug?'

'My what?'

'Ya ugly mug.' Jim pointed to his face. Crispin

felt his face. All he could ascertain without a mirror was that he hadn't shaved and he was a bit itchy.

'You've been giving free samples,' Jim said.

Crispin rummaged around in his valise and found a shaving mirror. He took a good look at his face. It was covered in red welts and as is the nature of mosquito bites, once you discover them, they itch like billy-o.

'Don't scratch, you'll make 'em worse.'

'Worse? Look at me.' Crispin was at panic stations.

'Steady Stitt. Jeanie has some of that lotion gunk here somewhere.' Jim rummaged about and found the old calamine lotion. 'It's pink, but we'll give it a burl.' He gave the bottle a shake and then began dabbing the bites. By the time he'd finished, Crispin looked in the pink.

'She'll be apples now.' Jim corked the bottle as Crispin studied his reflection.

'Apples, pffht.'

'Right as rain,' Jim thumped Stitt on the back and strode out the door like a man on a mission.

'I'll make the coffee, shall I?' Crispin said to the retreating figure.

The coffee was brewing, the bread cut and buttered and the eggs boiled when Jim returned like a conquering hero.

'Jeezus, isn't life beaut? Just did a ripper. When your bloody guts fall out. Really satisfying.'

'Oh.' Crispin wondered if it was appropriate to talk about toilet habits with your next-door neighbour.

'Know what I mean?'

'Um.' It was a subject Crispin had never really discussed with anyone.

'The wife knows what I mean.'

'You talk to your wife about bowel movements?'

'Doesn't everyone? She's my best mate.'

'Is she?'

'You bet. Bloody love her to bits. Don't you love yours?'

'Well, yes. Of course I do.'

'Well do you show her you love her?'

'Well, yes of course I do.' Crispin thought of the holidays, the jewels, the dinners at Giovannis, the plays, the house, the cars.

'I bite Jeanie's bum.'

It sounded like a much cheaper option. 'OH.'

'She loves it. Calls me 'the predator.'

'Does she?'

'Yeah.' Jim gazed into his coffee a contented man.

Crispin ruminated on the last words his wife had said to him. 'Why don't you just drop dead.' In no context could they be called terms of endearment.

'Now what's for slops, Stitt?'

Crispin rather enjoyed looking after the hut. He felt useful, wanted and appreciated. He took pride in his cooking and began to tidy around when his stomach gave a lurch and a grumble and he burped.

'Pardon me.'

'Great tucker Stitt.' Jim joined in the chorus and belched. There was something ominous about Stitt's burp that got Crispin thinking. He was a regular man. He never failed. But now, on reflection, he was at day two of not doing what comes naturally. When your body lets you down one can quite easily grasp the idea of panic and run with it, while others reach for antiseptic soap no matter their leg just fell off. Crispin was from the former camp. He had always been in robust health. His childhood was remarkable in that his father would say,

'That boy has the constitution of an ox.' His mother erred on the side of caution and set Crispin up for a life of worry and fret, so that, if in his adult life he felt a twinge, a niggle, a cough or as now, his innards weren't on cue, then it was time to panic.

'So, what do ya reckon we do today?' Jim asked. Crispin knew what he'd like to do and it required a bit of time on his own. 'Wanna go fishing?'

'Well, I…'

'Bonza. You know Stitt, I like you.'

'Thanks Jim.'

'Now, get out of ya fancy pants and we can really relax.'

'Well…it's just that I sort of, kind of…' Crispin didn't know how to tell Jim it was a choice of a dinner suit or a tuxedo.

'What?'

'I think I brought the wrong bag. You see I was already packed for a literary dinner and then…' Stitt concocted a lie so convoluted he almost believed it himself.

'Strewth.'

'So you see, I'm not exactly sure I can go fishing. I could just sort of stay around here and tidy up a bit and maybe just read.'

'Bull dust. Not a problem Stitt. I always keep a

few strides here. You can borrow mine.'

'Oh.'

When someone who is built like a bear gives someone who is built like a jelly baby a pair of trousers there is bound to be a bit of give in the seat. Crispin slipped on the pants and cinched his Carruthers and Sons exclusive leather belt tight over his belly.

'See, perrrrrrrfect.' Jim purred. With an old smelly jumper to complete the ensemble, Crispin looked every inch the odd cousin from Oodlawoopwoop.

'Now, let's go fishing.'

'Be with you in a tick. Just need to…you know.' Crispin pointed in the direction of the dunny.

'Not a problem Stitt. Meet me down at the lake.'

The dunny door was open and inviting. Crispin picked up the stick and gave a good whack at the door then ventured inside. He checked the rafters for Bob and once the all clear was called, sat down.

It wasn't easy to imagine he was home at Eden Grove in pristine conditions with proper facilities, but he tried. The flies were not making it easy. Once flies know that you aren't on the move they are all over you like a rash that was itching just to make matters more difficult. Crispin looked up at the roof and a pair of eyes in the gloom stared back at him.

'Jeez.' Stitt jumped then looked at the possum. 'For Pete's sake, what are you looking at?' Crispin sighed as Bob stared.

'You wouldn't understand Bob. Oh, that's right.

Mock me, why don't you.'

Bob blinked.

He tried to rationalise why he had failed.

'Obviously I haven't eaten,' he said to Bob. 'What goes in must come out.' The explanation seemed to mollify his worry bone. The solution was to eat.

'One olive and a few beans. Not enough to keep a man alive, never mind give his innards something to do.' Bob shifted on his rafter.

'A man needs a good meal.' Bob agreed with the statement and stretched.

'All it will take is food.'

A man can only sit on the dunny for so long talking to a possum before he realises nothing worthwhile is going to come from the exercise. Crispin came to the realisation and left Bob to ponder the imponderables and gingerly trod a path in the direction of the lake.

'Thought you'd carked it Stitt.'

'Pardon?' Crispin found a bare patch of earth and planted himself squarely in the middle.

'You know, ccrrrrrrrrriiiiiixxxxgh.' Jim clutched his heart and mimed a heart attack then laughed.

'Oh. No, I'm fine.'

'Bonza. Now we just need to...' Jim didn't finish as Crispin let out a scream and began dancing around whacking his trousers.

'What the?'

Crispin screamed an octave higher as he beat himself.

'Oh, you bloody silly galah. You stood on a meat ant nest.'

'Get them off me.' Crispin began to take his trousers off.

'Hang on. Hang on. Give me ya strides.' Jim took the pants. 'Cooee.'

'What?' Crispin stood in his silk boxer shorts with little golf club motifs, picking the ants off his legs.

'Swanky.' And Jim let out a wolf whistle.

'I'll have you know Broker these cost a fortune.'

'I bet they did.' Jim laughed.

'Well what do you wear?'

'Y-fronts. They have "scientific suspension and unique coverage",' Jim quoted from the advertising.

'Really.' Crispin said with a hint of derision

'You betcha.' Jim handed Crispin his trousers and stifled a laugh. 'You wanna go fishing Stitt?'

The water was a safer option that standing on an ants nest.

📖

Anyone who has been in a doctor's waiting room and cast his eye to the pictures on the wall will recognise the idyllic scene of man in the elements of nature, the sun shining, the three trout hanging off a tree on a willowy bank and the fisherman in waders casting his line with a smile on his face.

This has nothing to do with Broker's vision of fishing. His scene was more like Dante's inferno with mud, or Crispin thought so anyway.

'Right Stitt.' Jim explained how they were going to use his patented boardwalk to launch his homemade patented canoe and have some fun and get some tucker for slops.

Crispin looked at his loafers and just knew they were not going to be up to the job. The mud stretched for a good forty yards. Jim's boardwalk was nothing like a Bailey bridge. To Crispin's eye—and he wasn't an expert in these things, but the man in the street would be inclined to agree with him—the boardwalk that they began rolling out looked like an ill-conceived garden fence held together with wire.

'Are you sure it's up to the job?'

'Nothing to it Stitt.' Jim rolled and walked. 'Just gotta keep moving. This mud will suck the hairs off your legs if you get stuck.'

Crispin took the advice and jiggled around as he rolled the fence out to the water's edge.

'Er, what about the boat?' Crispin looked back at the boardwalk that was sinking.

'I'll carry on here. You get the canoe. She's a beauty Stitt. Real workmanship. I put my heart and soul into that canoe.'

An author rarely needs to run. It just isn't in the job description. Crispin looked at the boardwalk and did a quick reckoning on a sprint. Often ones capacity to over-estimate ones capabilities collides with reality and it usually hurts.

'Hurry, Stitt.' Jim yelled as he danced around, trying not to sink.

'Righto.' Crispin went as fast as his chubby legs would carry him. He lost his footing and a loafer to the primordial ooze, but like a trooper carried on.

'Made it,' he yelled, then turned to see Jim up to his knees, waving frantically.

'Just a jiffy.' Crispin hunted around for the canoe. He looked in the most obvious places. He looked in the not so obvious places.

'Er, Jim, where is it?' he yelled

'It's under the bed.' Jim hollered back

'Right.'

There was no way a canoe could fit under the bunk. It just wasn't possible. Nevertheless Crispin thought he should take a look. He grabbed a frying pan and banged it on the floor to frighten whatever might be under the bed, then got on his hands and knees.

'Ah.' He found a folded thing and pulled it out. Several spiders weren't so keen on being disturbed and ran for the nearest high ground. That the high ground happened to be Crispin was quite a shock to the system. He screamed and ran outside, throwing himself on the ground, then remembering snakes and other reptiles that were bound to kill, he jumped up.

Armed with a stick, the canoe was pulled outside and he made his way to the mud walk.

'Jim, I got it.' Crispin waved at Jim, who was now stuck up to his thighs. He waved back.

'Don't forget the paddle and the fishing rods. And a couple of beers wouldn't go astray.'

'Right.'

If you have ever subscribed to National Geographic, you will recognise those photos of women who carry things on their heads. Crispin subscribed to the magazine. He now put everything in an old large wash tub and stuck it on his head. With one arm free he wedged the paddle in his armpit and carried the canoe.

And so began the slow trip to the water's edge. The other loafer was sucked off, but Crispin was the hero of the hour. He made it to Jim and put his bundle down. It began to sink.

'You know, you could have just folded out the canoe and loaded it up.'

They looked at the tub slowly disappearing in the ooze.

'Beer?'

'Don't mind if I do.' Crispin popped a lid and squinted into the sun.

'Hot isn't it?'

'Thirsty work, eh?'

'Don't mind if I do.' Crispin popped another.

'You want to go fishing?' Jim asked as he began to assemble the canoe. 'I made it myself. A simple design, really.' Jim unfolded the canoe like an origami expert and put the washtub in place, fixed the paddle, and checked the fishing rods.

'All set?'

'Don't mind if I do.' Everyone knows if you drink alcohol on a hot day without a hat, it's bound to go to your head pretty quickly. Stitt giggled.

'I just gotta get out of the mud, Stitt.' Stitt giggled some more.

'For Pete's sake.' Jim pulled himself up and his trousers stayed put.

Stitt guffawed.

'Gotta get me strides, Stitt.'

Crispin let out a laugh.

If a tourist had a camera at that time the title of the picture might have been "The unusual formation of moon rocks on the shores of lake Wolluppy." Jim hoiked his trousers from the mud and covered his moon rocks.

'Shove off Stitt.' Stitt shoved. The canoe laden with an overweight author, beer enough for the British navy, and a naked man, moved an inch.

'Give it a good shove.' Jim moved to the front.

There is only so much shoving you can do with a small paddle.

'Change places.' Jim stood up and moved to the rear as Crispin tried to look elsewhere. There was a good deal of shove-offing and pushing and grunting, but slowly the two intrepid fishermen lightened the load by drinking the beer and they made it out into deeper water.

'I'll just wash me strides.' Jim waved his trousers in the water while Crispin looked at the cloud formations, the trees in the distance and the inside of his eyelids. They might do that sort of thing in Scandinavia, the outdoors and all that, but in Australia it was a bit more circumspect. There is just so far a neighbourly friendship can go before it gets a little creepy.

With his trousers back in place, the fishing line in the water and the last of the beer in his hand, Jim sat back.

'This is the life, Stitt.'

Damn it, nothing seemed to phase the man. He was up to his eyeballs in mud, he had lost his trousers, and he was still happy.

'How do you do it, Jim?'

'What?'

'That,' Stitt pointed to the smile on his neighbour's face.

'Life is what you make it. That's what my old man used to say. Life is what you make it.'

It was a maxim Crispin had yet to harness. It seemed to him he'd made a right hash of life up to now.

You either like fishing or you don't. There just isn't a midway point where you say, it's alright on a Wednesday when I've got my favourite shirt on. Jim looked like he could sit in the canoe all day and not care if he caught anything. Crispin kept checking his lure every minute, jiggling it, throwing it, readjusting it and couldn't keep still.

'Are there any fish in here?' The sun had worn a hole in his scalp and the alcohol was leeching out of his pores as he sat and sweated.

'Caught a woppa once. Biggest cat fish you'd see this side of Sydney.'

'Cat fish. Can you eat cat fish?' Crispin wrinkled his nose.

'Sure you can.'

It all sounded a bit too much like Huckleberry Finn. They might eat cat fish in the deep south, but in Australia it might be good for the cat. Crispin threw his line and tried to sit still.

'Ya shoulda brought ya hat, Stitt.'

'Yes.'

If there was one thing Crispin felt the hoi polloi needed schooling on, it was stating the obvious. Amanda would do it just to annoy him.

'Is that the manuscript?' she'd said as she stood in the doorway and eyed the pile of papers. 'Are you wearing that, darling?' she said as he finished tying his bow tie.

Crispin tried to smile, but his face felt tight, and his lips dry. He squinted, or it could have been narrowing his eyes in contempt. As the alcohol left him he wasn't in the mood to debate the point.

'Should get something soon,' Jim said, and as if to prove the point, his rod bent as the lure was grabbed.

'Cripes.' He sat up and began to reel in the fish. The fish was having none of it. It pulled and bucked and began to tow the canoe.

'Hang on,' Jim braced himself as they were pulled across the lake. Crispin sat back and watched the show. At least he didn't need to paddle.

The canoe was ferried to the other side of the water and they slowed.

'He's tired, I think I've got him.'

'Let it go Jim.'

'Yeah, I guess that's the plan. Would've been a monster though, don't you think?'

'Yeah, a monster.'

Jim reeled in the line and cut it.

'Ya know, Stitt. I like you.'

They drifted around a headland and Crispin sat up. He looked into the distance.

'Jim.'

'Yep?'

'What's that?' Crispin pointed to a mirage in the distance.

'That's Block 67.'

'Block 67?'

'Yeah. A sort of town. Got a shop, a petrol station and some crusty old fellas.'

'A town.' The word was said with reverence. To Crispin, it looked like the shining metropolis.

'Can we go?'

'We got everything we need. Don't need to go.'

'We could get beer?' Crispin was ready to become an alcoholic to get to the bright lights.

'I got something that will knock your socks off. I've been experimenting with a little recipe of my own. You're gonna love it, Stitt.'

'Oh.'

'How about toilet paper?'

'Nah, got it.'

'Matches?'

'Nope.'

'Toothpaste?'

'Nup.'

'Perhaps we should ring home, just to make sure everything's alright.'

'Relax Stitt. We're in paradise. Now, just paddle us back and we'll have a bit of my secret recipe with some sausages and eggs. Sounds bloody perfect, if you ask me. Bloody perfect.'

Crispin paddled back to the boardwalk, his mood darkening with every dip of his blade. He felt he was practically a hostage. Jim had lured him under false pretences. Jim hadn't explained what was required. Jim had led him astray. Jim was confining him to quarters, and it wasn't fair.

Eight

By the time the canoe reached the boardwalk Stitt had worked himself up into a temper. He pouted. He stuck out his bottom lip. Just Jim breathing annoyed him.

Jim, ever the eternal optimist sprang into action. He hoped out and waited for Stitt to stop sulking.

'Take it easy Stitt. I'll get things sorted.' Didn't the man ever have an off day? Crispin tried to pull a face, but as his sunburn had made his skin two sizes too small for his face, it didn't come off as planned. He harrumped out of the canoe and dashed for solid ground, only stopping to retrieve one Italian loafer that had popped up for air.

Jim whistled as he hauled the canoe to firm ground. He hummed a little ditty as he stowed the rods and washtub. He sang a libretto while completing his tasks.

'Hey Stitt,' Jim called. 'Whaddya say we fill this thing up and have a bath? Nothing like a bath to end a perfect day.'

'Together?' Crispin thought their friendship would be stretched to the limit. 'We're not in Norway, you know,' he mumbled under his breath.

'You go first. I'll get the hose connection I made. The latest thing in a Y valve. Works a treat. The girls liked the laundry tub, but I reckon the canoe's the ticket. Whaddya say, Stitt?'

'Alright.' How could you stay angry with the man? He was trying his best.

'Tell ya what. I'll get the laundry trough and we can watch the sun go down.'

'Fine.' Crispin sat in the hut, trying not to move his skin as Jim busied himself. Sunburn is one of those things that makes your skin crawl, eventually crawling right off your back or nose in sheets. It is itchy, painful, and around 5 pm when the sun goes down, it gets pretty darn hot. Crispin poked his head out once or twice to see how things were progressing, then perched on the edge of the bed.

'Won't be long.' Jim gambolled about the place.'You ready Stitt?'

Crispin stepped out wearing a silk dressing gown, a towel over his arm and carrying his sponge bag.

'Swanky.' Jim whistled.

'Amanda bought it for me.' Crispin looked at the water in the canoe. It beckoned him with its coolness, its small concession to civility in the wilds of Borneo—well outback Australia, but Borneo was how Crispin felt.

'You get settled, Stitt. I'll just get something to drink.'

'Look Jim, about the'

'Nothing to it, Stitt. Writing a book and all that, a man needs to unwind a bit. Don't you reckon?'

'Yes.'

'Start unwinding, Stitt.'

'Righto.' Jim left, and Stitt let his gown slip from his shoulders and then sank into the cool bliss. He went under and surfaced with a sigh, then squeezed his lilac shampoo into the bath and agitated it into a froth.

'Drink?'

'Don't mind if I do.'

The men settled into their bubble baths and sipped Jim's special brew that tasted like rubbing alcohol.

'Life is what you make it, Stitt.'

'Yes.' Crispin took a slug of rubbing alcohol and looked at life through the lens of 70% proof and bubble bath.

'You know Jim, I think Hemingway often had a bath in the bush.'

'A friend of yours, is he?'

It might have been a cringeworthy moment in different circumstances. Crispin smiled.

'No, just a fellow I read about once.'

'Sounds like my kinda guy.'

'Yes, I think you'd like him.' Crispin breathed deeply and swallowed a fly. He coughed it up and set the little fellow on his way, his cup of human kindness overflowing with something stronger than milk. His mood lightened with every drink as the two watched the sun slowly sink below the canopy of trees.

'Ever think about having little 'uns Stitt?'

Amanda had toyed with the idea, but she didn't think she was ready to look after *another* child, she had said.

'Yes, I'd like a bunch,' Crispin said.

'Best thing in the world, I'm telling you. Being a father is just great. Well, except for the wedding. That's for the women. I don't know my table settings from my cake decorations. Jeanie's a whizz with all that.'

'You're a lucky man.'

'You betcha. I'm the luckiest man alive.' Jim poured a drink. 'You know, when you get around to having kids, have lots.'

'I'll do that.'

'Let's drink to it.'

The men clinked aluminium picnic cups and sat back in their baths. The first mosquito bite made Crispin sit up.

'Never bother me. Don't know why.' Jim stood up and wrapped a towel around his nether regions. 'I'll get some tucker happening. You know Stitt, I like you.'

'Thanks.'

'Jeanie says there aren't many men like you.'

'Does she?' Crispin slapped his forehead.

'Yeah. She said you're certainly something different.'

'Really?'

'Ya know if ya rub some of that stuff on they might leave you alone.'

Jim disappeared into the hut whistling a happy tune. Crispin looked at the bottle of special brew.

'In for a penny, in for a pound.' He dashed alcohol liberally over his exposed parts. It stung like hell, but miraculously it worked. Apparently, even mosquitoes have standards.

As he sat in the soft evening glow he thought on his life. He had an ordinary upbringing. His parents were very ordinary. He hadn't excelled at anything. It wasn't the writer's curriculum vitae that seemed to be a necessity. His family wasn't even dirt poor.

How was a chap supposed to write the definitive novel if he didn't have any angst?

He stood up, doused himself in alcohol, cinched his silk robe around his waist, then strolled into the hut. Amanda's voice came out of the ether.

'You're not Noel Coward, you know.' Hang it all. Why was she such a a.

'Grubs up.' Jim interrupted the train of thought.

Crispin scratched his arm and pulled his sleeves down.

'Are they still bitin'?' Jim rubbed some more alcohol over Crispin's face. It stung the previous night's feeding frenzy, but it worked as a repellent.

'I wonder if I could bottle it?'

'That sounds like a good idea.'

And as with every drunk the world has ever known, everything soon becomes hilarious.

'Bottle it!' had them laughing until their faces ached.

'Patent it!' was a riot.

'Make a fortune,' had Crispin rolling on the bunk bed in stitches. Another bottle was opened and drunk.

'Don't mind if I do,' Crispin said and Jim was left in hysterics, wiping the tears from his eyes.

'Wanna sausage?' They ate, giggling at the tomato sauce and counting the beans on their plate.

'Wanna biscuit? Gloria made 'em.' Jim looked at the tin of biscuits his youngest daughter had baked.

'Gloria made them,' Crispin tittered, but the mood had broken, like the biscuits.

Drunks can go from madcap to maudlin in one drink.

'They're the best,' Jim munched.

'I love them too,' Crispin said, eating a broken piece.

'I know you do mate, I know it.'

'I love 'em to bits Jim.'

'Me too, and I'm their father.'

'I know you are.'

The men drowned their sorrows with biscuit crumbs and special brew/insect repellent.

'You know Jim, my wife hates me.'

'Never.'

'It's true. She loathes me.'

'No Stitt. I don't believe it.' The men were going through the various stages of a bender.

Merry, maudlin, and now melodramatic.

'She said I should drop dead.'

'She didn't?'

'She did.'

'And did you?' Jim slid to the floor.

'No. Although it was a close-run thing I can tell you.'

'I bet it was.'

A quiet reverie enveloped the hut as the mosquitoes buzzed, the bush rustled and cracked and the curlew screamed its nightly terrors.

'You know what Stitt. I'll tell you something.'

'What?'

'I wouldn't be dead for quids.'

'Me neither Jim. Me neither.'

Jim dunked a biscuit in his brew and went to the last stage of alcohol poisoning in quite blissful unconsciousness. Crispin went not with a bang, but a whimper.

Drinking practically non-stop for a week is bound to take its toll. Topping it off with a two-day bender in the bush is akin to becoming a Kamikaze pilot. There is just so much punishment the liver can take before it lets its owner know if he doesn't stop, the liver will.

Crispin was wallowing in alcohol. He was pickled, inside and out.

He woke up slumped half in-half out of his bunk and his stomach hurt, or as near to his stomach as his liver would get. The hut reverberated with a loud moan. Jim stirred on the floor and crawled to his bed, then went into a coma.

Crispin moaned a bit more and decided the next best thing would be some Alka-Selzer. It was kept in the bathroom cabinet. He slithered to the floor and tried to work out just where the bathroom might be. It hadn't occurred to him quite yet that he wasn't at home.

'Amanda,' he bleated. There was no reply.

With careful tread, he made his way to the door and pushed. Reality was still about fourteen hours away for Stitt. He felt his way outside looking for a hall light switch on the wall and tripped in the dark. It was an unsteady walk to the bathroom of his dreams, all the while clutching his stomach. You could almost hear his liver saying, 'I warned you, Stitt,' as it gave a wretched cramp and made Stitt yelp in discomfort. He doubled over and threw up.

Crawling over the leaf litter he found the canoe and for a fleeting moment a ray of clarity shone through. The best thing for a stomach upset is Alka-Seltzer, and he knew where the shop was located.

The canoe was hauled down the track, launched in the mud, and Stitt climbed in.

'Alka-Seltzer,' were the last words on his lips for about fourteen hours.

📖

Sometime around one o'clock, Crispin opened his eyes to bright sunshine winking at him through a canopy of leaves. He closed his eyes and sunlight filtered through his eyelids, reminding him he was still alive.

He wished he was dead.

His head ached, his stomach ached. and he thought he might have lost his tongue. A quick feel around his mouth, he touched something resembling a dried sea cucumber, which made him think of his trip to Japan in the heady days when he was the darling of the literary scene. He moaned and tried to bring some life back into his mouth.

What I need is a drink, he thought. The mention of drink made him whimper and clutch his head, then his stomach, then his head again. His liver said, 'What did I tell you!'

'Amanda,' Stitt yelled and tried to roll over. The sudden realisation that he was in a canoe on the water did nothing to alleviate his pain In fact, it added to the whole thing so much Crispin kept his eyes shut. And it wasn't long before he drifted once again into toxic shock with a little alcoholic poisoning on the side. Things like that are bound to happen when you drink insect repellent and then eat salt thinking its antacid.

He woke up and contemplated joining the human

race. He didn't exactly feel human, not just yet, so he lay in abject misery for another long doleful hour. Although it wouldn't be the longest hour of his life, it felt like it.

It took the laughter of a kookaburra to bring Crispin back to the land of the living. To him, it sounded like the laugh of ridicule. He cautiously opened one eye at a time and stared at the canopy of leaves. He felt his face and rubbed the growing stubble on his chin. Amanda said he was the hairiest man she'd ever know. He could grow hair overnight and sometimes shaved twice a day. He had once thought to let himself go and cultivate the 'he man' look. Hemingway had that look, but then the upkeep of a beard was too much. Everything he ate ended up all over his face. He tried a Clark Gable moustache for a little while, but Amanda only laughed. Now, without trying, he was growing something that Wild Bill Hickok would be proud to own.

The kookaburra resumed its torrent of abuse as Crispin surfaced into the late afternoon. The canoe rocked, and he grabbed the sides for support.

Some people when surprised are struck dumb, literally and figuratively. Crispin wasn't one of those people. He let out a howl that had the kookaburra launching into the sky, the lizards scurrying for cover, and the ants high tailing it home.

The plaintive cry of a man out of his comfort zone reverberated through the Australian bush.

There was no reply.

Crispin sat up and looked at his surrounding for the first time.

'Hello,' he yelled.

'Jim,' he called.

Silence.

'Help.' The cry sounded a little pathetic. Even Crispin thought he could do better. He cupped his hands to his mouth.

'HELP!'

Silence.

All he could hear with any certainty was the thump of his pulse as it raced around his head. A fly buzzed into his nose and upset the status quo no end. Crispin tried to dislodge the little explorer and set the canoe rocking once again. It swayed precariously, slopped water over the sides, and then began to sink.

Quick thinking was never one of Crispin's strong points. He sat as water, which was supposed to stay on the outside, was now on the inside. Although a rippa of an idea, as Jim said, a folding canoe has a couple of design flaws. The seams were only good for a few bends and stretches. They were now opening like a wet paper bag.

Trying to bail was a useless task, one that Crispin soon abandoned just before he abandoned ship.

Stepping into the unknown can be exhilarating or terrifying. Crispin plopped, clutched, fumbled and fell into the water to take up the Australian crawl. He went face first into the muddy water. It wasn't long before he found he could stand waist deep. What his bare feet touched had him jumping and screaming. It might have been funny if it didn't look ridiculous. Here was a grown man in a silk dressing gown with an almighty hangover, a sunburnt, mosquito bitten, dirty face screaming like an extra in an Alfred Hitchcock movie.

The mud oozed between his toes as he scrambled for the bank. Once on solid ground he turned to see the canoe slide gracefully under the water, never to be seen again.

Still, the enormity of the situation didn't ring an alarm bell in Crispin's brain. He sat on the ground and looked at the water, only to jump up when he was being bitten by ants.

'Help,' he whimpered. 'Help.'

Crispin stood on a small patch of green batting away flies, shooing ants and gave it one more try.

'Help.'

The kookaburra laughed.

After a bit of a whine, whinge and a few choice swear words Crispin got his brain cells into some sort of order. He took a deep breath, put on his man pants and looked rationally at his predicament. It wasn't exactly a rosy situation. He hadn't a clue where he was in relation to Jim's Shangri-La. He didn't have a canoe, or shoes, or clothes. Noel Coward was never caught out with just a dressing gown.

'Right Stitt,' Crispin began to give himself a stern talking to, but it didn't seem work. He felt his situation hopeless.

'You can't just sit here all day.' He thought he might sit. It was preferable to walking into the bush with flies, prickles, nasty things that could sting, bite, scratch, itch and eat authors for dinner. Someone would be sure to come and get him. He was missing, after all. If he just sat still, they would find him. His mother often said,

'Don't go gallivanting off. I want to know where you are.'

'Jim will find me. He knows about these things,' Crispin said to himself.

'Jim,' he yelled although to the untrained ear it sounded more like a two-year-old when their icecream drops on the ground.

'A search party,' he said to himself. 'They will send a search party. Dogs, helicopters, all that sort of palaver.' It was a small comforting thought. He added to the scenario with photographs of the rescue, an ambulance interview, perhaps a spot on television. The ego is an amazingly resilient piece of apparatus. Crispin's came in the extra-large variety.

As the shadows lengthened, Stitt still didn't have any bright ideas. A powerful thirst motivated him to move. With measured steps he tip-toed to the water's edge and looked at the brown water. It didn't look inviting. Little wriggly things danced around the edges, and who knows what unseen germs it held? He dipped his finger in the little pool and licked.

'Tastes ok,' he said. He cupped his hands and drank. His tongue came to life, and it wasn't long before caution was thrown to the wind and Crispin was gulping water like a camel after a hard three days in the Sahara Desert. His head stopped thumping and his mouth felt almost back to normal.

His thirst sated, Crispin looked up and studied his surroundings. It didn't look good.

'Hello.' It came out as a cry in the wilderness, one of many he would have in the near future. His stomach gave a rumble, just to remind him it was still around and expected food. He looked at his spare tyre sitting above his underwear. He wobbled it, weighing it in his hands. At a pinch, it would sustain him for a day or two. A doctor might have said, if push came to shove, it would feed a family for a month.

'What would Hemingway do?' He thought Ernest might pull out a whisky bottle and a pocket knife and get on with the evening meal. All Crispin had was a silk dressing gown and some rather expensive underwear.

There comes a time, so the psychologists say, when one needs to step up, fill out their man card and get on with it. Crispin took a very, very deep breath, let it out as a sigh and tied his dressing down a little tighter.

'Right.'

He knew the sun set in the west, only because he'd written it into his new manuscript. The sun obliged and began to dip. With a bit of boy scout knowhow, he deduced where north and south might be and drew out the cardinal points on the ground. He'd only been a boy scout for a few weeks—his mother thought the whole notion a bit too rough and tumble for a sensitive soul like Crispin. He had handed in his toggle with gladness. The scouts resembled the zoo more than dib, dib, dob.

Once he'd got his bearings, it was time to have a think. If he followed the shoreline, he'd be bound to find Jim's boardwalk sooner or later. It wasn't much of a plan, but it was all he had. Tomorrow, after a bit of a rest, he'd tackle the trek.

The sun dipped below the tree line. The mosquitoes come out to play and Crispin thought the safest place to sleep might be in a tree. He'd read in the National Geographic big cats do it in Africa. They ought to know something.

He climbed up a gum tree and wedged himself into a crook, tied himself to a branch with his dressing gown cord, covered himself as much as he could, and hoped he'd have about six pints of blood left by morning. He tried to get to sleep.

The brackish water had other ideas.

Words like hellish, horrendous and hideous flitted through Stitt's mind as he squatted not far from his tree. As dawn broke he wondered if he still had his lower intestine or had it been expelled sometime in the night and lay dying in the bush. He didn't want to look. And having a bare bottom half the night is just like sending out an invitation to every blood sucking creature that roamed the earth. Crispin was sure those creatures had taken up the offer, had their fill and left their calling card. He lay on some leaves and tenderly touched his arse. It felt like popcorn, all lumpy and hot. If he had the energy, he might have cried. As it stood, he was wrung out and blamed his misfortune on every person he'd ever met.

'Help,' he squeaked, and pulled up his underwear.

If he'd been in better spirits, he might have enjoyed the moment when the Australian bush wakes up at dawn. There is a crispness to the air, the birds begin their chorus and things are on the move.

The trees look majestic, their canopy catching the first golden rays, small droplets glisten, and it's good to feel alive. Crispin missed it all.

'I wish I was dead,' he moaned, groaned and rolled over onto his back.

It was only when the sun hit his face that the poor man roused himself and sat up.

'Follow the shoreline,' he said.

And so he did.

It wasn't easy. There was a fair bit of swearing, cursing, and stepping on things that hurt. But as the air warmed, Crispin sweated, and got the hang of avoiding prickle patches, ant nests, boggy ground and something that looked like it would bring you out in a rash. He made slow, thirsty progress. By late morning, he was gasping for a drink, a rest, a cigarette and food. When you have been married to the fridge for about a year and your stomach has become accustomed to the ritual, going without is a shock. Nicotine withdrawal is like a hot knife through your eyeball. Stitt's face gained a tick (not the bush tic, but a twitch). He sat on a log and looked at the lake. All that water. He licked his lips and massaged his growing headache. Perhaps, if I drank from the deeper water, it would be alright, he thought. Getting to deeper water would be the issue.

Armed with a stick, he poked the mud and waded into the lake. It was while standing chest deep something brushed past his leg and he screamed, losing his footing. He went underwater, taking a drink being the last thing on his mind. As he popped up for air, he turned, and if ever a man was grateful for 20/20 vision, he was that man.

In the distance, he saw a thin column of smoke and a building.

'Hey, hey!' he yelled and jumped up and down. Nothing happened. What looks like perhaps half a mile as the crow flies when you are desperate can be more like three miles as the crow flies. Crispin was desperate.

He began to swim. He was never any good at all those physical activities others enjoyed. Golf, chasing a little ball around in designer sweaters and getting a cool drink at the bar after—was more his line. He stopped splashing about and made a dash for the shore. He would need to walk.

Three miles as the crow flies was about eight around the lake. Motivated, he hiked through the day and as the sun dipped for the second day, Crispin sat down on a sandy patch near the water and listened to his stomach gurgle and churn. He grabbed his spare tyre and gave it a pinch. Surely it was getting smaller. He convinced himself he was practically wasting away. If they didn't find him soon, he'd be wafer thin.

'They will be looking for me. Jim would raise the alarm. People would be out and about.' It was a heartening thought. Much better than "Stitt, Stitt who?"

He drifted off to sleep imagining the headlines.

Author Lost in Bush.

Famous Author Found at Last.

Best-selling, Award-Winning Author has Harrowing Experience in the Bush.

World in Shock as Crispin Stitt is Missing.

They all had merit.

The warm sand was comforting and for one wonderful moment Crispin thought he was at home, in bed and he could smell coffee brewing. He rolled over and his face hit a stone. Something like that is a wake-up call.

Stitt sat up, yawned, inhaled a fly, swallowed it as pragmatism took hold and greeted the day.

'Help,' he said half-heartedly.

Where was the search party? Why didn't they have helicopters? 'Didn't anyone miss me?'

Crispin wallowed in self-pity. His stomach felt the same way. He bit his fingernails and looked at his belly fat. From where he was sitting, it looked to be shrinking. He gave it a familiar pat.

'At least it's keeping me alive,' he mused. Taking stock of his body, he studied his legs. They were bitten to pieces, red welts you'd be hard pressed to put a pin between festooned every bit of skin. Moving onto his feet, they were bruised and swollen. His bottom was sore, bitten, and itchy. His arms weren't much better. It was a good thing he couldn't see his face. Pock marked, sunburnt, bruised and a good candidate for the creature of the Black Lagoon. His beard was growing, and he had somehow collected a split lip in his travels.

Wading into the water, he decided to freshen up. If he was going to meet his public and probably the press, it was the sensible option. With his ablutions out of the way, Crispin took up the trek to civilization once again.

All was going well until the inevitable happened. The Australian bush is renowned for this type of thing. Crispin forgot to scream as a snake, disturbed from its morning duty slithered over his foot and hurried away. If he'd had anything left in his bowel it would have made a dash for fresh air. Some people have an aversion to reptiles. It's just in their blood. Crispin gave a shudder that came from the very depths of his core. He took his stick and carefully beat the ground as he trudged through the bush, the encounter never far from his mind.

It was slow progress. Although Crispin was living off his extravagant lifestyle cleverly disguised as a lump of lard around his midriff, he felt weak, faint and nauseous. Several times he stopped, just to listen to his stomach protesting. He began to daydream about sandwiches with an olive for decoration. Boiled eggs swam through his delusions, toast and roast lamb crowded his mind.

Having been a child of the war years, his psyche was attuned to food. Any sort, any amount. His father said it was unnatural to be thinking of food every waking hour. His mother gave him some small indulgences when she could.

Now the thought of food was driving Stitt mad. He tried to think of something else. It didn't work. Amanda's face was superimposed with a cream bun, his house was a trifle with a cherry on top, his golf club's sticks of celery poking out of a bloody Mary.

'Get a grip Stitt,' Crispin said to himself and slapped his cheek, hard. He picked a leaf and chewed. It didn't taste like a biscuit or a Christmas pudding.

A line of ants made their industrious way across his path. He watched them bring food back to their nest. It was a never-ending task and he thought of Amanda shopping. She was always inventive in the kitchen, making delicious things.

'For you, darling,' she'd said when they were newly married.

She still had a talent in the kitchen and tempted him with all manner of dishes. Crispin gave his flabby middle a poke.

'She did this,' he said. 'She tried to kill me with my knife and fork.'

People survived in the wild all the time. Cave men had been doing it for years. Stitt looked at his surroundings. If he was looking for an entrée he would not find it. He poked at the ground and nothing popped up like the vending machines at the train station.

His pace slowed to museum walking, then it fell down a notch to a dawdle. He spied a tree with reddish berries. The birds were eating them and not dropping dead. It was sound reasoning as far as Crispin was concerned. He picked a few and popped them in his mouth. They were sour, hard little specimens. He swallowed them whole. They might stave off his hunger for a few hours. He ate several handfuls and stood about, wondering how his life had come to this. In his state of mind, it must be someone else's fault.

'Hellooooooo,' Crispin's pathetic cry was a small last-ditch effort. He sat down on a tuft of grass and doodled in the dirt with his stick.

'A mirage,' he told himself. 'It was just my imagination playing cruel tricks. There is no town. Curse you,' he said to the trees, the sky, the insects. He picked at his feet. They were dirty, puffy, prickle infested specimens. He closed his eyes and dreamed of a turkey sandwich with pickle and a cold beer on the side. Amanda made an American pickle, her mother's recipe, which always reminded him of Christmas. She said she made it just for him because she loved him. She said she was trying to get him motivated when she slung small insults his way. She said she married him because he was so funny, so vivacious, so handsome.

'Amanda,' Crispin bleated. 'I love you.'

He sat and picked at his sunburn, which was coming off in sheets. It's one of those activities that can become quite absorbing. It's so satisfying getting a good run of skin. He was peeling, the ants taking the detritus away, and maybe hoping to renew himself with a new skin, figuratively and literally.

Floundering in self-pity is good for at least twenty minutes, forty if you push it. Crispin's time was almost up when he opened his eyes and sniffed the air. He caught a whiff of tobacco.

What he wouldn't do for a cigarette! He slapped himself, trying to dispel the fiction of wishful thinking. He stood up and gave his nostrils a workout. It was definitely tobacco.

The thought of meeting one's rescuers in your underwear had Crispin tightening his belt, running his fingers through his hair and generally making himself presentable.

'Hello,' he shouted into the bush. 'I'm over here.' He stood still and waited.

Nothing.

He didn't exactly have the nose of a beagle; Amanda said it often too far in the air, but Crispin tried to deduce the direction of the scent.

He needed to get to town that-a-way, only the

smell—as far as he could ascertain—was from "t-other-way", as his father often said.

'Help, help,' he blundered into the scrub forgetting plan A- the lakeshore, plan B- the town, and walked into the bush following his nose.

A well-concealed bark hut is hard to find. Crispin walked right past it, then turned and took another look. To a desperate man, it looked like the Taj Mahal. (forgetting that the Taj was built to honour the dead). He rushed up to the wall and walked around the perimeter until he found a door and tumbled inside.

'Hello, anybody, somebody.'

The place was one room, and it was empty.

A stronger man might have sat down and had a think. Crispin sat down and had a cry. Whether it was from despair or relief, he couldn't tell you, but he blubbered for about twenty minutes. His self-pity exhausted, he sniffed and looked around. The place had been inhabited.

He found a pair of trousers and a shirt and immediately put them on. They were a little on the tight side, but anything was better than a dressing gown, which now was the worse for wear.

The place was furnished with the chair he was sitting on, a bed, and what looked like a bottle factory. Some of the bottles were full. A thirsty man is a frantic man. Crispin rushed the bottles, popped a cork, took a sniff and then a swig. It was, euphemistically called an alcoholic beverage. He drank like a recovering alcoholic, a theme that had run through his life for about as long as it takes to write a novel.

It didn't take long before his stomach wanted

some of the action and food was a priority. The place was devoid of shelves or cupboards, but had what looked like an old meat safe hanging from the rafter.

'Please, please,' Crispin stood on the chair and opened the door.

Coming face to face with a snake, any type of snake, while standing on a chair hoping for a bacon sandwich, can be a bit of a shock. Crispin screamed, fell, hit his head on the end of the iron bedstead and party time was over. The lights went out.

Nine

Concussion, alcohol poisoning, dubious native flora and dehydration can knock you out for quite a while. Crispin opened his eyes to see a rugged face staring at him. The face smiled revealing one tooth and halitosis that might be considered an offensive weapon. Stitt cringed and groaned.

'Easy fella.'

The lump on Crispin's head throbbed.

'Am I saved?'

'Not yet mate, but I'm workin' on it.'

'Thank God.'

'You got that right.'

Len Gillespie, Gilly to his friends if he had any, was a man of convictions, judicial and moral. He was one of those blokes that once you put an idea into his head, it usually stayed there. The Chaplin at Pentridge gaol had suggested Len confine himself to doing the work of God rather than the devil. Len thought on that piece of advice and took it to heart.

'Steady there.' He helped Crispin to sit.

'Snake,' Crispin yelped as the memory came back to haunt him.

'Easy does it.' Len patted Crispin on the shoulder. 'You been at me special.'

'Special?'

Len hoiked his head in the direction of the bottles.

'Me special. Powerful stuff. I make it out back.' Len grinned and put his finger to his lips.

'Sorry, I had a thirst,' Crispin said.

'Ya can lead a horse to water, but he ain't burnt his bridges just yet.' Len smiled.

'What?' Crispin cringed at the mixed metaphor and wondered if the man was delirious. He certainly knew how to mangle the English idiom.

'That's alright son. We all get a thirst at some time in life. It's a mighty powerful urge.'

'No, I mean I was thirsty.'

'Yeah, I get thirsty too.' Len grinned and his halitosis washed over Crispin, giving his stomach a hard time keeping anything down. Stitt swallowed, and then swallowed again.

'I reckon you found ol' Len for a reason. One man's day is another man's dollar.'

Crispin winced as if he'd been hit with a thesaurus.

'Pardon?' Crispin was having a hard time keeping up. He licked his lips. 'I was lost, you see, and-'

Len took up Crispin's story, 'I know mate, but I found you and that's what I call luck. Don't ya reckon. It's lucky for you, lucky for me, lucky for bloody everyone.' Len threw his arms wide and smiled at all the "other" people in the room.

Crispin rubbed his eyes to get rid of the grand delusion, for he was sure he was hallucinating. He pinched himself to join the real world. Even though he had knocked himself senseless he found the man a bit disconcerting, never mind his dental hygiene. He looked his saviour over. He had a face only a mother could love, as the saying goes. With one tooth, one glass eye, and pock scars all over, he didn't instil confidence.

'Now, let's get you up and sittin'.' Crispin was pulled up and sat on the bed.

'Do you have anything to eat?'

'I got a bit of jerky. Do ya like jerky?' Len pulled a bit of dried meat from his trouser pocket. Crispin would have eaten shoe leather if it was offered. The jerky wasn't too far off the mark.

'Ya got ta chew it. I suck it like this on account of I got no teeth.' Len put the piece in his mouth and gave it a suck, then offered it to Stitt.

How hungry does a man need to be before he lowers his standards to take the food from another man's mouth, a mouth with only one tooth and wicked bad breath? There was a moment's indecision, then Crispin took the jerky and popped it in his mouth like he was eating one of Amanda's macaroons. He tried to chew, but with not much spit ,it was hard going.

'Nice, eh?'

'Mmmm.' Crispin swallowed and sucked his teeth.

'I make it meself. Possum.'

'Possum?'

'Yeah, kangaroos too hard to catch,' Len bounded around the hut like a kangaroo, emitting a manic laugh. The laugh sent a shiver up Crispin's spine. He could see the scenario. Killed in the bush by a one-eyed maniac with one tooth, his body never to be found. Amanda calling off the search. An empty coffin.

'Ya know,' Len said with his hands on his hips, looking at Stitt, 'I got a pair of trousers like them.'

Len pointed to the purloined pair.

'Really.'

'Yep. An' a shirt like that, too.'

'Amazing.' Crispin was getting the measure of Len.

'I'm Len. Leonard Gillespie.' He held out his hand. 'An' I know who you are.'

'Really?' Crispin wondered if his plight had reached far and wide, or perhaps Leonard was a reader.

'Yep, I know all about ya.'

'Well, that's just great.'

'You betcha,' Len slapped Crispin on the back. 'Ain't it the truth, and the truth is stranger than diction.'

Crispin winced at the mispronunciation and offered, 'Fiction.'

'What?'

'The truth,' Crispin said.

'You got that right.' Len nodded and grinned.

The grin from Len Gillespie had Crispin looking for plan C and an escape the first chance he got.

📖

Len packed up his burlap bag with a few bottles of Special while Crispin watched.

'So, Len, tell me. Where do you live?'

'In town.'

'And are you going back to town now?'

'Yep.' Len tied the string on his bag and hoisted it on his back. 'You ready?'

'I certainly am.' Crispin stood up, hitched his trousers, and put on an eager face.

'Where's ya shoes?'

'I don't have any.'

'Suit ya self.' Len walked out of the hut, closely followed by Crispin.

'What's the town called Len?' Stitt jogged to keep up.

'You know it as well as I do. Ya can't trick me like that.'

'No, I didn't think I could.' Stitt played along. 'You're a clever one Len, aren't you?'

'Ain't it the truth.'

'So, tell me, Len, who am I?'

'Ya want me to come right out and say it don't ya?'

'Yes.' Crispin caught up and matched Len stride for stride.

'Well. I reckon you're one of them wayward souls ya hear about. I found ya and I'm gonna save ya.'

'Right.'

They walked in silence for a while, each digesting the revelation.

'Len?'

'Yup?'

'What do you mean, save me?' The man was infuriatingly vague.

'Now I know ya got things planned for me. I kinda figured it out.'

'Did you?'

'Not talking to you, young fella, I'm just talking to Him.'

'Him?'

Len pointed to the sky. 'Him.'

'Oh.' Crispin nodded and trotted along.

Ain't it the truth.' They turned from the track

and Crispin saw an old tin shed. Across the lintel someone had painted IS C.R.A.P

'Here we are,' Len said. 'Home is where the rolling stones gather.'

'Pardon?' Crispin cringed at the malaphor. If there was one thing he prided himself on, it was his command of the language. This man was an affront to all that Crispin held dear.

'Home is where the rolling stones gather. Ya a bit deaf, eh?' Len put his hands on his hips and looked up at the tin shed.

'Where?'

'The Institute of salvation of children, rogues, aborigines and people.' Len stood back to admire the building made of corrugated iron sheets.

'People?'

'Mmmm.' Len nodded and made a face.

'Who exactly Len?'

'Them.' He beckoned Crispin to follow. They crept around the front of the building and Crispin saw Block 67 in all its glory.

'Them,' Len pointed to the petrol station/post office and a woman filling a drum with water from a hose.

'You mean women?'

'Them.' It was as far as Len would go in naming the she-devils. In his opinion, and that was the only opinion that mattered to Leonard in Block 67, the other fifty percent of the population were a blight, a bane, poison and the scourge of the world. He hated them with a passion.

'But you don't hate them, do you?'

'Every last one.'

'Why include them?'

'I'm charitable. I'm all for salvation. I can help 'em, but I don't need to like 'em. A scourge on humanity, if you ask me.' No-one ever would ask Len. He was the sort of bloke one crosses to the other side of the street rather than meet. His reputation in Block 67 was summed up with one nomenclature, Nutjob.

Crispin thought on Len's words. Women hadn't done him any favours. His mother had cossetted him to the point he was pretty much useless at doing anything, save colour co-ordination. His wife wished he was dead. His publisher felt nothing but contempt. His editor thought he was useless. His agent, well, she was only young. Plenty of time for her to mature into a she-devil. He was inclined to agree with Len.

Crispin looked at the petrol station. It was civilization. He could be rescued; he'd be back in the city in a couple of hours, and all this could be a memory. But something niggled him. Maybe, just maybe, those women in his life needed to be taught a lesson. What if he just fell off the earth for a bit? They would soon see he was part of their lives. They would miss him. It was a deliciously wicked scheme.

'Len?'

'Yup?'

'Can I stay with you? Just for a bit.'

'Countin' on it.' Len spat on the ground and Crispin jumped out of the way.

'Come on. I reckon we could do with a feed.'

Crispin hadn't heard such a beautiful word in what felt like a lifetime. He glanced at the petrol station. It was just across the road. He could get 'rescued' any time he wanted.

In the meantime, he could concoct a believable story. A spell of amnesia might work. Plan D had all the hallmarks of a devilish plot. He turned and followed Len to the Institute door, his moral compass not working in such close quarters.

The tin shed, aka The Institute for Salvation of C.R.A.P, held a bed, a camp bed, and a small kitchenette.

'Dunny is out back,' Len said and set down his sack, then deposited the Special brew under his bed. 'It's medicine.' He gave a cheeky grin. 'Make yourself at home,' Len pointed to the camp cot.

'Thanks.' Crispin sat down and picked a prickle from his toe.

'Ya know, I never saved anyone before.'

'No?'

'Nah. But I'm ready for it. First, I reckon we need a bit of somethin' to get us going.'

The thought of a session with the Special brew brought tears to Crispin's eyes. He felt his binge drinking days were behind him. His liver breathed a sigh of relief when Len pulled out a few eggs and began to light the camping stove. Some bread appeared. Len picked at the mouldy bits and it was chucked in the pan with a lump of lard. The crackle and spat were the most delicious sound Crispin thought he'd ever heard. He drooled as the smell of fried eggs wafted through the shed.

'I can't get me choppers around hard stuff,' Len grinned his one-tooth grin and served. The sight of food made Stitt want to dive on his portion like a seagull on chips. He licked his lips.

'Do ya wanna say a few words?'

'Please,' Crispin offered, and held his enthusiasm in check.

'Well, I'll 'ave a crack then.' Len said something like grace and took up a spoon.

'I only got the one.' He held the spoon aloft. 'Ya can have it after me.'

If you've eaten jerky that's been through halitosis hell, sharing a spoon is a piece of cake. Crispin watched every mouthful make its way to Len's mouth and gritted his teeth while he waited.

Len, he thought, might be as nutty as a fruitcake, and a man who had a hard time with a metaphor, but he was a decent human being. A person who might put a narcissist to shame. The salt of the earth. That thought led Crispin to his neighbour, Jim Broker. Jim would be frantic. He'd be wringing his hands in guilt at losing his friend. He'd be distraught. Crispin looked at the door and knew that rescue was just a few steps away.

'What's ya name?' Len asked as he polished the spoon on his shirt to hand to Crispin.

'My name?'

'Yeah. Only if ya wanna tell me. I know some blokes don't like to go by their real names. I met 'em you know.'

'Hmmm.' Crispin shovelled his eggs into his mouth.

'Light fingers Louis. Killer Stan, Muggsy Malloy and Animal.' Len shuddered at the last name. 'They weren't their real names you see. Sort of made up, if you know what I mean.'

'It's... it's Ernest. Crispin said, wiping his plate clean with his finger.

'Ernest,' Len said, trying it out. 'I like it. Ernest.'

'Ernest Hemm... Hemsworth,' Crispin said and rubbed his growing beard. What made him give an alias he couldn't say. It is not often one can be called a liar and a narcissist in the same breath, but Crispin was on the right track.

'That was fantastic, Len.' Crispin sat back. 'You wouldn't have a smoke, would you?'

'Sure.' Len handed over some tobacco and a papers. 'Nothin' like a smoke after a feed, eh?'

'Nothin' like it,' Crispin rolled a less than perfect cigarette and lit up.

'So, Ernest. I'm not gonna pry, but a man always has a story to tell. I reckon we found each other for a reason.' Len pointed to the roof of the tin shed.

'Pardon?'

'You know. Him. He works in them mysterious ways.'

'Oh. Him.' Crispin looked at the ceiling.

'Yeah.' Len grinned.

'What's your story Len?' Crispin was feeling a bit chipper with food and a smoke. He recalled an article he'd read about drawing on real characters for the art of writing. Perhaps he could draw on Len. He was certainly a character. For a fleeting moment Crispin thought it might not be all about him, but that fleeting moment passed.

'How did all this come about. Len?' he asked, thinking his fortuitous meeting was excellent character research.

'Him.' Len sucked his teeth and picked tobacco from his tongue.

'You mean He gave you a sign?'

'Nah. I got a magazine once. It said people need to go out and do stuff. To save the bush.' Len shrugged. 'So I did, and look,' he pointed to Crispin,' here you are, here I am, and I reckon that's about the size of it.'

'And I'm the first?'

'Yup. Only I'm not sure how. You got any pointers, Ernest?'

Crispin shrugged.

'Reckon we'll think of somethin'.'

'I reckon you will,' Crispin said with a smirk and stubbed out his cigarette. 'Just going to... you know.' He stood up and headed for the dunny out back. With food, his insides felt things were finally getting back to something they recognised. His regularity had gone haywire in the bush and he felt it was time to get things back on track. Natural flora, seeds, berries, and leaves can often have therapeutic benefits. The berries, which were fine for birds, hastened the experience of therapeutic benefits.

Crispin only just made it as the urge took hold and once again his body tried to expel his intestines. Crispin felt empty. He looked at his stomach and wondered if he had anything left to give. It gave a gurgle and gave it one last supreme effort, which left Crispin screaming as if he'd eaten a Grim Reaper chilli.

'Len,' he called. There was no answer. Not having toilet paper separates the men from the boys. Crispin gritted his teeth. He would have gifted his right eye for a corn cob at this stage of the proceedings. He pulled off his underwear.

'They came in a box, with tissue paper,' he said

as he gave them up for the greater good. Stitt sat and slowly recovered to resemble something human.

Some people do their best thinking while in splendid isolation. A creeping doubt about his plan surfaced and he could think of a number or reasons it was a bad idea. Staying incognito would be cruel to his nearest and dearest. It would make him look like a first-class cad. But, on the other hand, nobody loved him, anyway. He was weighing up his options when a spider dropped in his lap. It takes a brave man to sit still and wait for the little powerhouse of poison to move on. Crispin wasn't that man. He screamed and bolted out of the dunny straight into Len.

'Sometimes I feel like that, too. Reckon it's something to do with me Special brew. Powerful stuff.' Len held his nose.

'Anyways, I wus just coming to get ya,' Len said. 'We gotta to go an' help. It's an emergency.'

'Emergency?'

'Yeah. Come on.' Len repositioned his glass eye and strode off with purpose.

Crispin hoiked up his trousers and followed. They jogged over to the petrol station/post office/ general store/bottle shop/bar. A gaggle of people were milling about with sticks, whistles, and water bottles.

One man was directing the people to form groups.

'Shoes, mate,' the man pointed to Crispin's feet, then took a good look at the sunburn, the bites, scratches, welts and split lip.

'Right.'

'And hat?'

'I got some, Ernest. Under the bed.'

Crispin trotted back to the Institute and found a pair of old sandshoes. He slipped them on and joined the motley crew.

'C'mon Ernest.' Len gave Crispin a stick.

'What's happening Len?'

'We're looking for clues. Someone's lost.'

'Right. So you get to save two people,' Crispin said, amused at his own wit.

The quip was lost on Len as he shoved his hat hard on his head.

The residents of Block 67 formed up into two groups, then fanned out along the one road and began walking in opposite directions. Crispin followed the leader, but his ordeal, the heat, and chaffing of his backside took their toll. He soon felt weak.

'Mate? You better take it easy. You don't look so good.' A Chinese looking bloke slapped him on the shoulder.

'I'm just' Crispin wiped the sweat from his brow.

'Sit there. We'll be back soon,' an aboriginal bloke pointed to a patch of shade at the side of the road. The band of volunteers moved off and Crispin watched them leave, waving to Len. He leaned back in the shade and thought on the poor soul who was lost. A child, probably, wandered off into the bush, frightened, hungry. He knew all about hungry. In his daydream he was the hero. Some people can convince themselves of anything given enough time. Crispin got going lickety-split. He'd rescued the photogenic child. There would be grateful parents, a reward, a bit in the paper, perhaps a medal. It all looked just about perfect. He drifted off to sleep and rolled into the ditch.

'I found 'im.' Len shouted to his intrepid group of searchers while holding his eye in place.

Crispin was snapped out of La La Land and startled awake with a shake of his shoulder by Len.

'We thought we'd lost ya for a bit there.' Len laughed. 'Ya was sleeping in a ditch.' Crispin looked at the motley crew gawking at him. He waved and they moved on, satisfied he wasn't roadkill.

'Ernest, come on. We're going back.'

The walk back to Block 67 was made easier with the promise of a cold beer from the bar.

'Any luck?' Stitt asked.

'Nah.'

A bout of laughter rippled through the gang. Len almost broke into a trot the nearer they got to the petrol station.

Avis Varkov stood at the door and counted the men inside. From Russian peasant stock she was a woman of ample proportions and had a nose for chush' sobach'ya (bullshit).

'Nuzzink?'

'Nah. Been three days now,' the leader said. 'P'raps if we'd known sooner,' the man shrugged and went inside.

'Three days?' Crispin asked, following him in.

'Yeah. One of them city blokes. Just walked into the bush. Bloody crazy, if you ask me.'

'Tiz crazy.' Avis slammed the screen door and handed out cold bottles of beer from the Buffalo Bar.

'Ze papers.' She pointed to the newspaper.

'Walked into the bush?' Crispin said and frowned.

'You deaf or something?' the storyteller looked

at Crispin and gave his attire the once-over. He gave a sniff.

'I'm with Len,' Crispin pointed at Len.

'Figured as much.'

It didn't take Crispin long to work out he had been on a manhunt for himself. It would look pretty stupid to pop up now and say, 'Found him.'

He slithered his way over to the newspaper stand and picked up a paper. The front page was full of a cricket match. He didn't rate a mention on the second or third page. At page six, under the agony aunt column there was a small three-inch piece about a man who had gone missing. They didn't even call him a celebrated author, writer, or best seller. Probably keeping it low key until something definite. A body or some clue, he thought.

'Do youz vant to read it, youz gonna buy it.' Avis snatched the paper from Crispin's hands and folded it back on the stand.

'Sorry.' He looked at the date. It was two days old. No wonder he didn't rate a headline.

'Er, do you have the latest?'

'Vot you tink, we the big smoke here. Latest. Pffft.' Avis slapped Crispin on the back. 'It'z a good one. Some joke.'

'This is Ernest.' Len rescued Crispin with introductions and gave Avis a grin.

Avis hitched up her enormous breasts with her bra strap and opened the door to spit.

'Youz anozer Nutjob?'

'Me?'

'He's deaf, Avis. Repeats everything,' the leader of the search party butted in.

'I saze, youz nut job?' Avis repeated very loudly.

'Me?'

'Youz,' Avis jabbed Crispin in the chest.

'No. No, I'm not a nut job.'

'Well, that's a start. I'm Mal Franklin. The doc around these parts,' he shouted.

'A Doctor?'

'That's right mate. Doctor,' Mal said slowly and with emphasis.

Avis spat out the door, then returned to the conversation.

'He is 'armless. Just nut job.'

'Right.' Crispin's character research just stepped up a notch as he looked around.

The Buffalo Bar, so named for the big taxidermy Water Buffalo head above the bar, which, legend has it, was downed by Avis with one shot, was the hub of Block 67. Everything happened at the Buff, everyone met at the Buff, and nothing was worth mentioning if you didn't hear it at the Buff.

Avis stood behind the bar made from a single slab of wood and sniffed.

'Youz stink mate.'

'Me?' Crispin looked around for another culprit. Everyone was keeping a good distance from him.

'Youz stink,' Avis shouted.

'His names Ernest,' Len said. He took off his hat and smoothed his hair, hoping for another beer.

'Vell he stink.' Avis slapped the bar and put a pound note in her bra for safe keeping.

'Take him avay and be bloody quick.' Avis waved a dirty tea towel in Crispin's direction.

'C'mon Ernest.' Len pulled Stitt to the door. He turned back and said, 'them.' It was his last word on the female of the species. Crispin could well understand the sentiment. Avis wasn't exactly a shining example of the feminine. She screwed up her nose and pulled a galvanized water pipe from behind the bar, brandishing it at the pair.

'Out, Stinky.'

Norm and Ted, the regulars of the petrol station/ post office/Buffalo Bar gave a rousing cheer and laughed. Not much happened in Block 67, and it didn't take much to be classed as entertainment. It also didn't take much to be branded with a new moniker. Nutjob or stinky, these things stick.

Stinky and Nutjob looked a rum pair as they sauntered across the road to the Institute.

'Len, I wonder,' Crispin began, 'can I have a bath?'

'A what?'

'You know, a bath.' Crispin smelt his underarm and made a face.

'You mean like take ya gear off and sort of have a bath?'

'That's it.'

'With soap and stuff.'

'Yes.' What was normal practice for most of the population was an anathema for Len. He didn't like the idea of getting his body clean all at the same time. Some days he picked at his feet, other days he'd give his neck a wipe as the mood took him. It didn't take him often.

'You do have a bath, don't you. Len?'

'Not if I can help it.' Len smiled.

'No, I mean you own a bath or a shower.'

'Well, ya kinda got me on that one, Ernest.'

'Soap?' Crispin asked with a hopeful look on his face.

'There.' Len pointed to the kitchenette and a bucket.

The slither of soap had a hair in it, not the best start for Crispin who had been accustomed to hot water and plenty of it with perfumed soap and sponges from the Aegean Sea. He filled the tin bucket with water and retired out the back.

'Er, Len. Do you have a towel?'

'I got this.' Len held out a flannel that looked like it had seen action in the Napoleonic Wars. 'Ya really going to town Ernest.' Len watched the proceedings with a mixture of wonder and awe.

'Thanks.' Crispin shuddered at the thought of where the flannel might have been.

Washing in a bucket isn't exactly luxurious. Crispin's mother often said 'from base to apex'. He looked at the slither of soap and the flannel, then took a deep breath.

After two bucket changes, Crispin felt human again. He put on his/Len's clothes and hung up the flannel on a bit of wire to dry.

'I got some things might fit ya.' Len rummaged around and pulled out a pair of shorts and a lurid shirt with a palm tree and cocktail motif.

'Not exactly colour co-ordinated,' Crispin mumbled.

'Seems a waste to put on ya dirty duds.' Crispin took the clothes and changed.

'Goin' on holiday, Ernest?' Len gave a hearty

laugh while holding his eye in place. The joke fell
flat with Crispin. He hated to be the butt of ridicule
it had been another of those recurring themes in his
childhood. He gave a sour look at his benefactor.

'Sorry mate.' Len patted Crispin on the back. 'If
ya can't stand the heat, ya gotta take it lying down.
Didn't mean to offend.'

'None taken,' Stitt said, although it came
out through clenched teeth. If he heard one more
mauling of an idiom, he might not be responsible
for his actions.

'I reckon it might be time for a drink. How about
it, Ernest?'

The question was a simple one. A yes or no
would suffice. But there was more to the answer
than that. Crispin thought on what 'a drink' might
entail. He had wasted a good portion of the last year
in an alcoholic haze. He had wallowed, swallowed
and now felt it was time to turn over a new leaf. All
of his old skin was amost gone. Did he feel strong
enough to say no? Did he feel strong enough to say
'just the one'?

'I reckon we can sort this savin' business out
with a Special brew.' Len was ready to see the
guiding light at the bottom of a bottle.

'I don't think I need saving, Len,' Crispin said.

'What?'

'I really don't think I need saving.' Crispin smiled.

'Ah, get on with ya. I know ya testin' me.' Len
scrabbled under the bed and pulled out a bottle
of Special.

'I seen ya lookin' at me. I know ya think I'm not
up for it. But, see Ernest, I know ya need saving,
an' I'm the man to do it.' Len thumped his chest and

then pulled the cork and took a swig of the Special Brew. He shuddered and wiped his lips with the back of his hand.

'Bloody grand, ain't it?' He handed the bottle to Crispin.

Crispin took the bottle and sniffed. He ran his fingers through his hair and rubbed his new beard. Last time he had the drink, he'd woken up on a different day.

'Get it down ya neck and we can talk about it.'

'About what?'

'What's on ya mind mate.'

If only Len knew the half of it. Crispin looked at the bottle, then took a swig, and the warm feeling of an old friend slipped down his neck.

'I was like you, you know.' Len took the bottle for a drink. 'I thought I had nuthin'. Turns out I had it all, only I couldn't see the wood and the breeze. That's what a fella said, anyways.'

'The trees,' Crispin offered.

'Trees?' Nah, a bloke.'

'A bloke?'

'Ya know. Those blokes in church and the like. I met 'em when I was in the army .' Len took a deep breath.

'You been to war, Ernest?'

'Me?'

'Yeah.'

'No.'

'I have.' Len frowned and touched his eye. 'If they ask ya to go, just don't do it Ernest. It ain't worth it.'

'Wouldn't dream of it, Len.'

'Well?' Len snapped his tongue over his one

tooth. 'Are ya thinking to get it off ya chest, Ernest? If I'm gonna save ya, I need to know what ya need savin' from, if ya get me drift in a snowstorm.' Crispin flinched as if the metaphor was a hot poker aimed for his eye.

'Um.' Crispin prevaricated. How cathartic would it be to unburden himself of all his woes? Then again, he thought, he could weave a credible story. He was an author after all. It was tempting to reinvent himself. Perhaps he could meet fact and fiction half way.

'I just think no-one likes me.' It wasn't far from the truth.

'Sure they do Ernest. Ya just gotta show 'em ya true side.'

'But I did. And that's why they don't like me.' Crispin slipped into his bleating so easily. He stuck out his bottom lip.

'Take me for instance,' Len began. 'People think I'm some sort of nut job.

'Never.'

'It's true Ernest. But here's the thing' Len came in close and grabbed a fistful of Crispin's shirt collar.

'Yes?' Crispin held his breath against the bad breath.

'I'm the only sane one here.' Len laughed.

'Amazing.'

'Ain't it. All these blokes running around, doing stuff, "getting on" they call it, so they can have this 'n' that thing. What's it all for?

'I' Crispin began.

'When all ya gotta do,' Len smiled and waved the bottle in Crispin's direction, 'all ya gotta do is do stuff for other blokes. It's that easy, Ernest. I'd

give ya me last bottle of Special if ya needed it.'
Len looked at Crispin. 'Do ya need it?' Len asked.
Crispin shook his head.

'I let ya use me soap ,didn't I?'

'Yes.'

'I let ya stay here, didn't I?'

'Yes.'

'An' I ain't asked for nothin', 'ave I?'

'No. Nothing.' Crispin felt guilt creeping up his
spine and into his conscience. Len was correct. He
had been generous to a fault. He really was a decent
old soldier.

'So ya see. Who's crazy?' Len took a swig of
Special and scanned the room. 'I got it all if ya ask
me? 'cept for me eye.' Crispin was about to add
teeth, but thought better of the moment. They sat in
the tin shed and contemplated having it all with one
eye. Len's homilies were a bit too prickly for Crispin.
He scratched his mozzie bites. He knew he should
be grateful for all the things he had. But, when you
mix your metaphors and the light at the end of the
tunnel is a train with your name on it, it's hard to see
the bright side. His ego obscured the view.

'You ever done stuff, Ernest?'

'Oh yes. Plenty.' Crispin began with New York,
and started to count off his travels on his fingers.

'Nah. I mean stuff ya not proud of.' Len gave a
manic laugh and swigged his Special.

'Oh.'

At this stage in Crispin's reformation, he still
had the idea he was a model citizen. It was an
unequivocal 'no.'

'I done stuff Ernest.'

'Really?' Crispin was between a rock and a hard

place. Did he really want to know what Len had done? It might give him nightmares for years. On the other hand, what a gold mine for a writer.

'Oh yeah. I done stuff.'

The question as to what was left in the air like a hangman's noose. Crispin's imagination ran away with the information and once again his headlines were lurid and attention grabbing.

*Author dismembered.

*Famous author found in cage, half-starved.

*Best-selling writer ordeal *now serialized* near-death experience at the hands of a maniac.

Stitt changed the subject.

'Len, how did you lose your teeth?'

'I took 'em out with a pair of pliers. They were bothering me and I had nothing better to do.' Len finished the bottle and fetched another.

'Yours bothering ya?'

'No. No. Not at all. Just fine, thanks.'

Len gave Crispin's mouth a long, hard stare.

'Sure?'

Crispin nodded, clamping his lips shut, not daring to ask about his eye.

It wasn't long before Len passed out and Crispin was left to his own devices. He hunted through the Institute for something to eat and came up empty. Perhaps he could get something on credit at the Buffalo Bar.

A quick tidy of his hair, a shirt tucked in and he presented himself at the screen door. Inside was civilized society. People who weren't on the most-wanted list. People who didn't pull their teeth out because they had nothing better to do on a Saturday night.

He stepped into another world. Two regulars turned as the door banged shut.

'Stinky,' Avis said.

'It's Ernest, actually. Ernest Hemsworth.'

'Avis held up her hand.

'Alvays Stinky to me, or youz prefer Nutjob?' He was between that rock and the hard place again. It wasn't the worse name he'd been called in his life.

'Um, Stinky,' Crispin said and walked to the Bar.

'You vant sometink?' Avis hitched up her bra and waited.

'Do you have toilet paper?'

'Vot youz tink. We are savages peoples.' Avis gave him a hard stare.

'Well no.' Crispin said as the regulars tittered. 'Not at all. It's just that Len's run out.'

'Len.'

'Yes, over at the Institute.'

'You got some money, Stinky?'

'Well, no. but I will pay you back, I promise.'

'He promise. That good one.' Avis slapped the bar, which made Norm and Ted, the regular fixtures, jump. She packed a mean left hook on the odd occasion, so everyone knew to laugh when the time came.

'Please.' Crispin gave it one last shot.

'Nyet.'

The regulars looked at Crispin, waiting for the next volley. Avis waited.

'Ok then.' Crispin admitted defeat. He put Avis on his list of women who "done 'im wrong".

She was obviously someone who didn't have a charitable bone in her body.

'So Stinky, what it all about?' Avis settled in for the answer heaving her breasts on the bar, and waited.

'Well it's like this' Crispin began. So far he had avoided too many porky pies. Now he went to town as the lie got bigger in the telling. He could have been a number of things as he rejigged his history, his derring-do, his bravado. He became a colourful identity. One with a past that the government would like to rub out. One that sounded like a fictional character in a book called *Il Est Mort*.

His audience listened with rapt attention.

'So you see, I'm in' Crispin whispered, 'hiding.'

'Stinky, that one stink.' Avis laughed. 'It load of chush' sobach'ya.'

'Bullshit,' Doc said by way of translation as he came in the door.

'I give one drink for story.' Avis pulled a bottle from the fridge and handed it over. Crispin looked over to the toilet paper in the small shop.

'Nyet. Beer.' Avis said.

'Mate,' Doc patted Crispin on the back. 'A bit of advice about Block 67.'

'Hmmm.' Crispin sipped and took in his surroundings.

'People come to the Block for one reason and one reason only.'

'What?'

'Whatever it is, doesn't matter. They are here 'cause they don't want to be out there.' Doc hoiked his thumb in the direction of the road.

'He right Stinky,' Avis said. 'We all got to

running from sometink.'

'And hope like hell it doesn't catch up with us,' Doc added.

Crispin wondered how fast he could run before his past tackled him to the ground.

'Do you have a telephone?' Crispin looked around the bar.

'Vot youz tink? We all mod cons?' Avis winked at the doctor.

'Nah mate. You landed beyond the black stump. We only get a delivery once a week. Petrol for the generator, bit of food, papers.' Doc pointed to the two-day old paper languishing on its stand.

'Right.'

'Wanting to ring someone?' Doc asked.

'Well' Who did Crispin want to ring? He shuffled his feet.

'No, didn't think so,' Doc said and tapped his nose. 'You look like you need to sort out a few things before you go out there.'

'Out there?' It sounded like a jungle. Crispin thought on the doc's words. Was he that transparent? He picked some skin off his nose.

'You betta listen, Stinky. Doc know a thing or two. He got plenty up here,' Avis tapped her head. Doc smiled and raised his eyebrows in Crispin's direction.

Stitt felt like his skin was peeled back by the stare. He wanted to button it up before the Doc looked right into his soul. It was unnerving. He wanted to say he had a life, friends, golf clubs and a signed copy of a first edition Dickens. He might have pointed out he was considered a shining light in the literary world. A beacon of writing excellence. 'The most exciting voice from a writer we have seen in a long time.' But all that didn't matter in Block 67. The Doc probably never read a decent book in his life. What would he know?

Crispin's stomach gave a low rumble in indignation.

'You eaten?' Doc asked.

'Not recently,' Crispin said.

'Give him something Avis.'

'Vot? On ze credit?'

'I'll pay.' The Doc slapped a note on the bar.

'Take your money Doc. I don't need it.' Avis shoved the money back at Doc and he put it in his pocket.

'Never argue with a lady.' Doc smiled.

'So,' Crispin began between bites of a sausage sandwich, 'have you heard any more about that fellow who walked into the bush?'

'Nah. News was two days old. He could be anywhere by now. He could be sitting right here and we'd never know.' Doc looked at Stitt. Crispin tried to look gormless, it didn't take much effort.

'They might never find him. People disappear. It's the people he left behind I feel sorry for. You know, like his wife and family. Never knowing what happened. What was going on in his mind? If they might have said something different to change his mind? You know, that sort of thing.' Doc turned to Norm and Ted and they nodded in sympathy for those left behind. Crispin licked his fingers of grease and sat back.

'I'll pay you back.'

'Sure,' Doc said. He picked up his bag and walked out.

'What's his story?' Crispin asked. It's amazing how one simple sandwich can transform a man from almost having an epiphany back to an egotist.

'Youz don't learn fast, Stinky.' Avis took the empty plate.

'Oh, right,' Crispin tapped his nose. 'I get it. Secrets.'

'Stinky listen to Avis. Not secrets. Pffft. Everyone got secrets. We all got a long memories. From vay back.' Avis waved her hand in the air. 'It better the memory stay vay back.'

Crispin nodded and glanced at the newspaper.

'Next one not for five days,' Avis yelled.

'Five days,' Crispin repeated.

It felt like a lifetime. What could he do with five days in Block 67?

'You gotta be somevere hotshot?'

'Er, no.'

'Stitt was beginning to dislike Avis. She sounded a bit too much like his wife and the Doc pricked his conscience. He thought it wise to forgo the pleasures of the Buff Bar/petrol station/post office. He had five days to contemplate his navel (if he could see it) before the papers would arrive. Then he might see how plan D would play out.

Such is the optimism of a writer who was a one hit wonder and scaled the heights of the literati, he thought the papers might have a feature, an editorial piece and a nice author photo given by his agent.

Ten

Five days, Crispin thought. They might be the longest five days of his life. He suddenly felt exhausted.

Back at the Institute, Len had slumped to his bed and was out for the count. Crispin looked at his camp cot. He remembered his bed at home. Crisp sheets, monogrammed pillow slips, a soft, inviting mattress with his wife beside him.

'Amanda,' he said to his camp cot and lay down. It didn't take a heartbeat and Stitt was asleep. What he dreamt could keep Sigmund Freud busy for a decade as the ego and the id fought tooth and nail.

When one is out of one's comfort zone waking up in strange surroundings can be a little disconcerting. Crispin woke up with a start and fell off his bed.

'Ya up then?' Len stated the obvious, although Crispin wasn't exactly "up". 'Ya been sleepin'.' You should give the man credit. He had a knack for the obvious.

'Um.' Crispin tried to get his bearings.

'Been out of it for most of the day.' Len scratched and planted a bottle of special on the table. 'I started without ya,' he grinned.

'What day is it?'

'Today.'

'Yes.'

'Today,' Len said. The conversation didn't have the hallmark of intelligent written on it.

'Right.'

'I've been thinkin' Ernest.'

'Really?'

We could tell what Crispin was thinking as he raised his eyebrow.

'Yeah, an' I been thinkin' ya need to get it off ya chest.'

'Do I?'

'Yeah. They tell ya that at the Army hospital. Get it off ya chest, they say. You'll feel better.' Len took a swig.

'Did you?'

'Did I what?'

'Get it off your chest.' Crispin asked.

'Bloody oath I did.'

'And did it make you feel better?'

'Nup. I still hate 'em.'

'Women?'

'Yeah. Them.' Len sucked on his special and closed his eye.

'Perhaps you just haven't found the right one.'

The thought that there might be a woman in the universe that was the right one for Len was a long shot. Len glanced through the window at the petrol station and in a blinding flash of inspiration, Crispin saw it all.

Unrequited love in Block 67. Len was in love. That was the reason he hated women. His love hadn't been reciprocated.

'You know, Len, sometimes women can be

a man's salvation.' Crispin recollected Ernest Hemingway said it somewhere. Not that he believed it, but it sounded like he knew what he was talking about. Ernest Hemingway had hundreds of women practically hanging off his every word.

Len took a swig of Special and spat on the floor. That would be his last word.

Sometimes when you come across a problem, the solution isn't instantly obvious. But this solution was sitting opposite Crispin, and it was *so* obvious it was laughable.

Len needed a make-over. He needed Crispin like a pair of linen trousers needs a heat press. And if there was one thing Crispin knew about it was panache. That, and colour co-ordination. He was practically an expert in assertive flamboyance.

Len cracked open another bottle and sat back, enjoying the minutiae of life.

Crispin sat back and wondered how he was going to pull it off.

Crispin thought on plan E. He was a plotter not a panster, the latter being people who just wrote whatever came into their head at the time. If he was going to plot Len's love life, he needed pen and paper.

'Len, do you have anything I could write with?'
'What like?'
'Pen and paper maybe?'
'You mean to write stuff down and stuff?'
'That's the idea.'

Len waved his hand in the direction of the kitchenette and took to the bottle.

Scratching around in the kitchenette, Crispin began to tidy as he progressed from drawer to drawer. He found all sorts of treasures. Old bottle caps, hair nets, a can opener—broken, and glory be, a fork.

'Found a fork,' he said as he fossicked. Len slipped into a Special place and slithered to the floor. Crispin, with something to do, got stuck in and it wasn't long before he was having a bit of spring clean. He stopped to fry up some eggs and then continued his housework until it was too dark to see. Amanda always said he was very neat, ending with the qualifier; "for a man". She said he had nice habits. His mother had instilled a sense of order in his psyche from an early age. He finished up and lay down to think about how he could bring Cupid's arrow to Block 67. He contemplated Len's words. Doing things for other people, that's all it takes to be happy. Perhaps Len was right. Crispin thought bringing star-crossed lovers together might not be his life's work, but he had every confidence in his abilities. It would be five days well spent. Of course, he didn't think to ask Len or Avis what they thought of the idea. Anyway, if Hemingway could bring F. Scott Fitzgerald and Zelda back together, then Stitt could get a Russian and a one-eyed nut job to hit it off.

Crispin made a list by moonlight and lay in the dark, thinking of love. Perhaps he didn't hate all the women in his life. Perhaps he only hated some of the nasty ones. Maybe he didn't even hate them, because they were women after all, and everyone knows women are sensitive creatures at heart. You just needed to know how to treat them right. They were fickle, but with the right guidance, they could be a man's best friend, possibly, his salvation. In the dark, a long way from home and reality, a man will conjure up all sorts of notions. Whether they be a flight of fancy, they feed the positive bias of one's aggrandisement. Crispin's bias was stuffed. He fell asleep dreaming of his wife in the kitchen, cooking him meals because she loved him.

While Len slept through the morning Crispin busied himself around the Institute. He cleaned, tidied, and threw out things that might not be identified even if you had a thesaurus. It was around lunchtime when Len surfaced and blinked in the light.

'Ernest,' Len looked at the shed. He could see the cupboard tops for the first time. He never knew he had linoleum on the floor.

'Len. You want breakfast, or lunch perhaps?'

Len gave a nod and lay down.

Crispin cooked some eggs and threw in an onion he'd found. He laid the table and brewed a pot of tea. It was all very civilized and clean.

'Ready,' Crispin trilled and sat down. He'd been making notes, lists, and was ready to outline his plan to Len.

Len staggered to the table and sat.

'I just thought we ought to get a bit organised.' Crispin poured the tea. 'No sugar, I'm afraid.'

Len looked around with a frown and jumped at

the sight of the camp stove.

'Yes, I gave it a clean. It came up a treat.'

'Ernest?'

'Hmmmm?'

'Ya not one of them fellas that likes knittin' are ya?'

'Knitting?'

'Yeah, knittin'.' Len narrowed his gaze.

'I seen grown "men" if you know what I mean. In the hospital. They like knittin'.'

'Oh.' Crispin shook his head. 'No. I don't like knitting.' Stitt puffed out his chest and beat it, cleared his throat, then cracked his knuckles.

'Alright then.' Len took his tea and sipped. 'Not that they bother me or nuthin', but I just wanted to know.' He ate his eggs. 'Because, well, I don't know how to save a fella who likes knittin'. Not that they need saving like that, but they're just a bit different, if ya know what I mean.'

'I know what you mean, Len.' Crispin sipped his tea and tried to look like Johnny Weissmuller's Tarzan at the same time.

Having a bit of a whip around with a wet rag is all well and good, but Crispin threw his back into a complete transformation of the Institute. He tidied, found a broom and swept, found a mop and so it went, until he had the place looking half decent. Len sat and watched his life turn upside down. It was when Crispin was out the back, he discovered an old tin bath.

'Len,' Crispin sat down opposite and began, 'I

reckon you could do with a bit of a spruce up. I found a bath.'

'A bath.'

'You know, you'd feel a whole lot better if you had a bath.'

'I dunno about that, Ernest.' Len rubbed the back of his neck.

'Trust me.'

'Are you havin' one?'

'Yes.'

'Just one thing. I think we'll need some soap. Do you have any money for soap. Len.'

'Well.'

'How do you pay for things?'

'I get the army pension. In the post. Once a month.' Len smiled. 'An' I sell me Special.'

'I'll pay you back.'

'Alright then.' Len pulled a pound note from his pocket and laid it on the table.

There was so much promise in that pound note. Crispin could buy all sorts of things.

'Len?'

'What?'

'Do you ever eat vegetables?

'What?'

'You know. Like carrots, peas, potatoes. That sort of thing.'

'I had 'em once. Didn't agree with me. You eat 'em do ya?'

'Well, yes. I just think they are good for you. I saw a can of them over at the shop.'

'Nah. I wouldn't risk it.'

Crispin needed roughage. Eggs were all very well, but they didn't have what Stitt needed. He was beginning to worry about his regularity. If things didn't move along soon, he might be desperate enough to contemplate some red berries.

What Crispin failed to see was that he was living off the fat of the land, so to speak. With not much going in, there wasn't a need for it to come out as often. His reserves were taking care of keeping him alive, and he had plenty in reserve. He wasn't Tarzan just yet, and it wasn't a diet that might be in the women's pages, but with regular exercise, aka housework, and a low calorific intake, Crispin was slimming and trimming.

He took the money and walked across the road dreaming of sauté cabbage and bacon fat with minted peas.

Avis watched as Crispin sauntered over to the shop shelves and perused her offerings.

'Youz vant sometink?'

'I'd like a bar of soap please,' Crispin said.

'No more stinky, eh?'

'That's right.' Crispin tried to remain civil. Avis slapped a bar of laundry soap on the countertop.

'Er, do you have bath soap, perhaps?'

'This for everything.'

'What soap do you use?'

'This.' Avis pointed.

'Excellent. Miss Varkov isn't it?' Crispin smiled. If he was going to play Cupid, he needed to know where to point his arrow.

'Da, Varkov.' Avis narrowed her eyes. She smelt chush sobach'ya.

'I guess it's pretty busy, running this place all by yourself?' He waited for Avis to respond. She set her jaw.

'Youz vant nothing else?'

'Do you get lonely?'

'I got plenty nut jobs keep me busy.' Crispin thought she would be a hard nut to crack. He reminded himself that women were simple creatures. They just needed a push in the right direction. Well, most were simple creatures. His publisher, Plethora Carmichael, wasn't even human.

'And I'm sure you do an excellent job Avis. May I call you Avis?'

'Da.'

'Now, let me see.' Crispin tapped his finger on his lips and gave his cheeky grin. Amanda always liked that special way he had of smiling and the promise it contained.

'I think I need tooth brushes. Two Avis, if you have them?'

'I got,' Avis put two brushes with the soap.

'Um, any paste?'

Avis put a tin of toothpaste in the pile.

'And perhaps' Crispin raised his eyebrows 'a pair of manicure scissors?'

'Vot youz tinking Stinky? You set up barber shop?'

'Oh, Avis,' Stinky laughed. 'You're such fun.'

Avis hitched up her bra. 'You got money, Stinky?'

'Oh, certainly.' Crispin handed over the pound note and waited for his change.

'Well, lovely chatting Avis. We must do it again sometime. One rarely meets a charming, intelligent and funny woman.' Crispin laid it on thick. Avis thought he was a bit thick. It was the worst pick-up line she'd ever heard. And although it was absolute chush' sobach'ya, it was almost one of the nicest things someone had said to her in a long time. A very, very long time.

With soap, Crispin got cracking. He'd found a bag of clothes while housecleaning and now filled the bath and did the laundry. It was cathartic to throw oneself into everyday chores. Gone were the worries of the real world. Gone was the angst of producing another best-seller, pleasing everyone, and wondering if your wife still loved you. Len watched on and developed a twitch in his one eye. What was once a world he understood was becoming something he thought he'd run away from.

'Now,' Crispin stood with a clean towel and soap and pointed to the bath. 'Are you ready?'

Len looked at the bath full of warm water. He sucked his tooth and contemplated taking all his clothes off at the same time.

'I'll just sit outside for a bit. Take your time.' Crispin hummed a tune as he trotted outside.

Len peeled his clothes off and gently sat down in the water. It wasn't too bad. It brought back memories he'd long ago buried. He washed them away with the years of dirt. There was a lot of hollering and splashing as Leonard got into the swing of things. He began to sing a ribald ditty he'd heard while a young lad in the 14-18 war. He felt life might be alright. He had linoleum on the floor, money in his pocket, and Ernest, who gave him purpose. Len stopped singing and stared into the distance. The light that shone on his future beckoned.

'I've put out some clean clothes, Len,' Crispin yelled from the window.

Len slipped into a pair of shorts and shirt and wondered who was saving whom, as Crispin scooped the water out of the bath with a bucket and whistled.

'I took the liberty of purchasing a pair of scissors.' Crispin looked at Len's toe nails. They'd give a troglodyte a run for his money. Len looked at his talons.

'I pick 'em.'

'Well, I'm sure we can do better than that,' Crispin said.

To Crispin's way of thinking there was nothing better than a manicured set of toe nails. Your world might be falling apart, but clean, neat toe nails just about fixed everything in La La Land.

'Ya sure ya don't knit?'

'Positive.' Crispin got to work and whistled a happy tune. He sat back and admired his handiwork.

'You know Len,' Crispin tidied Len's fingernails, 'I had the idea my life was chush' sobach'ya. But now I find,' Crispin looked at Len, 'I find that it wasn't so bad after all.'

'I know what ya mean.' Len looked at his finger and toenails.

As the make-over progressed, Len and Crispin forwent the pleasure of drinking into oblivion. They talked instead.

Len's story came out in small snippets of anger, despair, and astonishment. A war, a young soldier with an even younger wife. He thought he was fighting for something good, noble, just. He thought he was fighting for a way of life. He'd given his all and then some. He'd given his eye, his sanity, his loyalty.

And when he came home, it was all gone. She'd gone.

'Them,' Len said, although the sting had gone from the word.

'So, tell me, Len, do you think you could find love again?'

'Nup.'

'Do you think there is a woman out there for you? Someone that might not misplace your trust.'

'Nup.'

'Someone that knows you're a good man.'

'Am I Ernest? Ya know I done stuff I'm not right proud of. Ya know I been in the big house for fightin'.'

'Yes. Len. You're a good man.' Crispin patted his friend on the back. 'A very good man.'

'It's not all chush' sobach'ya.'

It was very cathartic.

Five days flew by as Crispin sculpted a new man. Len got a shave, a haircut, and a new toothbrush.

Crispin began to school Len on the, finer things of life. He didn't need to spit on the floor for instance, or pick his toenails while eating tea.

'I think Avis would like it if you tried to be nice.'

'To one of them?' Len asked.

'They are not all bad, you know. Some of them just put on an act. They act tough. Women are just a bit fickle. Like a cat.'

'A cat that will scratch ya eye out.'

'No. No. Not at all. They need to be pampered and cajoled. They like flattery, and a little treat now and again.' It is amazing how a man can dish out any amount of advice on the opposite sex and not have a qualm about his blatant hypocrisy. Stitt had alienated just about every woman he ever met. He had belittled them, ridiculed them, cursed them and might have made a voodoo doll if he could find a pin. Now, he was the everyman encyclopaedia of women, most of the advice gleaned from Mr Hemingway's books and interviews. Ernest Hemingway had four wives. He ought to know something.

'What about Avis?'

Len made a face. It wasn't a nice one.

'She seems nice enough.' Crispin gilded the lily to the point one needed sunglasses. 'She's over there, all alone, probably dying for a bit of company. A woman needs a man, Len. Avis is a woman, you're a man.' Crispin raised his eyebrows knowingly.

'I don't like 'em and I don't trust 'em.' Len went to spit and Crispin held up a finger.

'Ah, ah, ah, no spitting Len.'

'Are ya sure ya don't knit?'

'Absolutely not.' Crispin cleared his throat, stroked his growing beard and puffed out his chest. 'Wouldn't know the first thing about knitting.'

📖

'Well?' Crispin held up a mirror. Len looked at the reflected face. He touched the scars on his cheek, and looked at his glass eye. It had had a bit of spit and polish too. He grinned. His one tooth was almost white.

'Is it me?'

'I think so.'

Crispin huffed on the mirror and turned it on himself. His face was thinner, a full beard sprouted, and his eyes bright.

'Reckon we could celebrate with a drink Ernest?' Len looked over the road.

'I think that is entirely appropriate Leonard. Entirely appropriate.'

Crispin put on his sandshoes, tucked in his Hawaiian shirt and smoothed his hair. Len licked his lips in anticipation. He had a powerful thirst.

The two dapper gents walked into the Buff Bar and Doc whistled.

'Get outta here.' He pointed to the door and smiled. 'You'll put us to shame.'

Len grinned and swaggered to the bar. He sucked his tooth and put some money down.

'Two bottles.'

Avis looked at him and pursed her lips. Crispin came up behind Len and whispered in his ear.

'Please,' Len added.

'You got the hot date?' Avis flicked the lids on the beers.

'One should make an effort in front of a lady. Isn't that right, Leonard?'

'Sure.' Len grinned at Avis and then downed his bottle without coming up for air.

Norm and Ted, the regulars, nursed their beers.

'Not drinking?' Crispin said, enjoying the moment of triumph when all eyes were on him. Try as he might to be humble, once an egotist, practically always an egotist.

He nudged his star pupil. Len harrumphed.

'She's a woman, you're a man,' Crispin whispered.

'I'll 'ave another,' Len swallowed, 'please.' Avis lined up the bottles and narrowed her eyes.

Conversations were stilted, the air thick with expectation.

'Is something wrong?' Crispin asked as he twiddled with his bottle cap.

'Always like this,' Doc said.

'Pardon?'

'Tomorra,' Norm said. Ted nodded in agreement.

'Truck's coming tomorrow,' Doc added.

Crispin had almost forgotten the import of that word. He'd been preoccupied, but now it all came rushing back. He looked over to the paper stand. He was hoping for a mention, an op-ed, or at the very least a photo. To be forgotten would be crushing.

'Always a good day, eh?' Doc added to Norm and Ted at the Buff.

Avis nodded and winked at Crispin. 'A good day.'

Eleven

Crispin was up at the crack of dawn, his ears pinned back for the sound of a truck. Every noise had him jumping.

'Sorry, I'm a bit on edge this morning.' Crispin took his cup of tea and sat near the window.

'About last night, Ernest,' Len began, 'I think it was the drink.'

Crispin looked at Len's burgeoning black eye. 'I didn't think she'd hit you. Well, not that hard anyway.'

Len touched his eye. 'You know, after she walloped me, I kinda realised she was not too bad for one of them.'

'For a woman, you mean?'

'Yeah, for one of them. I think she kinda likes me.'

Some men take a woman out. There is wine, flowers, conversation, and they get a sense of how they feel. Len got a black eye from Avis's mean right hook after he tried to kiss her, and now he was in love. Well, as in love as a man can be after thinking of "them" as a separate species, one that he didn't like.

'Perhaps take things one step at a time. Women like to be wooed.'

'Wooed?' Len winced as his eye throbbed.

'Sort of made to feel special.'

'I could give her some of me Special,' Len said.

'They like soap. Little trinkets,' Crispin said. Len thought on the object of his desire.

'Can you write poetry?'

'Nah.'

The conversation was cut short as a truck pulled into the petrol station. Crispin jumped up and sprinted across the road, closely followed by Len.

'Er, Len, could I just have some pennies for a paper? I'll pay you back.'

'Reckon ya good for it.' Len handed over some change and waited outside. He didn't' want to risk a busted lip at this delicate stage of his relationship.

Crispin walked inside, waited for Avis to take delivery of her packages and post then pounced on the papers.

'I'll have these please,' He put five days' worth on the counter with his money.

Avis counted the change. 'Something?'

'Oh, yes. I just want to know... um, about the... football.' Crispin said looking at the back page. He bundled up his newspapers and hurried outside.

'What's up, Ernest?' Len looked at the bundle.

'Just want something to read. You know, just to pass the time.'

Avis came to the door and looked at Len and his shiner.

She tsked, hitched up her bra and walked back inside.

'She looked at me,' Len said squinting into the sun. It wasn't quite Romeo and Juliet, but she didn't bring out the galvanized pipe or throw a punch, so things were looking up. Well, as up as one can look with a black eye squinting into the sun.

The papers were a couple of days old, but there he was, in the paper, on page three. There was a short piece about his book, and Plethora Carmichael had called him promising. 'A promising talent cut short.'

The next day there was a story with a picture of Amanda. She was wearing the earrings he'd bought her in New York. She looked wonderful in her grief. The paper mentioned Stitt's award-winning book was now on sale.

His publisher wasn't surprised at the resurgence of interest. His book was put on a list of 'one book you must read before you die'. Crispin had thought he'd died and gone to heaven. One could only dream of such a by-line.

Day three, and the paper showed his house, his unfinished manuscript, which Plethora said they would publish. Crispin nearly cried when he read that.

Day fours paper had his disappearance in detail. There was an extensive search over several days, the local people joining the hunt, but no clue was found. It was presumed Mr Stitt had gone for a canoe paddle and was now lost. And a paragraph at the bottom said, 'Stitt's neighbour is helping the police and Detective George Binks with inquiries. Binks had no comment when asked if this was a straight forward case of missing person, presumed dead or was foul play involved.'

The latest paper, two days old, had Plethora saying they were working to serialize his book for the paper. Sales were up, and just as soon as the police came to a conclusion, she would be publishing his latest work, prophetically named, *Il Est Mort ~ He Is Dead.*

That his wife was distraught, his neighbour was under suspicion, and the police were involved didn't matter to Crispin. His publisher, Raven & Square had called him promising and she said she was publishing his book.

Was it a clue, *Il Est Mort,* the paper opined. Binks had no comment.

To someone who thrives on attention, having great reviews in the paper and not being able to share is torture in the extreme.

'Somethin' wrong Ernest?' Len asked as he made his bed with army regulation corners.

'I...' Crispin left the word dangling.

'Ya bunged up, eh?' Often, ones problems come down to being bunged up, figuratively and literally. Why Crispin thought he needed to share the inner workings of his inner workings with Len is anyone's guess. A night on the Special brew often has that effect. Some call it talking seagull, others chush' sobach'ya.

'Want some Special?' Len smoothed his hair and ran his tongue over his tooth. He took several swigs of courage and winked. 'Just goin' over. Me cheque will be waitin'.' He hitched up his trousers and braced himself for a conversation with Avis. He walked over the road as a man with a purpose. Crispin thought he heard him humming a little tune.

The world was a cheery place as far as Stitt was concerned. He swatted a mosquito and put the kettle on, contemplating the accolades, the awards, the sheer talent to have...

The sudden realization that he couldn't partake of the tributes because he was presumed dead hit him like Avis's right hook.

The media don't look kindly on a fellow who is presumed to be dead and then pops up, very much alive, especially when they have just shelled out a bundle for the serialization of his novel. Stitt got to thinking on the widening circle of people who might gladly throttle him if he reappeared. The list grew like ripples on a pond. He shuddered as he imagined Plethora's face.

What would Ernest do? It was the question Stitt asked himself as he sipped his tea.

The only answer he could find was that everybody loves you when you're dead. Maybe he should stay that way. Anyway, people can't hate you forever. Such is the delusional optimistic thinking of a narcissist, albeit a nice one, when he tried hard to be a decent human being.

Stitt kept the papers under his camp bed, lest others see the story and put two and two together to make five, although by his reckoning that was the collective IQ of the patrons of the Buff bar, excluding the Doc. That man had Crispin worried. After he'd read his story, the accolades, the conjecture and the offer of publication one more time, he sat and tried to rationalise his decision. It came out as a list of things he'd often dreamed about, but never achieved. There were a few advantages to being dead.

Serialization in the paper.

Publication without begging. That was a biggie.

A notoriety that went far beyond the inner circle of literati, or Arty-Farty, as Amanda often said.

Five days in the news. That was worth more than a slap on the back and a canapé.

On the negative side. Crispin thought for a bit. Nothing came to mind. He thought a bit harder. Then, if he was being honest with himself, there were a couple of downers to resurrection.

Amanda would hate him for putting her thorough the agonies of worry when he popped up dead or alive.

Jim would hate him, probably never talk to him again, or invite him over, or let him drink his beer.

Plethora would probably kill him.

His mother might never talk to him again. He put that one on the positive list.

And somewhere, in the back of his mind, there was the small matter of the police.

Detective George Binks was on the case.

He was nudged out of his reverie by the sound of the truck shifting into gear. It was his one chance to redeem himself. He looked at the papers once again. What's another seven days in paradise? Crispin thought at the very least he would have seven days to concoct a story of epic proportions. Something to rival Agatha Christie's eleven missing days in '26. Stitt sat down, finished his cup of tea, and thought he was pretty damn clever. Of course, he hadn't met Detective George Binks, whose brain was admired at headquarters for being top shelf.

Twelve

Detective George Binks might have a brain that the scientists wanted to preserve in formaldehyde, but he missed out in the Mr. Personality stakes. George Binks didn't discriminate; he hated everyone.

A balding man with no charm, no style, no panache he was, throughout his life, labelled the fellow least likely to.

Now, Binks sat at his desk as head of missing persons and looked at the papers for the last five days and chewed the end of his pencil. This wasn't his usual type of missing person case. Usually there was a corpse, and the missing person, the suspect. But something about this case piqued his interest.

Although George hated everyone, he reserved a special hate for fraudsters, imposters, charlatans, swindlers, shams and hoaxers.

He chewed his 2HB and read the missing person's report once again. There was scant to go on. The neighbour was a blubbering, blithering idiot. The wife a cool customer, the publisher a rat with a gold tooth and the author... well, Stitt was one or several of the above adjectives Binks hated with a passion. He had a nose for this type of thing ever since he was duped as a young man into handing over his watch to a hypnotist/magician. You don't catch Binks out twice.

He decided he'd like to visit Mrs Plethora Carmichael of Raven & Square Publishing. On the phone she was too well rehearsed. A little one to one just might start the ball rolling.

Binks put on his jacket and checked the address of the publishing house. It was only a short walk from headquarters. He told the front desk he'd be gone for an hour or two and, grabbing his hat, set off.

As Binks walked, he window shopped. A display of Stitt's award-winning book caught his eye. He stopped and studied the author portrait. Stitt was suave, with perfect hair, a cravat, white teeth and a smile that looked genuine. He really did look happy. George went in and bought a book.

'Have you heard?' the shop assistant gushed, 'he's dead and we've had to go for a second print run.'

The book was a weighty tome. *He Lives*, a book for life, the blurb said. George opened it and read a few lines and that little twitch he often had in his left eye took up residence.

Envy is one of those deadly sins most keep hidden. George had kept his hidden for quite some time, but now it wriggled out and took up residence in his greenish eye. For although George didn't have a personality, he fancied himself as a writer of short stories about people with personalities. They say one should write about what you know, but George was breaking the mould. He wanted to be a short story writer, or perhaps a long story writer. He thought he had a novel in him.

George was a closet writer of hard-boiled western adventure. He thought that being on the spot in the world of missing persons would give him the edge when it came to the work of the sheriff to find the gun slinger. Of course, being at the coalface of missing persons is, for the most part, sitting at a desk, writing things in triplicate, typing with two fingers, and trying to get the suspect or close relative to say something incriminating.

George thought he'd write with realism. It's just a pity his real life was as exciting as picking fluff from your belly button. There was never a high-speed car chase, a gun pulled, a bar fight. Binks wrote his stories with the dedication of his work reports. To say they were dry would be like saying you needed galoshes in the Atacama Desert.

He looked at the author photo of Stitt and tsked. Who wears a cravat? It was one of those things right up there with hypnotists and swindlers that George hated, effete aggrandisement.

Raven & Square Publishing House was on the main road, a grand building with columns, marble and a concierge on the door. George stood back and took a long look at the edifice. Somewhere in his mind, he reserved a small spot for the moment he would step up those stairs as a fully fledged writer of hard-boiled western adventure. The concierge would know him by name, he'd be ushered in.

'May I help you?' Harold asked. As a job, the concierge was easy street. Harold had the temperament to suit. He could stand for hours with nothing on his mind, watching the traffic. If a man was born to a job, it was Harold.

'Oh,' George looked at Harold's livery. Gold epaulettes, shined shoes. 'You'd see all sorts come and go I'd imagine.'

'Yes.' This was Harold's favourite subject.

'Anyone famous?'

'Oh, yes. Some very famous people. I once opened the door for Mr Shute.'

'Shute, eh?'

'Yes. He's written dozens of books.' (Crispin Stitt could tell you how many, if you needed to know.)

'What about this fellow?' George held up the volume of *He Lives*.

'Yes. A very smart dresser Mr Stitt. Very smart, amazing colour co-ordination.' (Stitt's mother would be proud.)

'Seen him lately?'

'Haven't you heard? Dreadful business.'

'Do tell.'

'His neighbour went completely mad. Chopped him up with an axe. Body parts all over the place, but never found, they say.'

'Fancy.' Detective Binks raised his eyebrows.

'Yes, dreadful business. The wife was home at the time. He went on a fishing trip. Just disappeared. Like that.' And Harold clicked his fingers.

'What was this fellow like?'

'Polite. Some of them aren't, you know.'

'I can imagine. Seen him lately?'

'No, not for some time. Now his book is out, well, they usually come by. But he won't, will he?'

'Not if he's in pieces.'

'Quite,' Harold said. 'I always thought he was a bit, well, you know, theatrical.'

'Theatrical?'

'Yes. Nice and all that, but a bit... theatrical.'

Harold held the door for a young lady, and

Binks scooted in, yelling, 'business,' and headed for the lift.

Angel looked up from her typewriter as Binks entered her office. Being the gatekeeper to Mrs Plethora Carmichael, she had to be on her toes. Mrs C, as she was known around the office, was "exacting". It was the kindest adjective those who worked with her could find. Her catch phrase from the minions was, *never late, never wrong, never nice.*

'Yes?' Angel looked at the man holding his hat. He looked like someone who came to read the meter.

'I'm hoping to see Mrs Carmichael. I don't have an appointment, but, um.'

'Well, if you don't have an appointment.' Angel made an apologetic face.

George pulled out a card with his credentials which changed the tone in the room.

'Oh,'

'Well, if it's not convenient miss,' George said and the little innocuous meter reader got to work on Angel.

Plethora Carmichael's office was a large one. It had all the trappings of success. The big desk, the artwork on the wall, the plush carpet. She now sat at her desk and waited for Binks to be ushered into her presence. Although from different spheres of influence, Binks and Carmichael were quite alike. They held the human race in disdain.

Angel escorted Binks into the lion's den and he stood to take in the palatial surroundings.

'Detective Binks,' Plethora said and stood up.

'Mrs Carmichael.' Binks took a step towards the woman.

'Please, sit.'

George looked at the pair of white upholstered Barcelona chairs.

'They are the Barcelona chair,' Plethora said. 'Ludwig Mies van der Rohe designed the chair for his German Pavilion at the Barcelona Exposition of 1929.'

'Fancy.'

It may have been the must-have item of 1929, but with all things new, exciting, innovative, it may look good, but George found it uncomfortable, low, hard and it made him sit with his knees around his earlobes. He placed his hat on his lap and looked at all the titles on the prominent bookshelves.

'I can give you,' Plethora looked at her small, exquisitely expensive watch, 'twenty minutes.'

George dragged his eyes away from the books.

'Mrs Carmichael, when was the last time you spoke to Mr Stitt?'

'I told your little man all this. Do I really need to repeat myself?'

'I believe he asked you when you'd seen Mr Stitt. I want to know when you spoke to the missing person.'

'Missing? Not dead?'

'The date Mrs Carmichael?'

Plethora consulted her large leather-bound diary. George looked at the stationery and thought he'd like something similar when he was a proper writer.

'I really thought it was all cut and dried.'

George looked on with a frown.

'You know, dead.'

'Not without a body,' Binks said.

'Oh.' Plethora furrowed her brow. 'Here it is. I spoke on Wednesday 15th. He rang. He'd finished his book.' She looked at the detective and summed up his reading habits.

'Have you heard about it, Mr Binks?'

'Detective Binks.' George corrected Plethora. He may be only in the missing persons department, but the title mattered.

'Do you read?'

'Some.'

'He rang. We spoke. I said I was looking forward to getting the manuscript. Quite excited, actually. He is one of Raven & Square's rising stars.'

'And that's how you remember it?'

'Are you suggesting.'

'Nothing, it's just that I heard.' And here Binks looked at the door. 'I heard that you told him you were busy, and he might have a chance if he was dead. "A cheque in the post or check out".'

The words were barbs, meant to wound. Plethora kept her composure.

'Heat of the moment. Nothing in it.'

'Sounds like something to me.'

'I run a busy house, Mr Binks.' The slight was not lost on George. 'Stitt was late. I often encourage my stable of authors.'

'With death threats?'

'If that is all, Mr Binks?' Plethora looked at her watch.

'For now, Mrs Carmichael.' George rose and tucked his copy of Stitt's book under his arm.

'Like it?' Plethora asked.

'Haven't read it yet.'

'Would you like a signed copy?' She found a hardback and put it in George's hand.

'Let's hope Crispin, dear Crispin, is somewhere out there. But as time ticks by... hope fades.'

'Malcolm Sutherland. *The Clock Struck True.*'

'You *do* read, Mr Binks. Bravo.'

'I try tokeep up.

'Don't we all Mr Binks, don't we all?' Plethora said as she watched George walk out the door.

As soon as George stepped into the lift, Plethora sharpened her tongue. 'Angel.'

'Yes, Mrs Carmichael.'

'Do not talk to that odious man again.'

'No, Mrs Carmichael.'

'And what goes on in this office is confidential.'

'But he was the police. A detective. I didn't think I should lie to the police.'

'Am I surrounded by idiots?'

'Yes, Mrs Carmichael.'

'If anyone, and I don't care who, asks anything, anything at all, say you can't remember.'

'I can't remember,' Angel nodded.

'Yes.'

'Yes, Mrs Carmichael.'

'Did he say whether he thought Stitt was dead or not?'

'I can't remember.'

'Completely surrounded by idiots.'

Never one to squander money George made his way back to the bookshop for a refund.

No-one in their right mind needs two copies of *He Lives*.

He stood at the counter and quizzed the assistant on what she knew of Stitt as his refund was processed.

'We had him in for a signing. He was very smart. You know, one of those really well-turned-out people. I think he had a rather expensive hat.' The assistant conferred with her colleague.

'Yes, it was an expensive hat. And coat, Mabel, don't forget the coat.'

'Wool, I believe. Cost a fortune. Came in a car, too.' They recounted the event by the value of the items.

'Was he... nice?' Binks hated the word, but he couldn't think of any other to get to the nub of Crispin Stitt.

'Oh yes, very nice. Wasn't he nice, Mabel? Manners. That's what he had, manners.'

'Yes, very nice manners. We all got a small box of choccies.' Mabel's head bobbed up and down.

'Oh yes. He was nice. Pity he's dead.'

'But good for business. We've been busy, haven't we Mabel.'

'Oh yes, busy. Just as we were going to send back his remainders for pulp he goes and dies. BOOM!'

The last word made Binks jump.

'Sorry,' Mabel laughed. 'But we've been busy, very busy. Haven't we Ethel?'

'Yes, busy.'

George left the bookstore and ambled back to his office. The way he saw it, there was more to the plot.

No body had been found. Perhaps Stitt's lavish lifestyle was starting to pinch the purse. What better way to recoup one's finances than a magic trick?

And just like that, BOOM! as Mabel said. A new manuscript was at the printers and he was selling like hot cakes. It might be dumb luck (perhaps Binks had a better handle on Stitt than was first thought), or it might be a swindle that was just a bit too clever. Binks sat down at his desk, a small, paltry thing compared to Plethora's and picked up his pencil.

He made a list and distilled his thoughts. The list wasn't dissimilar to Crispin's. All the same characters were on it, the only difference being their motives rather than their reactions. Top of the list was Plethora. She'd certainly want Stitt dead or to stay dead. Uncomfortable chairs from Barcelona (Binks had no idea about the Bauhaus movement) don't come cheap. He didn't like the woman. She was rude, abrupt and probably hated humanity. She reminded Binks of someone, but he couldn't put his finger on who. On the other hand, she was shrewd, perceptive and astute. Again, he had the feeling he'd met someone similar. If Binks was prone to introspection, he might have recognised himself. But as he was as introspective as a lump of ear wax, he missed the nuance.

At day's end, George caught the bus home and settled in for the evening. He was a man of routine. He liked to get to his kitchen table, aka writing desk, by seven o'clock. His correspondence course on How to Write a Best Seller or your Money

Back, was a stickler for regularity. Binks sent his cheques regularly and received his course in return. He sat down and diligently wrote out his lessons on sentence structure, syntax and synonyms. He applied his lessons to his short stories and by the time he'd finished, they looked like something the war time censer practiced on with more holes than plot.

His lessons complete, he poured a cup of tea and settled down in his easy chair, Crispin's book on his lap. If he was to get to know Stitt, he felt this was where one should begin. The blurb ran something like this:

Man's journey through hell and back under the façade of the metaphor of a bad marriage and the existential threat of obedience to the soul of one's human complexities via an attempt at self-improvement. It wasn't what George considered light reading with tea and biscuits. He glanced at his latest western novel, *Something's Got to Go West!* It was a gripping read.

Self-control and George were made for one another. He rarely indulged in flights of fancy, the extra custard cream or anything that could be construed as a whim.

He read the first page of *He Lives* several times. He read it out aloud. It was all rubbish, arty-farty rubbish as his mother might say. He flicked through the pages and the book fell open at chapter six.

Crispin had slaved over chapter six. He thought it his best work.

'But Ambrose, don't you see, we all strive - but there's more to life than just livin' it.'

George read the phrase twice. It spoke to him. It

needled him as it has needled humankind through the ages from Socrates to Ernest Hemingway. The judges of the Arthur Crowther Medal for Writing Excellence had goose-bumps on the back of their necks at the premise.

Binks thought on those words. He read on,

'Goin' through the motions is not livin' Ambrose.'

And George applied Crispin's words to himself. Although to be fair, the premise wasn't a new one, but Crispin had given it a modern vernacular.

George sat back and sighed. Introspection is a dangerous topic when you have your life in order and you are a contented man. George found that he was not a contented man, after all. And he felt it was Crispin's fault.

Those words in chapter six were like barbs of truth and they pricked George like the devil. He took the book to bed and started again. Every chapter, every paragraph was a wound in George's side. One minute he was content with his lot, and the next he developed a scowl at the injustice to be handed a steady income, a house in an affordable suburb, loving parents and sober habits. Life was the absolute pits.

Now George felt the stirrings of dissatisfaction, he focussed them on Crispin.

'He did it. He made me unsatisfied with my lot in life.'

George Binks hated everyone, but now he hated Crispin even more.

The problem when you are an ordinary man in

an ordinary job is that no-one sees your pain. No-one mentions your angst or artistic temperament. George suffered alone. Because he wore a face that had never registered anything but disdain his work colleagues didn't notice his agonies of being ordinary.

As George's frump grew, he felt that Crispin was making his life miserable on purpose. He would find that man if it was the last thing he'd do. He would use all his brain power to get to the bottom of the case.

Amanda Stitt sat down and poured the coffee.

'Sugar, Detective Binks?'

'One please.' George wasn't accustomed to having coffee in the middle of the day, but Americans do things differently. Amanda Stitt fussed with the coffee pot and tossed her hair over her shoulder. She really was stunning to look at and had an air of intelligence. Stitt should have been happy to be married to such a woman.

'Sorry to bother you again, Mrs Stitt.'

'It's been days now, Detective. I've run out of tears.' Amanda looked at the picture of Crispin on the mantelpiece and bit her bottom lip.

'I'd just like to ask you a few questions.' George looked around the room. It was tasteful, understated, extremely expensive.

'Of course.' Amanda crossed her legs and her cotton trousers made a swish. She shrugged her cardigan over her shoulder and pulled a hanky from her sleeve.

'I read the station report, but can you tell me what his mood was like the day he left?'

'He was feeling a little flat.'

'Flat?'

'Yes. The muse had left him and he felt, well, flat.'

The news that Crispin might have been suffering sent a shiver of glee through Binks. If he was going through agonies, so should Stitt.

'And you didn't say anything to him?'

Amanda shook her head. Detective Binks didn't need to know she told him to drop dead.

'And his note? I'm leaving all this to you.'

'Crispin was always leaving notes. He...'

'Yes?'

'He thought they would be a sort of legacy. For when he was famous ,you see.'

'Right.'

'It was rather annoying, really.'

'Was it?'

'He could be challenging. Sometimes.'

'Could he?'

'You see I love that man to bits. Absolutely to bits, but sometimes he drove me nuts and when I said why don't you just drop dead...' Amanda stopped.

Binks almost raised his eyebrow.

'I mean...' Amanda un-balled her handkerchief and blew her nose.

'You know how it is, Detective.'

'I'm not sure I do.'

'He was such, um.'

'Was he?'

'Hmmm.' Amanda blew her nose again.

'Do you think he might have?'

'Oh no, Detective Binks. He wouldn't do that. Crispin loved life. NO, he'd never do that.'

'So, Mrs Stitt, if he loved life, where is he?'

'I wish I knew, Detective. I wish I knew.'

As the Brokers were next door, George knocked.

'Jim Broker?'

'That's he.'

George introduced himself, 'Detective George Binks.'

'Police?'

'Yes.'

At the introduction Jim brought out a man size handkerchief and blew his nose vigorously.

'Right, you better come in then.'

They sat in the front room, which was full of wedding paraphernalia.

'Daughter getting married. Lots to do. You got any?'

'No.' George thought on the disruption to his life others in it might bring.

'Best thing in the world, you know. Having kids. Best feeling in the world.'

George nodded. 'Now, Mr Broker, I'd just like to go over your trip with Mr Stitt one more time.'

'No problem. Tea?'

'No thanks.'

'I'll put the kettle on.' Jim blew his nose and disappeared into the kitchen, dabbing his eyes.

George had time to look around the room. It was chaotic. Full of sewing, presents, pictures of the family, and he saw one picture of Stitt. He was sitting outside, drinking. He looked perfectly at ease. He looked happy.

'Here we are.' Jim put the tray down on some sewing patterns and sat down.

'Terrible, really terrible,' Jim said.

'Yes. Well, Mr Broker, can you tell me what Mr Stitt's mental state was on the day before he disappeared?'

'It's all a bit of a blur, to be frank. He'd been knocking back my brew and had a few.' Jim brought out his hanky. 'If only I'd heard him leave.' He blew his nose.

'Was he happy?'

'Happy?'

'Yes, you know, happy.'

'Well, I don't think Stitt was ever happy. Weird fellow like that.'

The news that Crispin might be suffering made Binks feel better by the minute.

'He was a real nice bloke an' all that, but he wasn't happy. More like almost happy. He writes some rubbish or other, you know. Arty-farty stuff. I like westerns myself. Give me a beginning, middle and end. Something I can understand. Stitt writes... well, something my wife said is highbrow codswollop.'

'You like Westerns?'

'Oh yes, absolutely.' Jim fiddled with the teapot.

'Read any lately?' Binks sat forward on his chair.

'*Something's Got to Go West*! I think that was it.' Jim blew his nose.

The news gave Binks a warm feeling. There were people out in the world that liked westerns as much as he liked to write them.

'Detective?' Jim waved a plate of biscuits in George's direction.

'Eh?'

'Biscuit?'

'Thanks.' George juggled his cup and saucer and biscuit 'Now, do you think he might have...?'

'Oh no. Not Stitt He was one of those men that... well he wouldn't do that. It's not Stitt at all.'

'So where is he?'

The room went silent. The acres of tulle rustled near the open window. Jim blew his nose.

George sat at his desk and typed up his notes.

A search. A light plane. Dogs. The locals. And the man was missing. He left a note. He takes unsuitable clothes for the bush, almost like he knows he will be somewhere else. And he's missing as his book gets a boost in the ratings. The publisher wins, the wife wins, Stitt wins.

Where would a man go if he wanted to disappear?

If the clothes were a ruse, then a man wouldn't go far at all. Binks looked at the road map on his desk. He tapped his pencil on Block 67, a small dot with one dirt road in and one dirt road out. A dot in the vast outback, where no-one goes.

George hoped Crispin was happy, because he wanted to make the man as miserable as possible. No-one should suffer alone.

Thirteen

You can only organise someone else's life for so long before you need a break. Crispin needed some relief from the duties some of the population does daily from the time they are old enough to shell peas, until death. He moped around the Institute and grumbled when Len put a dirty spoon in the sink. It was the last straw, or the last spoon, as things stood, and Crispin saw red. He wagged his finger at Len and sounded like a shrew. It is one of the laws of human nature that some time in your life you sound exactly like your mother. Crispin sounded exactly like Mrs Bertha Stitt.

Len went bush to get away from Crispin. Cleanliness might be next to Godliness, but Len preferred the "lived in" look. Savin' people, he felt didn't include washing *every bloody day*.

Crispin wiped the camping stove one last time, folded the tea towel, and decided to go over the road.

He walked into the Buff Bar and plomped down on a stool.

'Youz vant,' Avis pointed to the fridge. Crispin shook his head.

'No monies, eh?' Crispin nodded and pouted.

'Too bad.' Avis shrugged.

'I could clean something if you want.'

'I don't vant.' Avis hitched up her bra strap. Crispin sighed and stared at the buffalo head on the wall.

Doc barrelled through the screen door and made his way to the bar. 'Line 'em' up Avis. I'm thirsty.' He slapped a few pound notes on the bar and sat down.

'I've been delivering babies.' He took the first beer bottle and downed it in one.

'Babies?'

'Yep. Six little beauties. Out west. Just got back.' Doc looked at Crispin and gave him a bottle of beer.

'Thanks.'

'No problem, mate.' Doc clinked their bottles and poured the beer down his neck.

'Six of the finest heifers you're likely to see.'

Norm and Ted and the others were treated to the blow-by-blow account of Docs trip out west. The weather, the flies, the dirt, the flies, the cows and the flies. Doc waved the money in the air and grinned.

'What's up?' He looked at Crispin and his dower face.

'Nuthin'.'Len's vernacular was slowly creeping up on Crispin. He'd be putting his duck out for greener pasture in no time.

'Well, I'll be back, Avis. Just gotta check on my place. Keep 'em cold for me, will ya?'

'Da, of course.'

'Ernest, come look at this.' Doc pulled Crispin out of the bar and into the sunlight.

'Isn't she a beaut?'

The men stood and admired the motorbike.

'She's ex-army. WLA Harley Davidson.'

The bike was in regulation khaki and had a sidecar attached.

'What's that?' Crispin pointed.

'Bloody machine gun.' Doc laughed. 'Bloody rusted on and can't get it off.'

'Does it, um, go?'

'Nah. Seized solid, but doesn't it look the business?'

It certainly looked the business to Crispin. He'd never seen such a monster of a motorbike, with a machine gun, and it gave him an idea.

'Get in,' Doc said as he went through the rather convoluted rigmarole to starting the WLA.

'Like this,' he said.

First the petrol was positioned to on. Then the advance on the handlebar was put in position. Choke, and kick her over three times. Ignition on, choke off, throttle kick and choke off. Crispin watched from the sidecar and didn't understand a thing.

'Nuthin' to it. Hang on.' Doc took off and headed out of town. He sang at the top of his lungs as he bumped and swerved down the unsealed road, his hair waving in the wind. Crispin held on and bumped along. He looked at Doc who seemed to enjoy himself. The man was happy. Crispin tried to smile. It hurt his face. He hadn't quite realised he was so miserable. Doc kept up a running commentary, although Crispin couldn't hear a thing as they powered down the road.

'Watch out!' The bike hit a pothole and Doc roared with laughter as Crispin was jiggled in the air. Crispin surprised himself by laughing too, which rapidly turned into a cough as a fly hit the back of his throat. Doc whacked him on the back and continued his conversation, often taking his hands off the bars to emphasise the point, which had Crispin hanging on that little bit tighter. They slowed for a corner and Crispin spat out the freeloader.

'Just up here.' Doc turned off and followed a small track to a copse of tea trees. 'Shangri-bloody-La,' he said and came to a halt, the dust settling over the pair. 'Come on Ernest, shake a leg.'

Crispin tried to get out of the bathtub. If you ever have the same problem the solution is to scrabble your feet, pull with your arms, wiggle your hips and slither. Crispin ended up half in, half out, then fell out the rest of the way and, cursing, trotted behind Doc.

'Sit. Won't be long.' Doc went off around the back of the shack and Crispin sat on the step and waited, pulling prickles from his clothes. It was peaceful out in the bush. Life and all its problems seemed so far removed from the gum trees, the buzz of insects, the bird calls and the flies it's just a pity Crispin didn't see it that way. He shooed flies and picked prickles with a scowl.

'Now, Ernest, can ya cook?'

'Well, I guess.'

'So go in there and whip something up. I gotta check on some stuff. Won't be long.'

The shack had three rooms, but they were neat, tidy and well stocked with books, food, and furniture. The new voice in literature looked at the bookshelves. It was a long shot, but he began to read the titles, looking for himself. There were quite a few textbooks on medicine, psychology and such, but nothing with Stitt's name on it. He ran his fingers over a large poetry section, well used by the look of it. Doc was quite a cultured man if his shelves were any indication. A noise outside made Crispin nip to the kitchen.

He found some ingredients and got to work, grumbling.

'Just whip something up, he said. Won't be long, he said,' Crispin parodied Docs happy demeanour. He rattled around in the small kitchen, working himself up into a frump. Granted, it was a change from Len's rudimentary arrangement, but once Crispin got frumping it was as if he had slipped on an old comfortable pair of slippers. He'd been in a frump, a funk, for nigh on a year and was practically an expert.

'So, Ernest, you all good?'

'Yes thanks.'

'Sure?'

'Yes.' Crispin snapped, although he wanted to say more. He bit his tongue to stop himself. When your favourite topic is yourself it's a hard ask to keep quiet.

They ate the pasta in silence as the night descended on the bush.

'I know I shouldn't ask, but...' Crispin began.

'Then don't.'

They sat and listened to the bush. Well, Doc listened, while Crispin swatted mosquitoes and practiced his frumping.

'Um, you don't think I could have a go at that, do you?'

'The WLA?'

'Yes.' Crispin collected the plates and took them inside.

'Sure.' Doc lit a cigarette. The aroma brought back all of Crispin's hankerings. He breathed in the smell.

'You want a smoke?'

'Um, no, that's ok.' The smell reminded him of his wife, his home, his life.

'You can ride a motorbike, I presume?'

'Oh yes. Definitely.' Crispin said it with such confidence he almost fooled himself.

'You can sleep here tonight. Take the ol' girl tomorrow. 'I'm gonna be catching up for a few days. Keep her for a bit.'

'Thanks.'

As Crispin lay under the mosquito net in his make-shift bed, he thought on the generosity of others. He'd yet to work out the giving part of the bargain, but he began to appreciate the receiving quite a bit.

'Now just ease her into it.'

Crispin let go the clutch and shot off down the road.

'She's got no lights, and the brakes are a bit dicey,' Doc yelled as the bike hurtled to near death, with Crispin in charge.

He eased off the throttle and tried singing. Opening one's mouth at high speed is just plain foolhardy. Crispin spat a fly and kept his mouth shut. He tried the gears, and by the time the Buff Bar came into view he had more or less got the hang of motorbike riding. It was the stopping that was tricky. The Harley sailed past the petrol bowser at speed and Crispin thumped the foot brake. It was made of marshmallow. He crunched down the gears, went bush with a wide U turn and came back past the Buff for an encore. Avis waved a tea-towel like a chequered flag, the regulars giving a whoop in encouragement. Crispin grated down to second gear and pulled on the brake with all his strength. The bike came to a juddering halt inches away from a huge old eucalypt in front of the Institute. It had been a long time since Crispin had felt so alive. A near-death experience usually has that effect on people. He stepped off the Harley and his legs turned to jelly.

'Bloody cramp.' He acted nonchalant to the audience and walked inside the Institute tin shed, then collapsed on his camp bed with a smile on his face. To think, all it takes is a brush with death to make a man happy.

'Len, pack your bags. We are going to town.' Crispin patted Len on the back. It never occurred to him to ask Len if he wanted to go.

'But-' Len looked at his new stash of Special. He had the next couple of days mapped out.

'Come on. I don't have all day,' Crispin said.

'But.' Len touched his black eye. Things were at a delicate stage, vis-à-vis Avis, and Len felt he should stick around.

When a man like Crispin gets an idea, and he thinks it's a good one, there is no stopping him. Crispin packed his toothbrush- that's all he had- and then it dawned he needed petrol if he was going to make the journey.

'Er, Len.'

'What?' Len said as he packed bottles of Special into a burlap sack.

'You got any spare money? For petrol.'

There was a moment of indecision. Len's face twitched. He went to his 'hiding place' (tea caddy) and pulled out some notes. Although Crispin's mother had scolded him on numerous occasions for snatching, she wasn't around now. Crispin snatched the notes so fast he could have worked for the tax office.

'I'll pay you back.'

'Nah, not a problem, Ernest. I reckon you got ya reasons and ya know what ya doin'.'

The chances of that were slim to zero. Crispin had an idea. A vague notion he needed to go into the city to see what was going on, to get a feel for how he might be received should he do a Lazarus. And, he wanted to bask in the glow of his popularity. The ego always needs feeding. There was no point in staying incognito if no-one missed you.

'Oh, it's you... been away, have you?' No, the vague idea was to snoop.

Len finished stowing his drink in the sidecar as Crispin went through the rather convoluted starting procedure. He gave the final kick, and the Harley came to life.

'Ernest,' Len looked through the machine gun sight, 'I like it.' He slithered into the sidecar and they rode up to the petrol pump.

'Fill her up Avis.'

'You got monies?'

Crispin flourished the notes and Avis picked off a few.

'You taking Nutjob?'

'Yep.'

Avis eyed Len sitting in the tub, nursing his burlap sack with a smile on his face.

'You better look after Nutjob, Stinky.'

'I will.'

'You better look after him good.' Avis spat on the ground.

'Of course.'

Avis patted Len on the shoulder. 'Don't you...' She wagged her finger at him.

'I won't.'

And they were off with neck snapping gear changes and ball breaking suspension on the rutted road.

'Er, Ernest?' Len shouted when they had been on the road for about half an hour.

'Yes,' Crispin yelled.

'Why are we goin'?'

Why indeed, thought Crispin. There were myriad of why's.

'Um, I need to get some money to pay you back Len.'

'Oh.' Len thought on that for a bit. 'Ernest.'

'Yes,' Crispin slowed so he could hear better.

'Ya don't need to, Ernest. I'm savin' ya. That'll do me and ya give us a haircut. The proof of the pudding is in the basin.' Len touched his head.

'Eating,' Crispin tried to be helpful.

'Nah. Not yet.' Len replied.

The conversation was becoming Kafkaesque

'I reckon ya me mate. Ya don't need ta pay us

anythin'.'

'Yes I do, Len.'

How Crispin was going to get money was another question entirely. One that might probably involve breaking into his house, then nipping back to the Block before the dust settled. That was a plan that he made up on the spot. And finding out if he was being missed. There needs to be something in it for the ego or what's the point? Of course, his superego—that critical, moralizing voice—was told to put a sock in it. This sort of thing was way out of Mr Super-cilious ego's league. Crispin wasn't usually a fly-by-the-seat-of-your-pants man. He liked routine, order and pressed underwear. Now he was, (as the French say) sans culotte and loving it. He was making it up as he went along. The plotter had become a stream-of-consciousness pantser. What could go wrong?

Fourteen

Two hours at normal highway speed may not seem a long time, but when you need to conserve fuel and travel at a leisurely pace, it can feel like eternity might get to the finish line first. Len dozed, clutching his bag of Special, and Crispin had all the time in the world to reflect, re-evaluate and resolve some issues. The only thing he did was think about what he might find in the fridge at home.

It occurred to him if it was a Tuesday, Amanda might be at tennis all day, unless she was grieving and lying in a darkened room with a supply of drugs from the family doctor and a large box of tissues. He wished for the former and hoped it was the latter. His mind ranged over a corn beef sandwich, pickles, mustard, and a glass of red that he kept in the wine cabinet under the stairs. It wasn't much of a leap to go to icecream and wafers. And before the cheese platter, the Harley and its occupants had reached the outskirts of the city.

Len woke up, readjusted his glass eye, and blinked.

'Are we there yet?'

And then our fly-by-the-seat-of-his-pants man had a slight problem. Crispin stopped at a petrol station and looked at his companion.

'Er, Len.'

'Yeah?'

'Where do you usually stay when you're in town?'

'Now let me think.' Len scratched his head. 'I recollect I stayed at a police station on the north side a couple of times.' He frowned. 'I had a stint at the big house.' He tapped his nose. 'And I seem to remember under a bridge somewhere.'

This wasn't helping.

'Wait here,' Crispin said. He hopped off the bike and jiggled his leg back into life, then hobbled to the petrol station kiosk. It was then he caught sight of himself in the plate-glass window and it was a bit of a surprise. The figure that stared back was rugged looking, a decent size beard, and although not sleek, he was slim (ish).

Crispin stood and looked at his reflection. It was quite pleasing. Not so pleasing for the cashier on the other side of the window.

'Oi,' the attendant shouted, 'what's your game?'

'Oh,' Crispin was startled out of his vanity. 'Can you direct me to a cheap hotel?'

'The Mission's down the road mate.'

'The Mission?'

The attendant gave Crispin the once-over and sniffed.

'Oh.'

'Down the road. Half a mile on the left.'

'Right.'

'No. Left.'

'Yes, got it.'

'And they got soap, mate.'

Crispin slowly backed away. He'd never been told he stank - apart from by Avis, but she was his friend.

'Stinky,' he said in her peculiar Russian accent.

'chush' sobach'ya.' It brought a smile to his face.

'What you grinnin' at' Len asked as he corked a bottle and stowed it in his bag.

'Avis.'

'Avis,' Len said, and a dreamy look settled on his face. 'Avis,' the name was repeated with reverence.

The Mission of Light was previously an office block and didn't look at all like the hotels Crispin had been accustomed to in his previous life. He parked the Harley and they looked at the sign.

The Mission of Light might have lit up once, but the light bulb was broken, as was the front door.

'Shall we try somewhere else?' Crispin asked as a man came out of the building swearing and cursing, then staggered down the street.

Len took a swig of Special He may not have been a customer of this particular establishment, but he knew enough to know these sorts of places were dry, very dry.

'Nah, she'll be right, Ernest.' Len took a long draught of his bottle and corked it. He stashed the burlap bag right to the end of the sidecar foot well; he had a feeling he'd be spending some of his evening in the car park.

Nutjob and Stinky fronted up at reception and were met by a bloke who had a chest two pickaxe handles wide. He smiled when Len smiled.

'It's not, is it?'

'You,' Len pointed and grinned.

'Leonard Gillespie.'

'Bruiser Brown.' Len pointed. 'It's Bruiser Brown.' Len pointed to Bruiser by way of introduction to Crispin.

'Where ya been Gilly?'

'Bush.'

Bruiser nodded. 'Bush.'

'This 'ere's Ernest.'

'Howdy,' Bruiser held out a meaty hand.

'Hello,' Crispin winced as Bruiser squeezed.

'Nice to meet you, Ernest. Any friend of Gilly's is a friend of mine. Now what can I do for you blokes?'

Crispin rescued his hand and explained they needed a bed for the night, maybe two.

'Well, you've come to the right place,' Bruiser said, and brought out his register.

'Name?'

'Ernest Hemsworth.'

Bruiser wrote it down.

'Len Gillespie.'

'I know that,' Bruiser laughed. 'Now, I can put you on the top floor. You ok with stairs?' He looked at Len's spindly legs.

They nodded.

'This way then.' They followed Bruiser through a maze of corridors and listened as he pointed out the highlights of the Mission.

'No lights here. Watch the broken wall. Look out for the hole in the floor.' Toilets, showers and dining room, which were all on the ground floor.

'We were lucky. Got the block for six months before it's gonna be knocked down. Top floor is a rippa. Grand views.'

They began to climb.

Cleaning a tin shed might be a bit aerobic, but it doesn't prepare you for a fourteen-flight climb.

Crispin felt the burn. Len was about to pass out when Bruiser picked his old mate up and with a fireman lift bounded up the stairs like a spring gazelle. Crispin became a mouth breather and hauled his body up one painful flight at a time. They reached the top and panting, Crispin hung onto the wall.

'Here we are,' Len was set on two feet and they looked around at the doors. 'Down there, second on the left.' Bruiser pointed then said. 'You ok to do kitchen duty?'

'Pardon?'

'We all got to pitch in, mate. Kitchen duty, five o'clock.'

'Oh, yes. Absolutely,' Crispin said, nudging Len.

'Yeah. Righto,' Len said, catching his breath.

Bruiser gambolled down stairs.

'Just showin' off. Used to be a boxer, in and out of the ring.'

Crispin listened to the retreating steps. 'A good man to know in a dark alley, eh?'

'Somethin' like that, Ernest.'

It was something like that which saw Bruiser as a next-door-neighbour to Gilly in the big house.

Crispin opened the door and could see a problem straight away. There was a double bed.

Len sat on the bed and sneezed. His glass eye popped and rolled on the carpet. It was one of those moments that isn't covered by Miss Elizabeth Mountjoy's book on etiquette for all occasions. Elizabeth didn't see this one coming, and neither did Crispin. He gave a little giggle which turned into a guffaw, which ended in a peal of uncontrollable laughter. Len retrieved his eye and without water, well, the only way to clean it of fluff was to just pop it in his mouth. This was too much, and Crispin collapsed on the bed and rolled around in a fit of hilarity.

I don't care what anyone says, laughter is infectious. Len was soon joining in, and they rolled on the bed like a couple of kids, giggling, laughing and it felt good. Len and Crispin hadn't felt this good for a long time.

'How did you lose it, Len?'

'I sneezed.'

'No,' Crispin giggled, 'How did you lose it the first time?'

'The war. Bloody shrapnel. Didn't see it comin' did I? I woke up in the ditch and a bloody duck was lookin' at me.'

'Really?'

'I can't be sure mate, but I think he got me eye.'

'What?'

'He bloody took it. Right there when a man's down on his luck, the bloody duck took me eye.'

Crispin stifled a laugh.

'They got me outta there, so that's somethin'.'

The mood turned maudlin as Len relived the past he had tried to forget.

'I'll never forget it, ya know.'

'I shouldn't think you would.'

'An' I'll never forget that note on the kitchen table neither. She just up and left. Said she couldn't live with a man like me.' Len touched his shrapnel disfigurement. Scars from war run deep and not all are visible.

'Still, it was quite a while ago.'

'Don't make no difference, Ernest. Not in here.' Len touched his heart.

'But now you have the Institute, and me.'

'Yeah,'

'And I think you're doing a splendid job, with saving me and all that.'

'Am I?'

'Yes, so things are looking up,' Crispin added, 'and Avis. Don't forget about Avis.'

'Avis,' Len said.

'So things are on the up.'

'It's 'bout bloody time,' Len said and lay on the bed.

'You got a watch, Ernest?'

'Nope.'

'Me neither. Reckon it's five o'clock?'

'I wouldn't have a clue.'

The kitchen was a hive of activity. Bruiser was directing traffic to and from the dining room, the oven, the sink and the pantry.

'Are we late?'

Bruiser looked at the clock on the wall. They were thirty minutes behind schedule.

'We ain't got a watch,' Len said.

'Not my problem, Gilly.' Bruiser handed two trays of bread and butter and pointed in the direction of the dining room.

Crispin was roped into cutlery and crockery. He set out the tables and marvelled at his life. One day you are wearing expensive underwear and called *The most exciting voice from a writer we have seen in a long time,* the next you're living in a shelter for men with a man who is convinced a duck took his eye. It somehow felt like he was living in the real world after a stint on the sidelines.

The men chipped in with chores, and it wasn't long before they were sitting down to sausages, mash, beans and lashings of bread and butter.

'Just a reminder,' Bruiser said when the meal was finished and the washing up done. 'The door closes at ten.' Crispin thought on the hours between six and ten. He could ride past his Eden Grove house in the dark and maybe catch a glimpse of his wife without being seen.

'Want to come for a ride Len?'

'Sure,' Len put his tea towel away and followed Crispin out into the cool night air.

'Hang on,' Len pulled Crispin and they went to a small room out the back. 'A bloke doin' the dishes said it's all for free!'

Crispin picked a jacket with lurid stripes on the sleeves, a pair of corduroy trousers and a purple jumper, Len a pair of overalls and a cardigan. They looked like they had been dressed by a blind man in the dark.

'Ernest, ya lookin' pretty sharp there,' Len said.

'You're not so bad yourself.' They giggled and walked to the Harley.

'One for the road, Ernest?'

'Don't mind if I do.'

Drinking and riding a motorbike should be exclusive activities. Put them together and you're asking for trouble. It seemed Crispin and Len were asking for trouble. They had polished off two bottles before they left the car park and were in high spirits.

Barrelling down the road, Len began to sing and wave at passing motorists. It's not the sort of thing you do if you want to remain undetected by the authorities. A police car did a U-turn and followed the bike. At this stage of the antics, it was only Len who had let his hair down. Crispin was intent on getting to his house, to scope the joint. He saw the police in his mirror and decided to take evasive action. Len saw the police and decided the machine gun would give them the fright of their lives. He sat up and took hold of the gun and waited until the car came alongside then let 'em have it with both barrels. He made the kak, kak, kak noise and laughed like a drain. The police didn't see the funny side at all. They are not renowned for their sense of humour. The officer motioned to Crispin to pull over. So he did, right down a narrow lane that a car could never follow. Len whooped with delight when the police were left behind.

'That was close,' Crispin said when he'd parked the bike in a recessed doorway and cut the engine.

'Ernest, I like you.'

'Len, I like you too.' The men sat in the dark and basked in their friendship. That the friendship relied on escaping the police, drinking rubbing alcohol and sharing a bar of soap only made the bond stronger.

After a goodish twenty minutes, Crispin went through the starting procedure about three times before he got it right, then they rode out of hiding and were on their way to Eden Grove.

The suburb was brightly lit as Crispin slowed and took the familiar turnings on Everard Drive. He rode past his house and took a long look. The upstairs bedroom window was the only light shining. Amanda must be in bed. He stopped in front of the Broker house and watched the family through the window. They were doing normal stuff, ordinary stuff, the stuff that makes life worth living. Life went on without him.

'Ernest?'

'Yes?' Crispin watched the bedroom window.

'You got a watch?'

'Nope.'

'Ya reckon it's ten o'clock?'

'I have no idea.'

Bruiser was just locking up when the two ran for the door.

'Just made it.' Bruiser put the padlock on and reminded them that the stairwell light didn't work.

The climb was torturous. Len had two bottles stashed in his overalls and at level six his legs gave out. He sat down and said he'd just sleep there.

'Come on Len.' Crispin pulled him up and half carried him up to level ten. They stopped for a drink to lighten the load.

'Not long now,' Crispin pulled up his mate and they made the climb to fourteen his legs burning with the effort.

'Thanks mate.'

'Come on Len,' Crispin opened the door and threw his friend on the bed, then plonked himself down and that was the end of that. Except sometime around two a.m. Crispin's bladder made the call. Fourteen flights in the dark wasn't a pleasing prospect. He knew they left the empty bottles on ten, but even that wasn't an easy option. Crispin looked at the window in the moonlight. If he just opened it, he could piss in the wind.

The office block had those windows that only open a fraction lest the workers get the idea that working nine to five for about thirty-five years isn't worth it. Crispin wrestled the window open and relieved himself. It was all going according to plan when a gust of wind banged the window shut, well. nearly shut. Crispin let out a yelp and fell to the floor. He rolled around in agony for a bit. He moaned for a while. He grabbed his crotch and sucked in his breath, then let it out and eventually, after he had exhausted every expletive in the dictionary, crawled to the bed and curled into a foetal position, eventually to sleep.

He woke to Len dribbling on his shoulder and when he tried to move, it reminded him of his exploits in the night. He moaned and pushed Len off.

'Ernest.'

'Yes?'

'Nuthin'.' Len smiled and rolled over.

An accident like Crispin's can leave a man with a lasting impression. Crispin looked under the sheets and didn't like what he saw. It had swollen to double its size, (contrary to what they say, big isn't always better) and was a nasty bruised purple. He lay back and willed the swelling to go down. It would take more than positive thinking.

Breakfast at the Mission consisted of sausages, beans and eggs with lashings of bread and butter.

Crispin looked at the meal.

'Donated,' Bruiser said. 'Once we had cornflakes with everything. A truck rollover or something.' Bruiser laughed.

After easing himself into a chair, Crispin ate with gusto. He hadn't realised how hungry he was for a bit of proper food.

'You alright, Ernest?'

'Hmm.' Crispin wriggled in his seat.

'Sure?' Len asked. 'Looks like ya need somethin'.'

Jim Broker's words echoed in Crispin's memory. It would take more than a decent dump to ease his unease.

'I have a bit of a problem,' Crispin whispered when he saw Len's solicitous frown. 'Down there,' Crispin pointed to his crotch.

What runs through someone's mind when they have a problem "down there" could form a long list. Len sniffed. Nope, it wasn't number one... or, as Len thought, number two. Third on the list was the dreaded zip.

'A zip?'

'Nope.'

Len was out of ideas.

'Bit sore,' Crispin said and made a face.

Len and Ernest had been together for a few weeks, and there was just no opportunity for a sexually transmitted disease. Asking about parasites at the breakfast table, well, even Len had standards.

'Bunged up?' Len asked, his standards slipping.

'Well...' Crispin shook his head. 'I...'

'You blokes leaving or staying?' Bruiser interrupted the moment.

'Er, I reckon we'll be staying one more, mate,' Len nodded and grinned in Crispin's direction.

'Hot water goes off in around ten minutes.'

Len didn't see the significance, but Crispin was right on it.

'C'mon Len.' They bolted their breakfast, collected some new clothes from the donations and hit the showers.

For someone who had been washing in a small tub with laundry soap, the sight of a real bar of soap almost made Crispin weep. The hot water hitting his little problem, or big problem if you looked at it, brought tears to his eyes. Len sang as he got into the swing of things, Crispin luxuriated in the hot water, perfumed soap and being grateful. The latter was a new experience, one that crept up on him. Being surrounded by genuine, kind, considerate people often has that effect. What he had yet to discover was that most people are genuine, kind and considerate, but when you've been concentrating on your own reflection for quite a while, 20/20 vision is a blur.

'Looking sharp, Len,' Crispin said as Len put on some golfing slacks and a hideous shirt with horseshoe motif and a jacket of prickly wool.

'Right back at ya mate.' Len said, looking over Crispin's stylish outfit of brown fleck suit trousers, a green shirt and the lurid jacket from the night before.

Suitably attired, the thought of going back to the room up all those stairs was put aside and they stepped out to greet the day.

'What's the plan?' Len asked.

'Well... perhaps we should...' Crispin began.

'I wanna get Avis somit. Somit for her. Nice like.'

'Shopping then?'

'Yeah.'

The Harley was pressed into service and headed for town.

What to get a woman who has everything? So the bill posters said on the front of the shop.

'That sounds like somit,' Len grinned and winked his eye. The purple bruise was now a nice mustard yellow, a reminder of the love of his life. They looked at the window dressing and Crispin clutched his crotch. It was not the time to be thinking of his wife, their marital bliss under the sheets and the lingerie he'd lashed out on her. He rubbed his trousers to the tsk of the foot traffic. Someone muttered, 'filthy man,' as his blood set up a throb which did nothing to alleviate his pain.

The men entered the lingerie shop and Len's one eye opened wide. He looked around at the lace, the bras, the petticoats and the suspenders.

'May I direct you?' A little woman in black met them at the door. Miss Dolly King had seen it all in her career as a shop assistant. She looked Nutjob and Stinky up and down and took their measure. The clothes, the beard, the glass eye and one tooth. Dolly knew just what sort of men had walked into her world. She'd seen Crispin from her throne behind the cash register, goggling at the window, and called the police.

'I think you will find the department store across the street will have what you are looking for.'

Crispin narrowed his eyes. He knew all about these officious little women who ran boutique shops. He knew how to handle little women like Dolly. He oiled his charm-o-meter and smiled.

'What a lovely shop you have.'

Dolly remained stoic.

'Oh, I'm sure we can find just what we want here, and so reasonably priced for such quality.'

Dolly licked her lips and narrowed her eyes.

'Is that French?'

She melted, just a little. The man was a pervert, of that she was certain, but even perverts have taste. No-one had recognised her French lingerie at a glance.

'From Paris. That's in France you know.' Dolly directed her gaze to her bra selection. She slapped Len's paw from pawing the merch.

'We are looking for something special. My friend here wants to make an impression on his lady friend.'

Len nodded and grinned.

'What is she like?' Dolly asked. It was a big ask. How do you describe a woman like Avis? A mean left hook, keeps a metal cosh behind the bar, spits, but a heart of gold.

'Big.' Len offered.

'I see.'

Len brought up his to hands and in that time-honoured fashion, showed Dolly how big with his fingers spread wide over his chest.

Dolly looked at the door. The police shouldn't be too far away.

'We have this.' She held up what looked like a sling for two boulders, something a landscape gardener might use to position the rocks as a feature on a front lawn. It wasn't far off the mark for Avis's features.

Len ogled.

'We have it in black.'

'I'll take it.' Len grabbed at the apparel and Dolly whipped it away.

'If you will just step this way, Sir, I'll box it for you.' Dolly glanced at the door. She couldn't keep this charade up for much longer.

Len thumped a large wad of pound notes down on the counter just as the police entered the shop and made a beeline for the 'pervert with a beard in a hideous jacket.' Even the police can pick a hideous jacket in a line-up.

'Oh,' Dolly looked at the money, looked at the police, and then looked at Crispin and smiled. Apparently, a bottom line trumps a pervert.

'He the one Miss?'

Dolly put her hand over the money and giggled. 'I think he went over the road, to the department store.'

'Are you sure?' the policeman said looking at Crispin's jacket. Surely there couldn't be two people walking the streets with a jacket like that.

'Hmmm.' Dolly pursed her lips lest she compound the lie.

'Right.' The police gave Crispin and Len the once over, then departed, but not before one said, 'My missus wants this stuff, says it's French. But I reckon it's just a hard sell.'

'It's from Paris. That's in France, you know.' Dolly shouted at the retreating officers.

Crispin grabbed his crotch as a wave of relief passed through his body. Dolly conveniently looked the other way and boxed the over-the-shoulder-boulder-holder, while Len looked on.

The Hurley-burley of lingerie was exhausting. Dolly watched the two misfits leave and put the kettle on.

Crispin waited for Len to stow his fancy box and took off towards Eden Grove.

Every bump in the road reminded him of his injury and he had the facial expressions to match.

'Ernest?'

'Yes?'

'You're a good mate.'

'Thanks,' Crispin winced as he took a corner.

The Harley rattled down the road and as the familiar sign-posts came into view, Crispin felt cheered, almost happy. If only he could bottle it, he'd make a fortune.

They pulled up at the end of Everard Drive and Len took the opportunity to pull on a bottle of Special.

'Ernest?'

'No thanks Len,' Crispin patted his mate on the back. 'I'm just going to look up a friend. Won't be long.'

'Want me to come?'

'No. Thanks anyway.'

Len settled back in the sidecar and took a swig. Crispin inched himself off the bike and crept up to his house, one oleander bush at a time. The good thing about breaking into your own house is you know where the spare key is kept. He ducked into the shrub Amanda had planted and then snuck through the side gate and scrabbled under a flowerpot for the key. It wasn't there.

He knew the toilet window would be open—it was always open—so moving to the back of the house, Crispin hoped to have a bit more success.

'Yes.' He punched the air. It was a small window, but with the pipes as footholds, he'd be able to squeeze inside. He plopped down onto the cistern and then landed on the part of his anatomy that really should be at home resting.

Several whispered expletives later he was able to stand upright and breathe.

Crispin knew exactly where to get his hands on his wallet. It was in his golf trousers back pocket, which, last time he was home, were on the gentleman's trouser press in the bedroom walk-in wardrobe. He cautiously opened the toilet door and listened. Nothing.

Creeping about in your house, you suddenly become aware of all the things you should have done. The floor creaked, the doors squeaked, and every footfall was amplified by the stark, minimalist décor. He stood still for a moment and looked at his house with new eyes. It didn't look homely. It didn't look warm and inviting like Jim's house the night before. It was missing some soul.

Putting his décor to one side, Crispin climbed

the stairs to the bedroom and peered through the crack in the door. Amanda wasn't there. Her handbag, which she always kept on the dressing table, was missing. The idea was to get in, get the money and get out, but Crispin was struck by the disarray of the room. The bed wasn't made, there was a wad of tissues on the floor, and his pillow had been used as a bolster. It looked like someone had been having a hard time. Crispin grabbed his wife's pillow and took a deep breath. It smelt of her. He nuzzled in deep and closed his eyes when he heard a car pull up in the driveway. Now was not the time to be sentimental. He momentarily thought about coming clean. Just waiting there and surprising his wife. She'd probably fall into his arms and they'd live happily ever after, if she didn't kill him first.

He put her pillow back and ran for his trousers. He couldn't dilly dally fossicking for his wallet so he bundled the trousers under his jacket, grabbed the spare change tin and legged it down the stairs, and just as the back door opened, he ran out the front.

'Hey,' Jim saw the intruder and gave chase. Later he would describe the fellow as having a beer belly, full beard and wearing a hideous jacket with green and puce accents and a slim cut. (When a man has spent the best part of a month listening to wedding chatter, some of the vernacular is bound to rub off).

Now, Crispin ran, which was quite a surprise, as he wasn't accustomed to the feeling of exercise. He threw himself onto the Harley and prayed that it would start. If only he could remember the sequence. He fiddled, he pulled and pushed, and then Len said, 'Get over.'

Crispin didn't argue. They changed places and

Len went through the procedure like a pro. Jim stopped running and squinted at the pair as the bike flew past him at speed.

Len whooped as he put the Harley through its paces.

'Where we going, Ernest?'

'Shopping Len. We are going to hit the town.'

There was a slap-up lunch at the pub. There was a trip to the stationers for notebooks and pencils. There was new underwear, toothbrushes, and soap. By the time Crispin had finished, there was hardly any room for Len in the sidecar.

'We need a haversack,' Len said as he tried to put his arm in the tub.

They walked into an Army Surplus store and Len's past came flooding back. He stood and his eye began to twitch.

'Len?'

'Mate.'

Crispin led Len to a seat and then fetched a bottle of Special.

'Thanks.' Len took a long draft and wiped his eye.

'We can go somewhere else, if you want.'

'Nah. I'll be right in a tic.'

'Can I help you?' a shop assistant asked.

'We need a bag for the Harley.' Crispin pointed to the bike parked outside.

'He ok?'

'Will be in a minute. Just the war. You know.' Crispin patted his mate on the back. 'Give him a minute will you?'

'Sure.' The shop attendant went to collect a selection of bags muttering, 'Bloody war. Bloody,

bloody war.'
'Len?'
'Thanks mate.'

Now the WLA Harley Davidson looked the business. It had saddle bags strapped to the seat, bulging with bags and boxes. Crispin was wearing fabulous riding gloves with gauntlets, Len had an Aviators leather helmet with earflaps and a silk scarf and found an eye patch that was worn by Rommel (or so the sales pitch said—hand on heart).

'You take care now,' the shop assistant said. 'No charge for a digger.'

The unlikely pair rode off and headed for a bookshop. Stitt needed to see if he was famous. He remembered the large one where he'd done a signing. Clonbrock & Dunn was the biggest in town.

He parked the bike, and with Len in tow walked to the shop and looked at the window display.

'Ya like reading, don't cha?'

'Yes.' Crispin looked at his books. He took up the whole window; not a Neville Shute in sight. They walked inside.

'Do you have Crispin Stitt's latest?'

'Do we have Crispin Stitt's latest, he asks me, Ethel. Of course, we do. Look at the window luv.'

'Oh, of course.' Crispin smiled.

'He's dead, you know.'

'Really.'

'Pickled, they said. In a barrel.'

'In pieces, apparently,' Ethel added.

'Never!'

'Well, it's not confirmed, but...' Mabel said.

'Imagine if he popped up now,' Crispin said and laughed.

'Lordy lord. What a thing to say.' Mabel took a good, long, hard look at Crispin. She took off her glasses and squinted.

'He'd be in pieces,' Ethel laughed.

'Pickled, like an onion.'

'Or an egg.'

'Oh, yes, like an egg.'

Mabel rang up the price. 'Anything else?' she narrowed her eyes at Stitt.

'Hang on a minute.' Crispin went for a second look. 'Er, Len, do you want something?'

'How about this one?' Len put *Something's Got to Go West!* on the counter.

'And that, thanks.' Crispin peeled off a pound note.

'You know, you look awfully familiar,' Mabel said.

'Me?'

'Hmmm. Doesn't he look familiar, Ethel?'

Ethel came in close and took a good look, then shook her head. 'Nope.'

Back in the day, Crispin Stitt would have given his eyeteeth to be recognised, fawned over and asked for an autograph. Now he stroked his beard and waited for his books.

'Awfully familiar.' Mabel handed over his books.

'Thanks.' Crispin pulled Len to the door and then in a show of bravado gave a wave to Ethel and Mabel.

'You know who he reminded me of?' Mabel said as she watched Crispin and Len leave.

'Who?'

'Neville Shute.'

'Really.'

'Yes, except for the jacket. Shute would never be seen dead in something like that. Green *and* puce. Some people must be colour blind. No, Mr Shute would never.'

'Hmm,' Ethel nodded. 'He's prolific, you know.'

They headed back to the Mission, mission accomplished. Crispin whistled, Len sang, and the world was a happy place. That is until they drove past the Mission and a police car was parked outside.

'Bugger.'

Fifteen

Detective Binks sweltered in his car. With a map on the passenger seat, he drove with dogged determination past the black stump to the middle of nowhere. His old Vauxhall Velox bumped and wallowed over the potholes and corrugations in the road. Binks took another look at his map, swatted a fly that had managed to bypass all the sealed windows, and gritted his teeth. He didn't like the bush any more than he liked his fellow man.

A T-junction came into view and he read the sign hanging on one nail like a criminal. Half the letters had rubbed away, but he saw a B and 7, which was good enough.

'Block 67,' George said and swung off to the right. He went for around thirty minutes before the road ended in the bush. A U-turn, and he took the other road and by the late afternoon, he drove into the metropolis of Block 67 and went out the other side in the blink of an eye. Another U-turn, and he eventually pulled up at the petrol station.

Avis came out and spat. George wound down his window, and a fly took the opportunity to investigate an inviting looking nostril.

Binks snorted, and the fly shot out to live another day.

'Is this Block 67?'

'Maybe.' Avis didn't like strangers. She waved a

fly away. 'You vant petrol?'

'Yes,' George said and wound his window up.

'You got slave at home, eh?' Avis stood with her arms crossed.

'Pardon.'

'You get out of car or I don't give petrol. Simple.'

'Oh,' George put on his hat and stepped into sunlight and plenty of it. The heat beat down on the dirt, the flies found fresh meat and Avis gave him a look that might kill.... quite possibly a water buffalo at twenty paces.

'You lost?'

'No.'

Avis filled the car as the pump ticked over at twice the price of a Fabergé egg.

George followed Avis inside and handed over the money, wondering if he needed to leave his kidney as well. He asked for a receipt.

' A Vot?'

'A receipt. This is work related expenses.'

'You tax?'

'No.'

She wrote out a receipt on the back of an envelope and handed it over.

'Thank you.' George filed the missive into his pocket and looked around. It didn't take long before he was weighing up the moral dilemma of drinking on the job or quenching a thirst with alcohol, because in a place like Block 67 the water was suspect. He erred on the side of caution and put his first beer down to prudence. The second was being sensible, the third was to be sociable. A man who was thought to have sober habits and an ordinary life was bound to cut loose at some point.

That point was a dot on the map with one road in and one road out.

'You inspector of license?'

'No.'

George settled in and leaned on the bar. 'Many people come through?'

'No.'

'No-one recently?'

'No.'

Avis waited.

'Nothing unusual?'

'NYET.' Avis hitched up her bra strap and looked at Norm and Ted. They found the buffalo head riveting to look at.

The block was one of those places where the Pope could be drinking right next to you, but if asked, you'd never seen him or his little red slippers.

'You vanting somezink?'

'Another?'

'Da.' Avis pulled the bottle lid off with her teeth and handed the beer over.

'Thank you.' George drank with vindication, knowing he was quite right in hating the human race.

But then, alcohol often has the effect of softening the edges, just a little. As he consumed, George found he could relax. Whether it was the drive, the flies, the heat, or the flies, he relaxed so much he found himself telling his audience he really didn't want to be a detective. He wanted to be a writer of hard-boiled western adventure. Ted and Norm listened as George expounded on his hopes and desires. Avis nodded in all the right places. She had seen this scenario play out on more than one occasion. Everybody had a story to tell. She had heard them all.

'Vot stop you?'

'Pardon?' George looked at the buffalo and frowned. He was sure it was stuffed, but here it was, asking him difficult questions.

'Mr Detective. Vot stop you?' Avis asked.

'I...' George was stumped. Avis shrugged and wiped the bar. 'You go home. You tink about it.'

George nodded. 'But Mr Detective, you sleep here tonight eh? No drink and drive, eh?'

George nodded. Avis nodded to Norm and Ted and they led George over the road to the Institute and put him to bed on the camp stretcher.

If only he'd known how close he was to his quarry. But writers of hard-boiled western adventure who have had way too much beer on an empty stomach can often miss the smoking gun in the second act. Sober... well, that's a different matter.

Sixteen

Because the police at the Mission of Light were in the dark concerning a fellow with a full beard and hideous dress sense, they left, having nothing to show for their efforts. Crispin and Len watched them leave, then went inside.

'They always come here first,' Bruiser Brown said, looking at Crispin's jacket. 'Looking for a bloke with a beard.' Bruiser stroked his beard and laughed. Crispin laughed along, thinking it was a close shave.

'You two up for dinner duty?'

'Absolutely,' Crispin said. 'By the way, Bruiser,'

'Yes?' Bruiser had heard all the opening gambits that the other side of polite society had to offer. He was wary of anything that started with, by the way, as it happens, you wouldn't believe it, and I don't know where I left it. He stroked his beard and waited.

'I noticed you take donations of clothes.'

'And?'

'Well, I know of an address. The woman might be wanting to donate.'

'We'll take anything.'

Crispin recited his address, the telephone number and the name of the woman. She'd be home now, if you want to ring and just arrange it.

'Thanks.' Bruiser went into the little office and made the call. He gave the thumbs up.

'Ya know somit Ernest?'

'What's that Len?'
'One man's trash is worth two in the bush.'
'Ne're a truer word has been said, Len.'

After a good shower first thing in the morning, and an appraisal of one's assets that was favourable regarding size, colour and pain threshold, Crispin was feeling chipper. It only hurt when he thought of his wife. So the thing to do was not think of her—much. He went into the small room and looked at all the clothes on offer. His clothes. He picked his Messer's Mondial & Plath trousers and found they were a bit big. He rummaged and saw his two-tone lucky shirt and his hacking jacket. He was quite fond of his hacking jacket. It had that author-at-work look, and quite possibly the Hemingway look.

'Another life,' he said and put it back on the pile. He felt an affinity for his hideous jacket and slipped it on. His clothes were all a little large, but they made him feel a million dollars.

'Len, look at this.' Crispin pulled a nice pair of tweeds from the pile and colour co-ordinated it with a tasteful blue shirt. He matched it with his hacking jacket.

'Looking snappy, Len.'

'Looking slick, Ernest.'

A fellow came in and picked a jumper Amanda had given him on his birthday.

'Looking good, mate.'

'Thanks.'

They set off in high spirits back to the Block. Crispin settled into riding as Len looked at the scenery. They were making good time about thirty minutes from the Block when a Vauxhall came out of nowhere and only just missed them.

Crispin pulled over and looked back at the idiot driver.

'Absolutely nuts,' he said.

'Could have killed us,' Len said.

They carried on, thinking they were the luckiest people on the planet. Life had given them another shot and they weren't about to waste it.

'Ya think she'll like it?' Len combed his hair and ran a bit of Brylcreem through. He adjusted his eye patch and for that last bit of panache, threw his silk scarf around his neck.

'Perfect.'

'Ya reckon?'

'She'll love it.'

Len hesitated.

'Go on.'

'Ya comin'?'

'I'll be over in a sec.' Crispin was stowing away his paper and pencils, his new underwear and sundries.

'Go.'

'I'm goin'.' Len took a deep breath and walked out the door.

Crispin looked at his bed. Someone had been sleeping in it. He checked under the cot for his press cuttings. They were still there, but someone had been rifling through. Probably someone looking for Len's Special, he decided.

He ran his fingers through his hair, hitched up his trousers, and with money in his pocket, walked across the road.

Len was sitting at the bar nursing a cold beer on his one eye.

'Stinky,' Avis made a face, then pursed her lips.

'Me?'

Len pointed to the over-the-shoulder-boulder-holders which were hanging off the buffalo's horns above the bar. He took the beer bottle off his eye and Crispin winced.

'I think she likes me.' Len put the bottle back and grinned.

'Here,' Avis handed a cold bottle to Crispin.

'You put Nutjob up to no good?'

Crispin shrugged and gave a grin. He pulled a few bills from his pocket and put them on the bar.

'Thanks.'

Avis looked over the pair, called it chush' sobach'ya, but she pulled a bottle, popped the lid with her teeth and handed it to Len.

'On Avis, Len,' she said and smiled, hitching up her bra strap.

The men looked at one another.

'She called me Len.' Leonard Gillespie grinned.

Crispin woke to the sound of birds and lay in bed, thinking. He counted the days he'd been away, the days he'd been without a cigarette, the days he'd felt something akin to happy, and it all toted up to a new man.

He made breakfast, and left early to deliver the bike to Doc.

Doc came to the shack's front steps at the sound of the Harley and waved as Crispin rode up.

'Got the hang of it then?'

'Yes.' Crispin hopped off and pulled a package out of the sidecar.

'Thought you might like this,' he handed over a large box. 'Open it.'

Doc looked at the surprise. A pair of gloves with gauntlets, a book on poetry and at the bottom, Stitt's book, *He Lives.*

'Thanks,' Doc tried on the gloves and smiled.

'Thank you.' Crispin sat down on the porch step and in the still of the morning the men listened to the bush. To Crispin it felt like it was for the first time.

'And here is the money I owe you.' Crispin tucked a few pound notes into the poetry volume.

'Did you find what you were looking for?'

'I think so.' Crispin shooed a fly and sat back.

'Sometimes you don't need to look very far.' Doc flicked through Crispin's book. 'The meaning of life is how you see yourself in it. Want coffee?'

'So, what's the plan, Ernest?'

'Well,' Crispin began, 'I might just hang about here for a bit.'

'And?'

'And...' The word hung in the air as Crispin tried to put into words what he thought he might do with his time.

He looked at Doc's bookshelves. 'Read.'

'Help yourself.' Doc threw his hands wide. 'Just come by anytime. I have an old bicycle you can use if you want.'

'Thanks.'

The offer got Crispin thinking. And thinking, when you are full of the milk of human kindness, can have lasting repercussions.

Doc dusted off the old bicycle and handed it over. 'Anytime.'

'Thanks.' Crispin cycled down the road, keeping his mouth shut, but singing inside, all the way back to the Institute of C.R.A.P. He was formulating a plan, and it was a doozy.

Seventeen

George Binks arrived at the Police station in the afternoon and went straight inside to make his report. His head was still throbbing from a hangover and his nerves jangled at the near miss when a fly wanted to explore the back of his throat and he could have killed a motorbike rider.

As he sat down he vowed never to visit the bush again. But, at his desk, he thought about his 'adventure'. He analysed it, looked at it from every angle, and came to the uncomfortable conclusion that it had been rather exciting, intriguing and different. It was what his correspondence course on writing called "life experience". Half a dozen beers and a fly up your nose might not be much, but to Detective Binks, it was a bit of an epiphany. So, this was what other people got up to when he was ironing his underwear. Alcohol might just be the answer. He wasn't the first person in the world to have had the same thought, but it was enough to lift his spirits sufficiently to think he was onto something.

He looked over his notes once more. No-one could call the man a slacker, and thought that, yes, he was definitely onto something.

📖

It was while standing on the department steps deciding if it would rain and would he be wise to wear galoshes that Binks overheard a uniformed officer.

'The most hideous jacket thing you ever saw. Green and puce and something else.' A laugh was heard.

Binks pricked up his ears. He'd seen such monstrous dress sense thirty minutes from Block 67. In fact, he nearly ran the wearer off the road, which considering their dress code, might have done the world a favour.

'Where did you say?' And Detective Binks got all the information he needed to put two and two together. His brain really was worth bottling.

There was nothing for it. Binks would need to make the long trip back to the Block.

This time he assembled a survival kit.

The chap at the Army surplus store put the haversack, the hat with fly screen, the "you beaut" insect repellent, the hunting knife (he was working on commission) and asked about shark repellent.

'No.'

'Right then, anything else?'

Binks looked around the shop.

'I've got something you might like. A bit of a souvenir.'

'Hmm?'

'Rommel's eye patch. It's not cheap, but these things rarely are, if you know what I mean.' The attendant winked. 'Worth a fortune in a few years.'

'Really?' Binks said. Although he wasn't born

yesterday, he thought an eye patch would add something to his 'life experience'. He could just imagine his author photo with the swagger of a man who lived life to the full. It would add that little bit of panache. Of course, it had none of that effete aggrandizement about it. Only real men wear eye patches.

Everything was bundled into the haversack and Binks stowed his booty in the car. He just needed to take his correspondence course lessons (he wasn't a shirker) and a change of clothes, and this time he would be ready for Block 67.

If he calculated all the imponderables, Stitt would be at home, he could have the case wrapped up in twenty-four hours, and he would have a 'life experience' or two up his sleeve for his homework.

But, imponderables are like flies. They never give up.

Eighteen

Mr. 'I-run-by-the-seat-of-my-pants' Stitt thought that although he was taking each and every moment as it came, he needed a plan. Once a plotter, always a plotter. He had the idea he'd write another book. Something that people wanted to read. Something with a beginning, middle and end. Ernest Hemingway had done it. Neville bloody Shute was doing it all the time. Crispin Stitt should be able to do it, too. He'd yet to work out the finer details concerning plot, pace and premise, but they were mere trifles. The thing was, he had an idea. Naturally, he thought it was a good one. His ego wasn't quite ready for an epiphany just yet.

Crispin set the table for lunch and woke Len.
'Lunch mate.' Len opened his eye as much as he could and smiled.
'You ok?'
'Yeah.' Len said and tried to wink.

'Are these vegetables?' Len poked his food.
'It's good for you,' Crispin said, and put some sauerkraut on his fork. 'See?' He ate with relish.
Len looked at the cabbage and carrot.
'Go on.'
It was a struggle, but Len chewed and swallowed.
'I think I prefer me Special.' Len pointed to his

one tooth. 'Not so much work.'

'How old are you, Len?' Crispin collected the empty plates.

'Don't remember.'

There was a moment of silence as they looked at one another.

'Len?'

'I was thirty-two in '17.' Crispin did the maths.

'Sixty-five then.'

'Is that right?' Len ran his fingers over his scarred face.

'Yes. You still got a lot of living to do.'

'Don't know 'bout that.' Len sat back and rolled a ciggie.

'I remember the day I signed up. Me mate, Johnno, and me, we thought we'd be home in a couple months. Thought it was a bit of a lark, really. A game.'

And Len talked his way back to his memories while Crispin listened.

'First time away. We were all so fresh.'

'What did you do? I mean, before the war?'

Len took a deep breath. He rubbed his scars.

'I was a painter. I worked for the brewery. Never ending job, that was. By the time ya finished one end of the sheds, it was time to start t'other. Johnno was me mate. We was painters.' The only sound was the bush as the men sat in silence.

'He didn't come back.' Len reached for a bottle of Special. 'Hardly anyone came back.'

Crispin washed the dishes deep in thought. He

hopped on his bicycle and peddled out to Doc's thinking. He sat in an old armchair on Doc's verandah and pondered. All this thinking had to go somewhere.

He would write a fictional account of Len's story. It would be called *Resurrection*. He would write it from the heart. Crispin took a deep breath and his ego sat back and kept its mouth shut. Sometimes an epiphany can do that.

Of course, he didn't think to ask Len if he wanted to go through the agonies of remembering. He hadn't got to the point of thinking if those at Block 67 wanted the spotlight, and the problem of his own resurrection was lurking somewhere in the background. Crispin Stitt needed more than a moment of sudden and great revelation and tacit permission to pull it off. He needed a healthy dose of empathy, probably taken three times a day until the patient's narcissistic rash clears up.

Crispin still had a nasty rash as he thought of another Arthur Crowther Medal for Writing Excellence.

Doc's bookcases held Crispin captive all afternoon as he dipped in and out of poetry, anatomy, animal husbandry and psychology. It was the last subject that played on his mind as he rode back to the Institute. Reading about personality traits can be enlightening. One invariably studies the text with friends in mind. Crispin saw just about everyone he knew. By the time he had skimmed through the tome he felt he knew quite a bit about the ego, the superego and the id.

As he rode into town ,Crispin saw a car parked at the Institute. He recognised it as the same car that tried to run them down.

Probably came back to apologise, Crispin thought.

George Binks sat at the kitchen table with his fly screen hat on and waited.

'Ernest,' Len pulled Crispin inside and sat him down.

'This 'ere is George. He wants to be enlightened.'

'Does he?'

'He said he's lookin' for answers.'

'Is he?' Crispin narrowed his eyes at George Binks. He had the look of a man who doesn't scare easily.

Binks narrowed his eyes back at Crispin. To meet the man who is responsible for all your earthly woes is quite a moment.

'Tea?' Len put the kettle on and sat back down.

'This 'ere is Ernest. He wanted to be saved.'

Binks blinked.

'I saved 'im. Aint that right Ernest?'

'Yes.' Crispin watched the man for any twitch. He tried to peg George into a character trait. It wasn't easy. He looked perfectly ordinary. To George, that moniker was the bane of his existence and it was all Crispin's fault.

'Ernest, is it?'

'Yes,' Crispin blinked first.

'Now, George, do ya take milk and sugar? We got both, ya know.'

'Milk and sugar.'

Len fussed over the mugs of tea. He couldn't believe his luck to get another wayward soul through the doors of the Institute. Souls were dropping like flies (the ratio was about 1,877:2), but Len didn't let that get in the way of a good simile.

If Avis had been there at the kitchen table, the whole thing might have been cleared up in a jiffy. As it was, Len prattled on about the Institute while the two combatants eyed one another over tea and biscuits until George said, 'I read a book recently called *He Lives.*'

'Oh. Was it any good?' Crispin could feel his heart thumping out of his chest.

'I thought it was interesting.' Binks stared at Stitt and raised his eyebrow. Binks wanted to say more. He wanted to tell Stitt his dissatisfaction with life was due to his words. He might have said Stitt's books settled on his once contented life and poked its nose into the corners, under the hall rug and found George Binks a very ordinary fellow indeed. He wanted to grab the man by the scruff of the neck and boot him to Kingdom Come.

'Ya like books then. Ernest here, he likes books. Isn't that right ,Ernest?'

'Yes.'

'Read anything recently?'

'No.'

'He bought a book. You bought that book didn't ya Ernest? I reckon it was the book George was talkin' about.'

'Really?' George looked through his fly mesh and hoped Crispin Stitt was sweating under his collar. He hoped the man was going through agonies at his little ruse being discovered. He longed for

Stitt to crack under the strain. Under normal police procedure, Detective Binks would tell his quarry the game was up. He would wait for them to throw themselves on the mercy of the constabulary and the judicial system. Most criminal types had a brain that the scientists didn't want to bottle in a jam jar. Now, Binks wanted to hunt his quarry, to tease, to make him squirm.

'Oh, that book. I gave it to a friend.' It wasn't a lie.

'I heard the author went missing. 'round these parts.'

'Did he?' Crispin reminded himself to keep his wits sharp. He didn't like this fellow one bit.

'Hmmm.' George was enjoying himself.

'Ernest and I went lookin' for a bloke a while back. Just walked into the bush they said.'

'And then,' Binks began.

'Yes?'

'His books started to sell, he got a publishing contract for his second boo,k and by the look of it...'

'Yes?' Crispin leaned in.

'All his troubles were over, just like that.' Binks clicked his fingers. Crispin jumped.

'Amazing.' Crispin sat back.

'Well, I reckon this calls for a drink.' Len fetched a couple of bottles of Special and plonked them on the table.

'Now George. I don't wanna pressure ya, but sometimes a bloke who needs savin' needs a drink. To loosen up.'

'It helps,' Crispin said, passing around three jam jars.

Binks looked at the brew. It looked evil. It

looked like something that might be used on a carbuncle and give a nasty hangover. He weighed up the offer. On the one hand, alcohol was the gateway to life experiences. It was de rigueur as an author to have life experiences. The added bonus of alcohol, Mr Stitt would surely fall foul of the carbuncle concoction and spill the beans. Binks just had to be mindful of his consumption. It was all a matter of restraint.

Len began proceedings with a swig and passed the bottle to Binks. George looked at Len's mouth, which had, just moments ago, been clamped around the bottle.

'It'll loosen ya up, George.'

Binks poured a little in his jam jar. Len topped it up and winked. 'Ya got things on ya mind. This'll help.'

Binks looked at Crispin.

'It's not poison,' Crispin said.

'Git it down ya neck.'

Binks took a swig and swallowed. It felt like rubbing alcohol and soap in his mouth and went down with the afterburn of a jet fighter. George coughed and was sure he'd received third-degree burns.

'Ernest?'

Crispin filled his jar and took a sip, keeping his composure. If he was going to get to the bottom of this fellow, he needed to show some restraint.

'So, George, what brings you to Block 67?'

'If ya tell us, George, then we'd know just how to go about savin' ya.'

'Yes, tell us George,' Crispin said and supped his drink.

'I'm looking for...'

'Him?' Len interrupted and pointed to the tin roof. 'We're all lookin' for 'im George.' Len polished off his jar of Special and grinned. George, he thought, was a tough nut to crack, but with his special blend of therapy aka Special brew, the truth would come out.

Binks cast a long look at Stitt. A very uncomfortable long look.

'Drink George?' Crispin filled the detective's jam jar. 'It does wonders for your internal plumbing. It's restorative, informative and rehabilitative.' George took a sip and eyed Stitt over his jam jar lip.

'There now. Don't that feel better George?' Len relaxed into a second jar and sat back. 'Ya know, I thought I had nuthin'. Turns out I had it all. That right, Ernest?'

'Yes. That's right Len.'

They looked at George and urged him to partake of life. He sipped. It didn't burn too much on the way down.

How much alcohol it takes to get plastered really depends on more than one thing. But for an ordinary man of sober habits, it only takes about three jam jars. George finished this third, and it suddenly was so clear to him-what 'it' was exactly, might be up for debate, but at the time, *it* was crystal clear.

'You,' he pointed his finger at Crispin's chest. 'You,' he said again, just in case anyone had any doubt as to who.

'Me?'

'It's all your fault. I see it all now.' George tapped his nose and narrowed his eyes.

'That's the way, George. Get it off ya chest.'

George poked his chest and held out his jar. A man can work up an awful thirst when he gets going. As far as Detective Binks was concerned, he was on top of the situation. He was firing on all cylinders and had everything under control.

Crispin's stamina vis-à-vis alcohol wasn't in the same league as Len, but he was on the leader board.

'Now, George. What have I ever done to you? We only just met.' Crispin laid the bomb on the table and waited for it to go BOOM! If he knew anything about being drunk, he knew enough to bet his Mont Blanc that George would go Boom.

Stitt didn't need to wait long. George took his jam jar and pointed at Crispin.

'S'all your fault.'

'Is it?'

'Yes. You and your ideas- putting ideas into a man's head.'

Len basked in the glow of his therapy. He liked to see a man get it off his chest.

'You. More to life than just living it,' George scoffed.

Crispin recognised the words. He remembered the day he wrote them. How full of hope he'd been. How he thought he'd found a universal truth.

'It's not my fault I have nothing to show for it.' George whined.

'Don't you?'

'I didn't want to be in the police force you know.'

'Didn't you?' Crispin should have been alarmed at the word "police", but after five Specials, things weren't so restorative, informative or rehabilitative, never mind clear.

'No,' George said, 'I did not.' Binks poked his

finger in Crispin's chest.

'What did you want to do, George?' Len asked. 'I used to paint.'

George looked at Len and all at once, he knew he'd fallen into Beatnik territory. A painter with an eye patch, a writer with a beard, a commune arrangement in a tin shed.

'I suppose you play the ukulele,' Binks said. He really needed to get out more (FYI Beatniks played bongo drums and guitar).

Len opened a fourth bottle. 'Mate,' he grinned. 'So ya wanna play the ukulele, do ya?'

'No.'

'The piano?' Crispin offered.

'No.'

'Do the police play the piano?' Len asked.

'I don't know.' George was trying to follow the logic.

Crispin filled everyone's jar. 'George, George, what did you want to do?'

Binks looked around the room. To the casual observer, it looked like he was hunting for an answer. Something like that I spy game. He sighed and frowned.

'A duck?' Len asked, scanning the darkened corners of the Institute.

'No.'

'You wanted to be a duck?' Crispin asked, and studied the man. He didn't look anything like a duck.

'No.' George took a swig for courage. Somewhere in the back of his brain he thought he might store this moment and file it under "life experiences". Some fellows who don't drink for a living often think that they will remember everything. After all, it happens all the time in normal circumstances. George closed his eyes and pencilled in the memory. It was rubbed out just as quick.

'A duck?' Len asked, and his eye began to twitch.

'No. I want to be a writer.' There, he'd said it.

'Well now,' Crispin said. That's a co, a co- a coincideny 'cause you know, I wanna to be a writer too.'

'Me too,' Len said. At this stage of Len's therapy, he would have agreed to wanting to be Field Marshall Rommel.

'And what do you write, George?'

'Well, not many people know this but, hard-boiled western adventure.' George got it out in one breath. That little voice in the back of his brain told him to shut up, but now he had said it, he felt in good company. These beatniks would understand his creative side.

'I got a book ya know. *Somethin''s Got to Go West!* Ya been there, George?'

'Where?'

'West.'

Crispin's brain wasn't working well at all. His ego? Well, it couldn't help itself.

'I wrote a book once.'

'I know.'

'Ya didn't!'

'It was a bestseller.'

'I know.'

'Was it?'

'Not many people know this, but I wrote another one.'

'Get outta here!' Len said, then added, 'That

deserves a drink.'

They toasted the good fortune to know a man who had written two books.

'So George, you written anything?'

'Well, here's the thing.' George leaned his elbows on the table. 'I don't know how.'

'I reckon it's like the ukulele, George. If ya can play that, ya can do anything.'

'You just need to have a beginning, a middle and an end.' Crispin said.

'They're the ones I like.' Len nodded.

George began to laugh. It was infectious.

'I think Hemingway had a ukulele,' Crispin giggled.

The mood degenerated into hysterical laughter.

'Did he have a duck?' They laughed like drains.

'I never seen a duck play a ukulele.' Len was crying from laughter.

'I'm a detective you know.' That had them rolling on the floor.

'I'm supposed to be dead.' Crispin guffawed. George got the hiccups from howling with laughter.

'You know, I came out here to look for you.' Binks wiped his eyes.

'Me?'

'That's right.'

'Why Ernest?' Len tittered.

'I shouldn't tell you.' George put his finger to his lips.

'Get it off ya chest, George.'

'Well, he's s'posed to be dead. Only he isn't.' George poked Crispin in the chest to prove the point. That piece of information had them giggling uncontrollably.

'Looks like a furphy to me.'

'A furphy,' Len spluttered.

'A furphy,' Crispin giggled. 'I was meant to be dead.'

'You were s'posed to be dead,' George slapped Crispin on the back.

And that was the last word as Len slowly slipped to the floor, Crispin slumped on to the table and George staggered to the camp cot and flaked out. Chances are, in the cold light of day, everyone would wish they were dead. Hangovers show no mercy whatsoever.

Nineteen

It was late morning—well early arvo, really. Ok, it was around five pm when George surfaced and wondered if he was alive. He popped his eyeballs back in and tried to swallow. Life experiences can leave a nasty taste in your mouth.

He had a vague notion he should be somewhere, doing something, but couldn't at that moment think what that something might be. He lay still, hanging onto the sides of the cot as the tin shed revolved above his head.

If this was living, he wished he was dead.

Crispin had the same thought as he tried to move his head. It was stuck to the table with dribble. He pulled his face off the Formica table top and winced. As hangovers go, his was off the scale. He touched his tongue and moaned. George moaned in response, which gave Crispin a jolt into reality. He looked over at George, who stared back.

A small sliver of sense wormed its way into Binks's superior brain.

'Stitt.' The word came out like 'thit.' Tongues have a really hard time while hung over.

'Huh?' Thit blinked. 'The Ukulele player,' he said and frowned.

Len came to life.

'I'm blind. I'm blind. He groped the leg of the table. 'Oh lordy, lord, I'm blind.' Crispin leaned over and snapped the Rommel eye patch off Len's good eye.

'Bloody miracle.' Len slumped to the floor.

There was a longish moment as the three musketeers looked at the day, what was left of it and wondered if it was worth the effort to partake of life and all it had to offer.

Len erred on the side of caution and lay back on the floor. Binks rolled over and cursed the person who invented gravity and found out the earth rotated and Crispin's liver coughed once, flexed its muscles and sent a message to the brain. Stitt stood and held the table for support.

'Coffee, anyone?'

Two moans echoed in the Institute.

'I'll take that as a yes.' Crispin made his way to the camp stove and quietly went about the process of living. It was a slow, painful process for all three, but as the sun dipped for the day they came to life one corpuscle at a time. The mosquitoes kept their distance. It's only the females that bite and they had more sense than to risk a blood alcohol level that acted like rocket fuel.

Around seven p.m. George's tongue decided to work sufficiently to ask what day it might be.

'Dunno mate,' Len said.

'Wouldn't have a clue,' Crispin added.

'Need to be somewhere, mate? Ukulele practice?' Len asked.

'No.' George's superior grey matter began to function—you can't keep a brain like that in the dark for long.

'Stitt' George pointed.

Crispin pointed 'Detective George Binks.' His

brain was also coming up for air.

'How do. I'm Len Gillespie. Gilly to me mates.' Len smiled like he was meeting his room-mates for the first time. Knowing his brain, which was a bit pickled already, it might have been the first time. Everyone looked at everyone.

'Well, I wonder if this calls for a drink?'

You just can't keep a good man down! Len brought out his Special and plonked it on the table.

'No.' George eyed the bottle.

'Not for me, Len,' Crispin eyed Binks.

Len corked the bottle and slumped. 'I don't reckon it'd be right to drink alone.'

There was an awkward silence as the tin roof ticked and creaked after a hard day in the sun.

'George?' Crispin picked up a pencil and doodled on a sheet of paper.

'Hmmm?'

'I don't know who you think I am, but I do know you have a deep-seated desire and it's not being fulfilled.' Reading a book of psychology all afternoon, something is bound to penetrate the ol' grey matter.

'Ya just gotta practice ya ukulele, George. All it takes is practice.' Len nodded at his sage words.

George slumped at the kitchen table.

'What he needs is a good...' Len began when Crispin held up his hand. Jim Broker might put life's deep-seated desires down to being fixed by a good bowel movement, Len Gillespie might think life is alright as long as you can have a sit and a think, but Crispin knew that was not the answer. He'd tried.

'I know who you are Mr Stitt.' George sat back with a satisfied air. He stared at Crispin ,looking for a bead of sweat, a swallow, a confession.

Crispin was made of sterner stuff. He stared down Binks and then asked, 'Who?'

'Crispin Stitt,' George almost spat the last syllable.

'This 'ere is Ernest, George,' Len offered.

'I don't think so.' George had come to his senses and was getting tired of the shenanigans.

'This here is Crispin Stitt. A man who disappeared with the intention of defrauding the public, gaining publicity, wasting police time and money, not to mention giving people a sense that their lives have as much meaning as a bath plug.

'We've got a bath,' Len said.

'Really?' Crispin thought on his rap sheet. It sounded impressive. It sounded like something that might get you room and board at the Big House.

'And is your life as meaningless as a bath plug, George?

Binks narrowed his eyes and set his jaw.

'I see. And it's all this fellow's fault, is it?'

George let a sneer creep over his lip. Crispin thought he was practically up there with Jung and Freud and an expert psychoanalyst.

'It's this fellow Crispin's doing that you have an unfulfilling life? It's Stitt that made your life a misery, is it?' Any normal man might have snapped out an answer. George thought he had the answer to the question. He might have raged that yes, yes it was all someone else's fault. But the trouble with a superior brain is that it can see the nuance.

'Well, George?' Crispin knew he had the

detective on the run. He knew the feeling of blaming others so well, he could understand the agonies George was going through.

'Hmmm?'

The three men studied the tabletop. Len broke the silence.

'All ya gotta do is do stuff for other people. It's that thing. Ya can't lead a horse to water but he ain't burnt his bridges just yet.'

Crispin winced. 'Can't make him drink.'

'I dunno about that, Ernest.' Len popped a cork and took a drink. He wiped his mouth and handed the bottle to George.

'No thanks.'

'Ernest?'

'Not for me, Len.'

'George.' Crispin put his elbows on the table. 'Perhaps you are not looking for this Stitt fellow. Perhaps you are looking for...

'Life experiences,' George squeaked. It was a hard pill to swallow.

'I reckon he's lookin' for a beginnin', middle and end.' Len took a drink.

'Are you?' Crispin put his hand on George's shoulder.

'Yes.'

'So vot stop you?' Crispin took up Avis's inflection.

It was a question George had asked himself many nights as he toiled away at his kitchen table. There was always a convenient excuse.

'You know George, I think I could help you.' Crispin pulled out a pencil and a sheet of paper.

'See, I told ya. All ya gotta do is do somethin'
for someone else. That's all it takes. There's more
than one way to bury a dead horse.'

'To skin a cat.'

'I ain't got a cat, Ernest.'

'No.'

'Ya can always play the ukulele, George, but not
with a cat.'

'Or a dead horse,' Crispin added.

George pulled in his chair and rummaged
through his bag for his correspondence notes. He
pulled out his eye patch and Len looked at it with
the wonder of watching a magic trick.

'It's Field Marshall Rommel's actually.' George
looked at Len's eye patch.

It didn't take a superior brain to work out they
had been duped. Ordinarily, George would have put
Army Surplus salesmen on the list of people he hated
more than other people he hated, but the swindle
didn't hurt so much, the dupe didn't sting, and it
was all just the milieu of life and its experiences. He
smiled. Len smiled. George giggled. Len laughed.

'Ya reckon he wore 'em both at the same time?'
Len gave a guffaw.

'You never know.'

Stitt knew of the trials and tribulations of being a
writer. He knew what it felt like to toil alone, never
knowing if you're wasting your time or throwing
pearl after swine. He knew of the drought when
words would not come, the agonies of wringing
every word written in blood. He also knew a thing

or two about sentence structure, syntax, pace, story arcs and characterisation.

'Hard-boiled western adventure.'

'Hard-boiled western adventure,' George nodded in agreement.

Len looked on with benevolence. He had saved two people in one day. It deserved a drink. Or maybe two. It wasn't a big call to predict Len would quietly slip into familiar surroundings once the second bottle of Special was empty. George and Crispin watched him slump. Crispin put him to bed, tucked in his mosquito net and came back to the table.

'George?'

'Ernest.'

And as the evening fell into night a new chapter was begun.

Twenty

It's alright getting sentimental at the thought of George finally breaking free of the daily grind, Crispin doing something for someone else and Len saving wayward souls, but George still had a job to attend, Crispin still had a book to write and Len was still looking for love. One sober night does not make the world a better place.

But it was a start.

George slept in a makeshift hammock and woke to the sound of birds chirping, the tin shed creaking and cracking as it warmed to the day and the buzz of flies. He looked at his watch and thought he should get ready for work. Superior brain or not, it was a rude shock to discover he was sleeping in his underwear and over his prescribed time. He sat up and fell out of his hammock. For a man who was of regular habits, had never missed a day of work and prided himself on punctuality, his situation gave him a moment of angst. What would his superior say when he didn't turn up? (It would take two days before they noticed George was missing. He was a bit like wallpaper.)

Crispin sat up and rubbed his beard. He felt different. He felt energised. He felt like a decent human being.

'Morning George. Coffee?'

George was a "cup of tea, a soft boiled egg and a

piece of toast" man. He'd eaten the same breakfast most of his adult life.

'Coffee,' George nodded.

'You know, my wife drinks coffee at all hours.'

George remembered the occasion. Amanda Stitt had offered him coffee in the afternoon.

He looked at Stitt. The beard was a convenient disguise, but you can't fool a man with 110% brain power, even in the early morning in his underwear. He could wrap the whole thing up right there and then. He could collar Stitt and take him back to the city. He'd file a report, go home, put the kettle on, sit at his kitchen table and... the thoughts swirled around in his head. It would be certain death to his creative side. A side he'd just managed to crack open last night.

'Coffee will be just the ticket.' George smiled, pulled on a pair of trousers, and sat down at the kitchen table. It was about time he took a holiday. He'd telephone the office, take a few days off, and who knows, perhaps get started on a bestseller. He looked at Stitt busy at the camp stove. A wealth of writer knowledge right at his fingertips, and he was willing to give it all to George. It was an opportunity too good to miss.

'You ready for a bit of breakfast Len?' Len opened his eye and sucked his tooth.

'I'll take that as a yes.' Crispin busied himself as George looked over his notes, and Len watched a fly.

It wasn't a big step from a restorative coffee and eggs to 'what shall we do today?'

Crispin looked at his star pupil and felt he needed to organise George's life. He was good at this sort of thing. He'd managed to get Len looking human and just about married, so Binks should be a doddle.

There is a fine line between being bossy and being helpful, just like there is a fine line between generosity and self-congratulations. Crispin outlined the plan for the day to Binks and sat back waiting for the rain of accolades. It was a little dry in the Institute. Binks was a man accustomed to doing things his way. He liked to ease himself into an idea, a project, a situation. All this 'can-do' stuff had him on the hop.

'Er, I think I'll look over my notes if you don't mind.'

'Right.' Crispin had the idea he would be a mentor, a guiding hand, on-hand at all hours of the day or night. To be sidelined before the main event took some of the steam from his boiler.

'Er,'

'Yes?' Crispin leaned in expectantly.

'I wonder if you have a phone.'

'A phone?'

'Yes, a telephone?'

Len scratched his head and sucked his tooth. 'A telephone, eh?'

'Yes.'

'Nope.' Crispin shook his head.

'Over the road, perhaps?'

'Nope.'

'Down the road, surely.'

'Nope.'

'Oh.' Binks looked at his watch. He should be walking through the front door of the station at this very moment.

'Are you sure?'

The men looked at one another.

'Yep.'

This put a different slant on things. George drummed his fingers on the table. On the one hand he wanted to stay, get some writing done, experience life and all it had to offer. On the other hand, he had a job he would rather like to keep, until the royalty cheque took care of the day to day.

'Positive?'

Crispin nodded and Len spat, and that was the end of that.

With the dishes done, the tabletop wiped and teeth cleaned, the three sat down and contemplated the day. Len looked at the stash of Special under his bed.

'Too early ,Len,' Crispin said.

'Right.'

George glanced at the door and squirmed in his chair as his conscience pricked him something awful.

'It's out back George.' Len pointed to the thunder box in the backyard. 'Nuthin' like a big...'

'Len!' Crispin shook his head.

'Well, just sayin'. Fixes everythin' if you ask me.'

'What?'

'A dump, George. Nothin' like it.'

Crispin pursed his lips and frowned. It was a homily that somehow rang true.

'Really.' George looked at his companions. Old habits die hard. He knew he didn't like people for a reason.

'I'll just go over the road. Sort of, over the road.' George scraped back his chair and disappeared.

'Someit eatin' him.'

Crispin shrugged.

It didn't take more than a minute for George to find out that Avis didn't have any petrol, that there wouldn't be a delivery for another five days, and she didn't like him. She spat as she stood at the screen door and watched him slink across the road

'Chush' sobach'ya'. She went back inside.

What to do with five days? It was a re-occurring theme. George slunk, shuffled and cursed his way back to the Institute. He took a scathing look at the Buff bar and re-affirmed his attitude to the human race. One can get quite worked up if you put your mind to it. George was in a funk by the time he walked through the Institute door and plonked himself down at the table.

'George?' Len offered his own brand of homily. 'I may not be the smartest bulb in the room, but I reckon ya need the hair of a llama.' Len held a bottle of Special.

'The dog. It's the hair of a dog.' George said.

'I don't 'ave a dog, George.' Len took a swig.

'Never mind.' George huffed.

'Want to work on your writing?' Crispin offered.

George spun around and gave one of his scathing looks at Crispin. All his old habits sat down next to him and jabbed him in the ribs. Stitt was the cause of his predicament. Stitt was the man who made him unsatisfied with his lot. Stitt got him drunk and needled his hopes and desires out of him. Stitt was a pain in the neck.

'There will be no petrol. That women.' And here George pointed with a stubby finger, 'that woman who has as much personality as a hairball said it will be five days before a delivery. I have...' George stopped to draw breath, 'I have a job...' he faltered. He sounded like a bit of a whinger.

Crispin and Len watched his meltdown with fascination. There isn't much to do in Block 67, so any drama was a diversion.

'Ya wanna go home?' Len caught the drift.

'I...' George stammered.

'It's only five days George.' Crispin sat down and folded the tea towel. 'I know just how you feel.'

Binks looked at the man who was put on this earth to make George Binks life a misery.

'Do you?'

'Oh yes. But then I thought I should make the most of the opportunity.' Crispin looked at his watch and stood up. 'Got to go. I've an appointment with the doc.' He gathered his notebooks and left. When Crispin was in the mood for writing, he kept regular hours, a habit his mother instilled and had never left him.

'I saved 'im ya know.'

'Did you?' George picked up a pencil and doodled on a piece of paper.

'Yeah.' Len sat back and started at the beginning.

George licked the end of his pencil and took notes. Lots of notes.

A famous author (gunslinger), a missing person, a search (in a one-horse town), a ruse, a stolen identity, a handsome, wily detective who might be a sheriff on the case, and a cast of misfits. It had the makings of a story. A jolly good one.

'Tell me more.'

'Wanna Special?'

'Don't mind if I do.'

Meanwhile, in the metropolis where life was predictable, monotonous and conducted within the hours of nine to five, the papers were having a field day.

The Mercury was running a feature on missing persons throughout history. There was a reward, (a very small one) for information. There was a subscription reward of a book token, and anything that would boost circulation was fair game. (Advertising departments in newspapers have salaries linked to performance, so you can't blame them for trying.)

As the hype intensified, Stitt was spied all over the place.

And then... a crack reporter who smoked a packet a day and drank vodka like a Russian heard that a detective had gone missing looking for Stitt. It was too good to be true; an adage over the world that makes reporters prick up their ears.

Of course, the news wasn't exactly new, and the report came from a woman who lived next door to Binks and just happened to overhear a telephone conversation through her thin walls (a glass up to the wallpaper is a helpful addition) that Binks was on the Stitt case, but a reward is a reward, albeit a small one.

WHERE IS HE NOW? was the headline that greeted the public and the police.

The police read the news with interest. It was news to the department. A superintendent actually answered,

'Who?' when quizzed by a reporter. But eventually, as the police read *The Mercury*, as is often the case, (if you don't read the paper, how the heck do you know what's going on), the situation was given their undivided attention.

No-one went as far as driving to the Block to look for Binks. Boris Niblobski, investigative reporter for *The Mercury Daily*, wrote an opinion piece that was none too kind to the boys in blue.

The police force was stupid, or Binks wasn't terribly important in the scheme of things, and this reporter would like to know... where is he now? Do we have our own Bermuda triangle out there?

A file was plonked on Detective Binks' desk with all the details. That he was supposed to be investigating his own disappearance was lost on the constabulary. Order over chaos was the police way of doing the job. They were the purveyors of procedure over ad hoc, and above all else, paperwork, which translated into passing the buck, dropping the hot potato or not my monkey, not my circus. Someone with pips on their shoulders fumed that if this Binks fellow thought he was going to swan off to Bermuda at the drop of a hat, he had another think coming (The upper echelons of power live in another world where the oxygen levels stunts the brain... The lower echelons knew this to be a fact).

The police went about their business, safe in the knowledge that the procedure had been followed. Boris went about the business of keeping his job. Boris poured over a map of the area that was searched. He saw a small dot and circled it with a pencil. There was one road in and one road out.

He packed for a trip to Bermuda, aka Block 67. A change of underwear, and enough vodka and cigarettes to corner the black market. Growing up on the streets of Moscow, Russia, he knew the value of more over less, but didn't have a clue about the Australian bush.

Twenty-one

When you haven't been anywhere near the Australian bush, it can be a steep learning curve. Boris, or Nibs as he was known around the office, drove into the outback like he was driving to the shops. A pothole brought him up sharp and he cursed, in Russian and English and a bit of Ukraine (on his mother's side).

Getting out to take a look at the wheel he swallowed a fly and brushed up against a prickly bush that had him itching and scratching. When a snake slithering near your two-tone leather brogues just adds to the joy of the outdoors, it made Nibs scream like a girl. He jumped into this car, slammed the door, and spat out another fly, before reaching for a vodka bottle and a cigarette.

He drove with determination and the windows wound up until he saw a sign. Half an hour, half a bottle of vodka and several cigarettes later, he did a U-turn and back-tracked, eventually coming to a halt at the Buff bar/petrol station/post office/general store.

Avis looked at the stranger who staggered through the door and headed for the bar.

She waited as he lit a cigarette, took a look at the décor and the clientele. Nibs then cast his eye over Avis. She hitched her bra strap and pursed her lips.

'Do you perhaps have Vodka?'

Avis narrowed her eyes.

'Vodka?' she repeated his accent. 'Vohd-ka'.

'Yes.' Nibs took a good look at Avis.

'Vohdzya-ra?' He tried the nickname for vodka.

'Dah.'

And as the regulars looked on, Avis blossomed. She had been waiting for a countryman to walk through the door since she took over the lease of the Buff bar sometime after the poker match had finished and she'd reloaded her M1 Garand standard issue rifle.

Boris laid on the charm with a trowel as two vodkas appeared on the bar. There was the clinking of glasses, the exchange of toasts, the slamming down of the shot glass and a general feeling that the world was a better place if two Russians were in the same room and a bottle of vodka was between them.

Len walked through the door and felt the world would be a better place if the fellow wasn't so close to Avis. He walked to the bar and sat down to scowl at the intruder with his one good eye.

Avis glanced in Len's direction and then back to Boris. Boris had a way with women, and had had his way with women quite often. He was tall, handsome and had white straight teeth, more than one as the comparison was obvious, and a head of hair. It was a winning combination, as far as Avis was concerned. She looked at Len, then at Boris, and it was a painful. There is nothing like a bit of rivalry to liven up ones fighting spirit. Len tsked. The only thing vying for Avis's attention in all her years at the Buff bar had been a leaking pipe and a broken fridge compressor. Boris sat and sipped his vodka, never taking his eyes off Avis. Len sat and studied the beer mat.

Drink? She tapped the bar and Len looked up.

'Yes please,' Len stared at Boris who was nursing his vodka. If it took a whole crate of beer, Len would outstay the fellow.

'Drink, Hot shot?'

'Da.'

'Vodka, maybe?' Avis smiled.

'Da.'

Len glued himself to the bar stool. It would be a long night.

With nothing to do except lie around hating the human race, George decided he could hate everyone just as easily at the Buff bar. He wasn't one for binge drinking, and to be frank hadn't had much experience in that field, but alcohol did seem to be the catalyst for joie de vivre. If all it would take was a bender, then the joy of living would be in every alcoholic's blood. He sauntered over and plopped down on a bar stool with a sour face.

'Ah.' Avis pointed.

'Ah yourself.' George said.

'This 'ere is George.' Len patted George on the back.

'HA!' Avis spat the word.

'George?' Boris looked at the small man who had trimmed fingernails and a sunburnt neck.

'Yes?'

'George Binks?'

'Actually, it's G. Ranger.' George picked his pseudonym when he first decided to write westerns. He felt it had a certain ruggedness to it and a whiff of the prairies.

'G. Ranger?' Nibs sucked in his top lip. He knew Binks was lying, but why?

'That's right.'

George looked at Nibs with an analytical eye. He took in the accent, the city shoes, the pale complexion. 'And you?'

'Boris.' Nibs held out his meaty hand. 'Boris Niblobski.'

'Niblobski?' Avis echoed.

'Da.'

'Niblobski Moscow?'

'Da.'

'Niblobski, mother Rita Niblobski?'

'Da.'

George and Len followed the conversation like watching the Australian tennis final.

Avis slapped the bar and the assemblage jumped. In usual circumstances ,it meant the cosh.

Nibs sat back and studied Avis. He cast a critical eye over her face.

'And you?' Nibs said, 'are a Varkov.'

'Da.'

'Cousin.'

'Cousin.'

This revelation put Len at ease. You could almost see the fellow straighten his spine as his rival in love became one of the family.

There was a round of drinks as the cousins toasted their good fortune. There was another round of drinks as the cousins toasted their relatives, the boat that brought them to Australia, the Government that let them stay, the people that helped them get settled and the good fortune to survive the war. Two bottles of vodka, eight cans of beer and everyone was related to everyone. By the third bottle of vodka, everyone was brother and sister. George, although hating the human race, thought Russians were particularly nice.

'When a Russian drinks, everyone drinks. Nasdrovia!' was a maxim Len rather liked.

Crispin and the Doc walked through the door and Len repeated the phrase adding, 'Nasty drivin ya.'

There was a lengthy debriefing on the turn of events and more toasts.

'It's nas-drove-ia, Len,' Doc said.

'Eh?'

'Nasdrovia,'

'Ah away with ya.'

Doc looked at Leonard and frowned.

'Len?'

'LEN,' he shouted.

'Wot?'

'Can you hear me?'

''Course I can.'

'How about now?' Doc put his hand over his mouth.

'Eh?'

'Hang on a minute.'

Doc fetched his haversack and brought out an array of tools of the trade. That they were made for animals was lost on the audience.

'Len, let me take a look at your ear, will ya?'

'Not bloody likely, Doc.'

'Your ear, man. Your EAR!'

'Oh.' Len gave a giggle. I thought ya said me...'

'Yes, we all know what you heard,' Doc said. He found a torch and a thing-a-me-bob that can see into a horse's ear.

'Brains?' Avis asked as Doc took a good look and the light didn't come out the other side.

Len sat still like a model patient.

'Tweezers.' Doc held out his hand.

Crispin acted as nurse, and then as if a magic trick had been performed right there in the Buff bar, Doc pulled a small yellow ball from Len's ear.

'Vot?'

Doc put the thing in an ashtray and went to work on the other ear with the same result.

'I think it's cotton wool,' Crispin said and took a good gulp of beer. He didn't have the stomach, like a two-year-old's mother, for miscellaneous foreign objects from miscellaneous body cavities

'Cotton wool ya say?' Len repeated the sentence perfectly. 'I recollect I put some cotton wool in me ears in the war. The guns an' all that. Bloody racket when ya tryin' to sleep.'

'You're kidding me,' George said.

'Nope.' Len turned to the crowd. '1917 I reckon.'

They all looked at the yellow balls in the ashtray. As I said, entertainment is thin on the ground. A blob of cotton from someone's ear might not be the lights of Broadway, but you had to be there to appreciate the moment.

'A bloody miracle.'

The vodka was passed around. Russians are renowned for finding any reason to drink a toast.

As the evening darkened in Block 67 the Buff bar was swinging. Avis fried some sausages, George decided that he must be of Russian descent— they were such decent people, Len went googly eyed for Avis, hanging on her every word, which was clear as a bell, and Crispin, Doc and Boris began a philosophical discussion on Russian poets and authors.

'But don't you see? Dostoyevsky makes suffering and guilt noble.' Boris smoked a cigarette and looked at the ceiling.

Crispin took those words and tattooed them on his chest. He felt noble. He felt he suffered for his art, just like Dostoyevsky.

'Guilt isn't noble,' Doc waded in, 'love is noble.'

'Ah, what we do for love eh?' Boris said.

'We do everything for love.' Doc slugged back a drink.

'We Russians suffer for love.' It was the definitive answer from Boris.

It was a short step from Tolstoy to what makes a man turn his back on 'out there' and live in the Block. There are stories that must be told, stories that should be forgotten, and stories that are every bit as good as War and Peace. Vodka reserves a place for them all. Nibs sat back and listened. He had the knack of making people talk.

Avis told a grand tale of escape, a journey through unimaginable hardship and a ticket to freedom.

Len talked about how he suffered for love and how his heart was wrenched from his chest and lay beating on the kitchen floor the day she left.

George told of a life of solid devotion to a job he didn't like, looking for people that didn't want to be found.

The vodka coaxed Doc to talk of snapping a sacred Hippocratic oath for love, and now treating animals with the same respect he once treated his patients, and Crispin revealed his epiphany: all he had to do, was do things for other people.

'Vino Veritas,' Nibs said, raising a glass.

'Yeah, ya said someit there,' Len concurred.

'Vino Veritas,' Crispin toasted.

'In wine there is truth,' Doc translated and threw back a shot of vodka.

'Da,' Avis smiled.

After talking themselves sober sometime around three in the morning, the men staggered over the road to the Institute and that was the last anyone heard for a good twelve hours. Anyone, that is, except a Russian who had a cast iron constitution and was practically weaned on potato vodka and herrings. Nibs woke up with a spring in his step, a cigarette on his lips and a keen eye for detail.

Snooping around the Institute, he found more than enough to concoct a story of grand proportions. A story that would stretch over several editions. All he needed to do was get back to the big smoke and start typing.

Boris turned the key in the ignition and a red warning light came on. He was low on fuel. He looked at the bowser over the road.

Of course, we are privy to the information that Boris had to find out the hard way. Avis shrugged as she pulled her housecoat a little tighter over her chest and swatted a fly.

'Four days.'

'Da.'

The population of Bermuda just added one more.

Twenty-two

The Institute was getting a little crowded. Four blokes sat around the kitchen table and supped tea, smoked cigarettes and nursed hangovers of varying degrees.

'There is no petrol,' Boris said and lit another cigarette.

'We know.'

'For four days.'

'We know.' George supped his tea and winced at the effort of swallowing. He hung his head and idly wondered how he could go from practically a teatotaller to alcoholic in less time than it takes to fill out an AA form. He'd give himself a stern talking-to the minute his brain was back to normal, although the way he felt he might just as easily shift the blame to the company he was keeping.

A collective sigh wafted to the tin roof.

'Four days,' Crispin said. It felt like a dead ine.

Len looked at his stash of Special. 'Reckon I might need to go bush.' He licked his lips. 'A bit of brewin' needed.'

'You make this?' Boris looked at the empty bottles on the table and sniffed.

'Sure do.'

'Chush' sobach'ya. I show you how to make vodka. A family recipe.'

'Ya kiddin' me?'

'A Russian never jokes about vodka.'

'So what do you do, Nibs? I mean for a living? Sort of a job?' Crispin folded his dishcloth and raised an eyebrow.

'Me?'

'Hmmmm.'

'What do I do for a living?'

'Yes.' Crispin wiped the edge of the table.

'A job?'

'Yes.'

George looked at the man who was evading the question. He'd seen enough people dancing around the truth in his job to know when someone was cagey, evasive or lying.

'Yes Boris, what line of work are you in?' George's brain was running at 90%.

'Oh, you know, sort of this and that.'

'Go on.' George sat forward.

'The usual nine to five, really.'

'Yes. And...'

Boris's rather large Adam's apple bobbled around as he swallowed. He weighed up his options. The detective, or G Ranger, would come after him with a posse. Crispin Stitt, or Ernest as he was known, would read about it and curse him until the snows melted on Kilimanjaro. Avis would call his chush' sobach'ya (and no-one needs to cross a cousin), plus he might never get an opportunity for the inside scoop, ever again.

'As a matter of fact...' And Boris didn't stop until he had painted a picture of braving the wilds in the slim hope of getting a scoop with a subheading of *in their own words!*

That last bit was the clincher. Everyone loves to

tell it "in their own words".

Crispin hung off those words like a recovering media tart. The publicity. A new book with a beginning, a middle and an end. George thought this was his chance to make his words count. He might paint a picture of a man who suffers for his art. The publishers would beat a path to his door, for didn't everyone love a good hard-boiled western adventure? Yeee-harr!

There was silence as the imposters thought on the opportunity. It would necessitate coming clean. Crispin bit his fingernails and George's leg jiggled.

'Of course I had hoped to find the world-famous author Stitt, but I guess he will just live on as a literary legend. We may never know.' Boris shrugged and blew a smoke ring. They watched it rise to the ceiling. 'And they haven't a clue as to the disappearance of Detective Binks of the missing persons department.'

'Crickey,' Len was riveted to the story. 'Ernest and me went lookin' for a fella a while back. Remember Ernest? Just up an' walked in to the bush so they said.'

'Really?' Boris cracked the lid on a bottle of vodka.

'And now ya reckon this detective bloke's gone missin'?'

'That's about it.'

'Jeez. Like findin' a needle in the eye of a camel.'

'It's a haystack Len,' Crispin said. 'A needle in a haystack.'

'That'd be for the camel then.'

'What?'

'To eat or sommit.'

There was no getting around Len's logic.

The roof ticked as the sun went down. Boris let his quarry stew. And stew they did. George squirmed in his seat.

'I'm tellin' ya, George.' Len hoiked his head in the direction of the dunny out back. George took the opportunity and almost galloped to the back door and away from the uncomfortable feeling that he had been caught at high noon and he was out of ammo. He sat down and contemplated his next move... literally and figuratively.

How to tell the story without sounding selfish, entitled, whingy and whiney and looking like a complete pillock was quite a big conundrum. Crispin started on another fingernail.

'Cigarette?' Boris held out the packet.

'Thanks.' That first inhale was carcinogenic bliss. Crispin savoured the moment and it transported him back to his home, his wife, his life. If he was honest, he missed it all, especially Amanda.

'Boris,'

'Yes?'

'When you said in your own words, is that sort of... well, in your own words?'

Hook, line and sinker. Boris smiled.

'Naturally.'

'Right.'

Binks came back and sat down.

'Better, mate?'

'Yes. Much. Thanks Len.' George felt he liked the fellow. In fact, after a good think he was feeling magnanimous towards the human race. They couldn't help being so obnoxious. He would just need to make allowances.

'Didn't I tell ya George? It's a miracle of nature, it is.'

'I believe you're right, Len.' George looked at Crispin, Boris and Len and smiled. It didn't hurt his face too much.

Boris sat and waited. Russians know all about human suffering.

Crispin stubbed out his cigarette and took a deep breath.

'My name is Crispin Stitt and I'm an author.'

It wasn't so much a statement of fact as a confession.

Len looked at Crispin with a wide eye.

George coughed.

'I am Detective George Binks and I am an aspiring author.'

Len shook his head and looked from one man to the other. He was the only person in the room that had a surprised look on his face.

'Len Gillespie,' he said, then added, 'an' I'm an alcoholic.'

Hook, line and sinker.

📖

Four days isn't a long time when you need to write a book, get cracking on a ripsnorter of a western, make vodka and put together a four-part series for a daily newspaper.

Block 67 might have its high moments, (ear cotton wool, et al), but for the most part, from sunrise to sunset it was conducive to peace and quiet.

Boris took pen and paper to the shack and, between showing Len how to make a still, wrote what his editor would later describe as the biggest load of poppycock this side of the black stump. It would give Nibs a raise in salary and a new typewriter ribbon.

Crispin went to Docs on his bicycle every morning and reappeared in the evening to mentor George, who was immersed in Hangman's gulch. It was all go at the Institute until the last night before the delivery truck would arrive.

Len came back from the bush with a stash of Special and a smattering of Russian poetry to woo his true love.

He sat at the kitchen table and smiled at his companions.

'Reckon life's pretty damn fine.' It was a shared sentiment and yet there was a feeling of gloom at the table.

'Tomorrow,' Crispin said and refolded the tea towel.

'Tomorrow,' George doodled on the Formica tabletop.

'Tomorrow,' Boris said, then added, 'Discrimen.'

'Pardon?' Len asked.

'Discrimen. It is that instant of perilous and excruciating tension when the achievements of a lifetime hang in the balance.' Nibs was well versed in languages, having been at the top of the academic tree before the war. He lit a cigarette and sat back.

'He's got smarty trousers.' Len patted his mate's back and adjusted Rommel's eye patch.

'I believe he does,' Crispin said.

Twenty-three

The morning dawned hard and hot. What little breeze there was had departed. The flies took to the shade, the dirt road shimmered and the Institute roof cracked and groaned at the thought of another relentless day in the sun.

Crispin put the kettle on and listened for the truck. George stirred and sat up in his hammock, the effort bringing out beads of sweat on his top lip.

'Morning George.'

'Morning Stitt.'

The kettle boiled and coffee was made.

Boris woke up from the easy chair and lit a cigarette.

'Coffee?' Crispin asked.

'Lovely,' Boris stretched and blew a smoke ring.

Len rolled over to size up the day.

'A stinker,' he said.

'Stinking hot,' Boris clarified.

'Yep.' Len sat up and took a coffee from Crispin.

'So ya goin' then?'

'Yes.'

'An' ya not comin' back then?'

'Not for a bit.' Crispin sipped his coffee. 'Once things get... back to... normal.'

'Right.' Len nodded.

'An' you goin' an' all?'

'Yes.' George came to sit at the table.

'An' I s'pose ya not comin' back for a bit neither?'

'No, not for a bit.'

Len looked at Boris.

'No.' Boris shook his head and offered a cigarette.

'Right.' Len looked at his mates.

'Any eggs?'

'Certainly.' Crispin got cracking.

The breakfast was a sombre one as each man waited for the sword of Damocles to drop in the form of a diesel truck driven by Stan.

Crispin washed the dishes, George wiped and Boris gathered his notes.

'What's the time?' Crispin asked.

'Quarter to,' someone said and right about then they heard the delivery truck come up the road, brake at the Buff bar and its engine stop.

'That'll be Stan.' Len opened the door to check the fact. 'Yep. Ya know, I never heard 'im before. Bloody miracle, if ya ask me.' Since Len's miracle everything was an act of God. He could hear clearly for the first time in a long time.

Crispin folded the tea towel, picked a small crumb from the camp stove and looked out to the road.

Boris gathered his cigarettes, his jacket ,and notes.

'I should fill the car with petrol,' he said to no-one in particular.

'Yes, I should do that too.' George jingled his keys. 'You riding with me, Stitt?'

'Thanks?' Crispin scooped up his first draft and pencils, his toothbrush, then his lurid jacket.

'Len.'

'Hmmm.'

'You want this?' Crispin held out the jacket.

'Nah. You keep it, Ernest. It looks good on ya.'

'Thanks Len. Thanks for everything.' The lump in Crispin's throat felt like a boiled egg.

'Ah get on with ya. I was just doing me job. That's all.'

George shuffled his manuscript and put it in his bag, set his hat on his head and held out his hand.

'It's been a pleasure, Len. A real pleasure.'

'Mate. Any time.' Len shook the offered hand.'

'You'll come to the city later, I hope? I have a bedsit. You're always welcome.

'I'll burn that bridge when I come to it.'

'It's cross...' Crispin began, then caught himself just in time. The men looked at the truck parked over the road. Stan was talking to Avis and handing over the letters and packages that kept Block 67 anchored to the real world of 1950.

'Len,' Boris slapped Len on the back. 'I make you an honorary Russian.'

'Ta very much.' Len smiled and took the cigarette packet on offer.

'You are a man in a million, Gilly. One in a million.'

'Nah.' Len shoved his hat on his head, and they all walked into the blinding midday sun.

Avis stood and counted the money as George fiddled with his petrol cap.

'Mr detective. You come back some time, da?'

'Yes.' George waited for Crispin, who was talking to Doc.

'Make it count,' Doc said. 'Make every day count.'

'I will.' Crispin and Doc shook hands.

Boris sat in his car and smoked. Avis thumped the bonnet and pressed some food on her cousin. It reminded him of home. Russian hospitality wasn't worth a rouble if it didn't include food.

'Spasiba. Bal'shoye spasiba.' Boris said thank you, a big thank you, and kissed Avis's hand. 'Dosvedanya, until we meet again.'

'Da,' Avis wiped her eye with her sleeve and blew her nose on an oily rag.

Crispin watched the exchange.

'You got somevere to be, hot shot?'

Crispin smiled. 'Da.'

'Get outta here, Stinky.' Avis waved a fly away and Crispin leaned in and planted a kiss on her cheek then hopped in the passenger side of the car and all that was left was a cloud of dust that settled on Block 67.

'Dosvedanya,' Avis spat out a fly. 'Nutjob, youz want a drink?' Len cantered after his true love itching to try his Russian poetry. Avis looked like she was in the mood for a typical Russian poem of angst, pain and suffering.

Twenty-four

The road is a long one when you need to account for your transgressions. Crispin had quite a list. He sat and looked out the window and thought while George drove ever closer to their reckoning.

George didn't have such an extensive rap sheet, but he felt his life needed a little reckoning of its own.

'Who wants to be stuck looking for people who don't want to be found?'

'Pardon?' Crispin took his eyes from the road and studied George.

'Who wants to be stuck in a dead-end job? Who I ask you? Not me, that's who!'

'So what will you do, George?'

'Hmmm?'

'Do. What will you do for a job?'

'I'll... I'll...' Binks hadn't got down to the finer points of the plan.

'Perhaps you could transfer to another department.'

'Dead man's shoes, I'm afraid.'

'Dead man's shoes?'

'You know, Stitt. The only time an opening opens up is when someone dies.'

'Oh. Rather snappy title though, don't you think?'

'What?' George swerved around a tree branch that was on the road.

'A good title for a story. Dead Man's shoes.'

George stopped the car. He turned to Stitt and began to smile. A big beaming grin spread across his face.

Crispin frowned, then caught the nuance.

'It's a great feeling, isn't it? That feeling when you just know.'

George nodded.

'When you can feel it in your bones. A novel. A story busting to be written. It's rather wonderful, isn't it?'

George shook Stitt's hand.

'Thank you. Thank you.'

'Pleasure.'

Boris stopped his car and walked to Binks's parked car.

'Everything ok?'

'Yes absolutely fine. Finer than you can imagine. Perfect in fact. Just about perfect.' George gushed as he felt the muse take up residence, rub its hands together, hitch up its trousers and say. Let's get to work.

'Say, I was wondering-' Boris lit a cigarette and lounged on the door window.

'Yes?' George beamed.

'I have a few loose ends vis-à-vis the *in your own words*. Any chance we could go somewhere and hash out some facts.?(Even a journalist needs some facts to pepper a good story.)

If Crispin thought he'd just pop home, put the kettle on and see what's in the fridge, he didn't think too hard. Boris had been thinking hard. He had a plan.

'I know just the place,' Crispin said.

The neighbourhood wasn't your average manicured lawn, concrete driveway and peonies in a garden bed. The Mission of Light was still doing business, the bulb over the banner still broken, the front door now hanging by one hinge like a drunk to a light post.

'Here?' George looked up through the windscreen. Boris parked and walked to Crispin's window.

'Here?'

Crispin nodded.

The three men fronted up to reception and were greeted by Bruiser Brown.

'Hello,' Crispin said, 'remember me?'

'You,' Bruiser smiled, 'back again.'

'Yes.'

'How's me mate, Gilly?'

'He's just fine.' Crispin looked at his companions. 'We'd like something for...' Stitt looked at Boris.

'Oh, I don't know, two nights?'

'Two.' Bruiser wrote it down, then handed the book over for the men to sign in. 'Whatever ya feel comfortable with.'

George was G. Ranger, Boris signed in Cyrillic script just to confuse the issue, and Ernest finished with a flourish.

'Right. Now kitchen duty at five and no drinking on the premises.' Bruiser looked at the bag Boris carried.

'Naturally,' Crispin said. 'Five sharp.'

'I only got the one room on the fourth.'

The men followed Crispin up the stairs, dodging the hole, the missing banister and a nasty something that looked like it was once a meal. He opened the door to their premium accommodation.

'Stitt.' George looked at the double bed and his companions.

'Well, we just need to wing it,' Boris plopped down on the bed and lit a cigarette. 'Perfect.'

George took the right side and Crispin the left, and they lay looking at the ceiling, smoking and listening to Boris outline the plan.

And what a plan he had formulated as he drove to the city. George interjected as he could see a few snags and loopholes—you can't keep a brain like that from wheedling out possible hiccups.

At the stroke of five they presented themselves in the kitchen and served a multitude of misfits and those the world forgot. Sausages and a mountain of sauerkraut were consumed, the leftover from a German convention. Stitt saw quite a bit of his old wardrobe parading through the hall. A pair of once-crisp beige trousers here, a tartan cardigan there, his tweed jacket matched with his Bermuda shorts, which Amanda purchased and he never quite liked—all had an airing. Crispin thought on Len's homily as he served. All it takes is doing something for someone else. It felt good, He felt good. He looked over at George who seemed to be enjoying himself. Boris had found a compatriot and was conversing in Italian, and life was marvellous, excellent and wonderful.

'Any more of them snags mate?'

'Certainly, my good fellow. Take all you need.' Crispin was so full of the milk of human kindness he could have opened a dairy.

The word exclusive will gladden any newspaper editor's day. Boris threw the word around with gay abandon as he sat by the pay phone and outlined the three or four-part story for *The Mercury*. His editor licked his lips and doodled dollar signs on his ink blotter.

'And I said it would be in their own words,' the journalist and editor laughed like a couple of politicians who'd just promised tax cuts.

Timing and organisation are key components in any campaign. Boris had both in abundance, plus an advertising/marketing department who were whip smart and on the ball. (Commission makes a man work just that little bit harder.)

As the paper gets printed overnight, Crispin and George went to bed safe in the knowledge that Boris had their best interests at heart. Their story would be *in their own words,* George would come out of the escapade as the man of the hour, Crispin's adventure billed as Australia's very own Agatha Christie mystery.

Boris lay between his pigeon pair and smoked his last cigarette for the day. He had his finger on the pulse. Everything would be dandy.

There is a saying in the cut and thrust world of newspapers when one paper has a scoop and the other gets the leftovers. *The Mercury* had "got the jump" on its rivals and was basking in the early morning run, hitting the streets with a very large headline.

FOUND

The word took most of the front page, and you had to admit it was eye-catching. The marketing men were congratulating themselves on a winner. The who, what, when, where and why was on page three. Well, some of the who, what, when, where and why, because you don't want to give all the game away. *The Mercury* could milk a week's worth of story out of the discovery.

Having the jump on the other papers requires a level of stealth and cunning. Mick O'Day, *The Mercury* photographer had about as much cunning as a house brick. He left the office the night before with his instructions, met an old mate who worked at the Enquirer, had a drink, may have said too much, went to get fish and chips, and met a bloke who worked at the Bulletin and chatted about jobs, then in the morning drove to the Mission of Light at the head of what might be described as a cavalcade. Of course Mick was oblivious and more intent on getting some breakfast.

Boris tiptoed downstairs and came back with the early edition and three stale doughnuts. He met Mick at the door and ushered him inside, offering him a doughnut.

'You gonna eat those,' Mick pointed to the other doughnuts as he hoisted his camera over his shoulder.

'Take 'em.' Boris said, and they started the climb to the fourth floor. The snoops from the Bulletin and the Enquirer got together and shared a cigarette. What goes in must come out... eventually. They could wait.

Twenty-five

Plethora Carmichael was one of those people who get up at the crack of dawn. (They do exist, apparently). She picked up the paper from her front lawn and the headline jumped out and hit her right between the eyes. The subheading of STITT IS ALIVE, had her scurrying back inside, her jiffy slippers hardly touching the grass. By the time Plethora had brewed her coffee, eaten her soft-boiled egg and toast, then made ready for the day, she had formulated a plan. Stitt was just beginning to make some money for Raven & Square, and Plethora wasn't about to let all that go up in smoke, dead or alive. Stitt had contractual obligations to Raven & Square. Stitt belonged to R & S from his Winsor knot to his Italian brogues. She had a loathing for journalists and journalism in general. They murdered the English language, but she would put her prejudice aside and ring *The Mercury* and put them straight on a few things.

She rang her secretary at home at the ungodly hour and snapped out some instructions to the poor girl, who was half asleep. Angel, (and you really had to be an angel to work for Mrs Carmichael sometimes) yawned and picked up a pencil and paper.

'Yes Mrs Carmichael. No, Mrs Carmichael. Straight away Mrs Carmichael.'

By the time Plethora sat down at her desk, she was ready to do battle with whoever was brave or stupid enough to walk past her crosshairs. The first victim was the Editor of *The Mercury*, Dorell Rotherhill.

'And Mr Rotherhill,' Plethora ended, 'Stitt is ours. Whatever you may have had planned is irrelevant. R & S's publicity department, who are world renowned, will take it from here.'

'It? Don't you mean Stitt.' Dorell might have been an editor as far back as the first draft of the Ten Commandments, but he still had a beating heart and people were his bread and butter, or manna from heaven, depending on your persuasion.

'Semantics. It, Stitt. You will inform your journalist, this Nib-bobble fellow, that our author is under a contractual obligation.'

'Niblobski.'

'Yes, yes.' Plethora hated Dorell and she'd only just met him. 'And as such, Stitt will be required to fulfil his obligations.'

'Really?'

'Yes, really, Mr Rotherhill.'

'Well, I'm sure just as soon as you find him, you can tell him.' Dorell sat back in his chair and a sly smile crept over his face. Plethora hung up, and it wasn't a smile that crept over her face, but something that might not look out of place in Hades. She bellowed for Angel.

Now the obvious place to start when looking for a missing person would be the missing person's department of the police station. Angel called and was put on hold.

'We can't seem to find him,' was the answer.

There was a small moment when Angel thought she might inform Mrs Carmichael of the turn of events, but it was a very small moment, miniscule, infinitesimally small, almost non-existent really. Angel tapped her teeth with her pencil and thought on the problem.

The problem was flicked to marketing. Azid looked at Angel and frowned.

'C'mon, you must know someone on the paper?'

Azid swivelled in his chair. He would do anything for Angel if he could. Unrequited love has that effect on people. His mother wanted him to marry someone Indian, but Azid's heart was already taken.

'Pleeeeese,' Angel bleated.

'Ok.' Azid smiled and hoped Angel would smile back.

She patted his arm, 'Ol' misery guts will have me guts for garters if I don't have some sort of something by the end of the day or sooner.' Working in a publishing house you'd think some of the finer points of the English language would rub off. Not so, it seems.

Azid looked at the door Angel had just walked through and touched his arm. 'Anything,' he said, with a dreamy look in his eye.

Mick O'Day's photographic job done, he gravitated to food, and it wasn't long before he was sitting in a café with a cheese sandwich and a milkshake. The competition were sitting at a table outside, watching O'Day's every bite. No-one would admit to it, but someone had the bright idea they would purloin O'Day's camera and get the scoop on the pictures. It was a 50/50 split with the Bulletin and the Enquirer. *The Mercury* might have the words, but a picture is worth a thousand words, or at least a bonus of about ten pounds, five shillings and sixpence.

Azid rang his cousin, who worked at the Indian take-away next to *The Mercury* print site. From there, the query went to a fellow who always had a naan and a poppadum with his lamb curry lunch. One free naan later, Mr lamb curry was ringing his daughter who worked in the typing pool upstairs. She rang her girlfriend, Lisa, on the fifth floor in accounts and it transpired that O'Day and Boris had put in a chit for expenses, and since Rotherhill had instigated sweeping reforms vis-à-vis 'expenses', everyone was being scrupulous, exact, and hoping their ploy would make the whole thing sink back into cigarettes and a bottle of scotch. So, Boris had rung in for three stale doughnuts, O'Day for a sandwich and milkshake. The where and when was part of the deal.

It was around three in the afternoon when Angel had the answer for Mrs Carmichael. Plethora was apparently the last to know.

The Mercury were scrambling, holding the afternoon edition for the photographs. They were sorely disappointed as the Enquirer and the Bulletin 'got the jump'.

'How much did you say your camera was worth?' Lisa asked as O'Day paced the room and wondered if he would need a camera once he was fired.

Boris looked out at the car park and wondered how it happened. There were cars, people, cameras and as he watched ,a television crew drove up and began to unwind electrical cables. The Mission of Light was well and truly in the spotlight.

'What's happening?' Crispin looked out the window, keeping well back. He didn't want a repeat of the last time he put a body part out the window.

'I can't understand it.' Boris scratched his head. 'Wait here.' Nibs scooted downstairs and bumped into Bruiser Brown.

'Know what's goin' on, do ya?' Bruiser asked. Nibs shrugged and went to the pay phone.

He was seen nodding, making a face, frowning, and then hanging up.

'Trouble?'

'Nothing I can't handle.' Nibs took the stairs two at a time to the fourth floor.

'So,' he began. There was the part where the opposition had got the jump. There was the bit where O'Day had lost his camera. There were a few words to say about Mrs Carmichael and then the ultimatum from the editor, Dorell Rotherhill.

'Anything about the police?' George asked.

'Nothing.'

A drama is unfolding, you're at the epicentre of the quake and no-one even knows you're missing. George flopped down on the bed and tried not to mope.

'Did you say contractual obligation?'

'That's what Rotherhill said. The devil hath power to assume a pleasing shape.'

'Shakespeare?'

'Carmichael,' Boris said.

'I know just what he means. '

The cut and thrust of media is basically digging up anyone who has had any association with the drama unfolding. Then a microphone is thrust in their face and they are asked their opinion. Not that their opinion makes a dot of difference to the story, but it gives that impression.

So it wasn't long before Amanda had people knocking at her door and asking for her reaction to the news that her husband was found, he was alive and that for some reason he had hideous dress sense.

'Is this your husband?' a reporter thrust the picture of Crispin in Amanda's face. She was looking at a full beard, a svelte physique and the most God-awful jacket you could imagine.

'Well...' she took a long look. The reporter could see the headline.

Wife has doubts

'I...' Amanda started when Jim Broker from next door ran up the drive.

'Is it true?' Jim panted as he reached the front door.

'Jim, come inside.' Amanda grabbed the evening paper, then Jim by the collar and slammed the door on the reporter.

'Did you get that photo of her face?' the reporter asked her photographer.

'Sure did.'

Plethora bellowed as Bruiser Brown told her in no uncertain terms, using the words sweetie, dearie and luv, that he could not divulge the names of his guests. He hung up and chalked one up to the little man. All afternoon he'd been fielding enquiries on the same theme. He looked out through the front door at the growing crowd. If ever there was an opportunity to pass the hat around, this was it. Bruiser found two 'guests' and sent them into the throng, cap in hand.

Crispin wondered if he would ever get his life back. Not that he didn't appreciate the hullaballoo, the front page and the photo ops, but he felt like a prisoner of his own popularity and... he missed his wife.

'Do you think I could see Amanda?' Crispin asked.

'I'd like to go home too.' George piped up.

Nibs sat and poured a vodka into a paper cup.

'All in good time.'

Crispin looked out of the window and they heard him groan.

'What?'

'It's Plethora.' He pointed to a smartly dressed woman who was gesticulating while talking to a television technician.

'That's your publisher?'

'Yes.'

George came to the window and watched as the woman barged, pushed, and shoved her way to the door.

'She'll be livid. I just know it.' Crispin drank

a vodka straight from the bottle and lit a cigarette.

'She thinks she's got first dibs on you, Stitt. Does she?'

'Well, I don't know exactly, but I do recall my contract was sort of, kinda, terminated.'

'Well, what are you worried about? She's got nothing. And she's just a woman.'

'You don't know her.'

'All women are the same Stitt. I've met 'em all. They all just want one thing.'

'And what's that?' George asked. He'd like the inside line on what a woman wants, never having had one before.

'They want our....' Nibs smiled. 'Right in the palm of their hand.'

'Really?'

'Hmmm.' Nibs pulled hard on a cigarette.

Crispin crossed his legs and took a drink.

'The trick is to let 'em think they have them.'

'Let them think they have them,' George echoed, nodding.

'Tell 'em what they want to hear.'

'Tell them what they want to hear.' George took it all in for future reference.

'You don't know Plethora.' Crispin stood and put his ear to the door.

'Shall we invite her up?' Nibs stood and went to the door. 'I'll be back.' He opened the door and was gone.

'She'll kill me.' Crispin plopped on the bed and clamped the vodka bottle to his lips, trying to wring some comfort in alcohol. It wasn't working like it had in the past.

George tidied his manuscript, straightened his

collar, and reminded himself that he was a detective, he was the head of his department, and he wasn't afraid of Plethora Carmichael and her chairs from Spain. But on the other hand, she held the beacon of light to a bright future as an author. It felt like a Faustian pact.

Nibs opened the door and Plethora stood and took in the scene.

'Plethora,' Crispin rose and planted a smile on his lips. He looked like a dog who has just realised he's going to the vet for the chop.

'Detective Binks.'

'Mrs Carmichael.' George stood up and saw Nibs mime the tinkling of two bells behind Plethora's back.

'Mr Nib-bobble has just been telling me all about your little adventure. I must say, I was rather surprised at your tenacity, your bush craft, your stamina.' Plethora looked George up and down. 'Naturally, your story will be exclusive to *The Mercury*, but I'd like to talk about a book... in the future, perhaps.'

George almost genuflected. He caught himself just in time.

'Plethora, may I call you Plethora?' Nibs asked. She nodded. 'Plethora had a fabulous idea about capitalising on the man of the moment. It's not something I would have thought of, but I think Plethora is the only person who has the expertise, the know-how to pull it off.'

'I wrote a book,' Crispin held up his manuscript trying to get some attention. 'This one is good.' He flapped it about.

'Resurrection,' Plethora read. 'Interesting.'

'Yes isn't it?' Crispin gushed. He went into his lengthy synopsis. 'Of course, Raven & Square has first refusal.' Crispin put his testicles on a platter for Plethora.

'Naturally.' Plethora eyed George, who hovered with a bundle of notes.

'I...' Binks tried to smile and look humble at the same time. It came out looking simple. 'I've written something, too.'

'Really? You fellows have been busy.'

'Well...' George blushed, 'It's my first time you understand, but I think...'

'Detective Binks. It is not what you think, or I think, but what the reading public think.' Not that Plethora thought much of the reading public's intellect, but they often forked out a few shillings for a slice of entertainment, education or culture. 'One tries to elevate the public to literary heights, but frankly, I find it is beyond their scope.'

'It's hard-boiled western adventure.' George had yet to feel Plethora's squeeze.

'Mr Binks. It cannot be both. Hard-boiled _or_ western adventure. Perhaps it is neither.'

'Pardon?'

'Perhaps you are under the illusion, as many an author is,' And here Plethora threw a look at Crispin, 'that your time and effort will reap a reward. Perhaps dross is the word you seek.'

'Oh.' Binks felt a tightening of his nether regions. Crispin almost said, "I told you so", but could see the man was suffering torment enough at the hands of Mrs Carmichael. He patted George on the arm and took his manuscript from him and put a vodka in his hand.

'Thanks.' George downed it in one and knew he didn't like the woman for a reason.

'I hate to break up the party,' Boris lit a cigarette. 'But we have a date with the public.

'Quite.' Plethora looked at Stitt and shuddered at his sartorial elegance.

'I like it.' Stitt stood his ground. The jacket had become a talisman of sorts. It was a reminder of all he had been through, his personal growth, the excising of his demons.

'No,' Plethora made a seeping gesture with her hand.

'It stays,' Crispin felt his backbone straighten.

'Stitt?'

'And another thing, Mrs Carmichael.' Crispin pulled his balls off the menu and reinstated them in their proper place. 'You don't own me. My contract was at an end. My residuals and my second book probably paid off my advance, and I don't owe you sixpence.'

George swallowed a second vodka and stood behind Stitt. He poked him to egg him on.

'And another thing. Don't go dashing a person's hopes and dreams with one remark. You haven't read George's book, you don't know the first thing about his talent, and I'm not sure I want Raven & Square to publish my book, if you are at the helm.' Stitt took a deep breath.

'People have feelings, Plethora.'

This statement was like a bolt out of the blue, or a bolt off the old block, as Len might have put it. The woman grabbed her handbag a little tighter and set her face in stone. (It wasn't much of a leap.)

'People, people,' Boris came between the pair.

'We have a job to do.'

'Quite,' Plethora pulled a hanky from her handbag and blew her nose, then dabbed at something in her eye.

'It's not easy, you know.'

'Plethora, please,' Boris begged, 'not now for the love of Pete.'

'Being a woman in a man's world isn't easy you know.' She dabbed.

'Can't this wait?' Boris lit a cigarette off the end of the one before and pace the room. He had a deadline. Rotherhill was waiting on the big reveal in conjunction with the early evening edition in front of the television people. Boris was hoping for the big reveal in his pay packet, but this was harder than herding cats.

'People. We need to move.' Boris looked at his watch, then glanced out the window.

'You don't know what I've had to do to get where I am. I have feelings, Stitt, but feelings don't get you to the top.'

'Have you tried to be nice?' Crispin handed her a paper cup.

'Yes nice?' George echoed, pouring the vodka.

'Nice. Nice people don't win.'

'Yes they do.' Crispin said. 'They win respect, admiration, affection...' He looked at Plethora and gave a concerned frown. 'Love.'

Plethora blew her nose and threw back the vodka like a woman who knows a thing or two about drinking out of paper cups in hotel rooms. George topped her up.

'I hated everyone,' George said, by way of a

confession. 'But I don't now. Not *everyone*. Just some people.'

'Look, I hate to break up the confessional, but I've got to be in front of the camera for the early evening edition. That gives us just five minutes to get down there.' He parked his three cigarettes on his bottom lip and began to push people to the door.

'And smile,' Boris said as he shoved George out and shut the door.

The descent to the ground floor was peppered with small talk. Crispin apologised for snapping. Plethora said she was sorry she was so abrupt with George and yes, she'd love to see his manuscript. George said he hardly hated anyone at all when he thought about it.

They emerged to the flashing of cameras, as a paperboy thrust the evening paper in Boris's hand and the headline said it all:

EXCLUSIVE, STITT TELLS ALL

Boris looked at his watch. People, those with or without literary aspirations, would see the television and rush out to buy the paper. It was genius.

'You know Mr Nib-bobble, that headline should have an ambient 'it'. Stitt tells *it* all.'

Boris thought Stitt could have all the ambient its he wanted. Nibs had pulled it off.

He pointed to George and introduced him as Detective George Binks, the head of missing persons who, through prolific police procedure and superior brain power, located the author. The flash bulbs went off.

'You can read all about it in *The Mercury*,' Nibs added, waving the paper in front of the camera. More flash bulbs.

Crispin held Plethora's hand and smiled.

'He's back, and there will be another book,' Plethora gave it her best shot, and smiled.

The reporters, journalists and public called for Stitt to speak.

'I'm just glad to be back amongst friends.' He waved and smiled straight to camera. The flash bulbs outdid the sun.

And in Eden Grove, on Everard Drive, Amanda Stitt watched the news. She was one of the few people who didn't have a smile on her face. Crispin was holding Plethora's hand when he should have been holding hers.

Twenty-six

'I think I'd like to go home now,' Crispin said as the last of the television crew packed up and left. 'George?'

'I think I'll just go home too and pop by the department in the morning.'

'I can drive you if you like.' Plethora held her car keys up and jingled.

'I have my car.' George said pointing up the road.

'Oh.'

'Well,' Crispin drew a circle with the toe of his shoe, 'I guess this is goodbye.'

'Yes.'

'It's been... a real pleasure, George. A real pleasure.'

'Yes.' George shook Crispin's hand.

'I'll take this,' Crispin pulled *Dead Man's Shoes* from George's grasp. 'I'll see she gets it.'

'Oh, right. Thanks Stitt. Thanks for everything.'

When there is a feeling of euphoria, it is hard not to get a whiff and feel that all is sweetness and light with the world and your place in the said world is wonderful and delightful.

Nibs waved off the three, and thought five days of the serialization of Stitt should pull it up. They'd get pictures of his house, his wife, his dog if he had one. Of course, one brilliant idea can easily make the ol' grey matter leap and bound to another. Nibs walked to the train station thinking he was a genius.

📖

Plethora pulled up in front of Crispin's house.
'You want to come in?'
'No, I don't think so.' Plethora looked at the house, the street, the normality of suburbia. It all looked so lived-in. She lived in her house, but it wasn't a home. Since Mr Carmichael had left, she hadn't felt like making a home.
'I'll leave this with you.' Crispin placed George's manuscript on the seat. 'And this too.' He added *Resurrection* to the pile.
'Thank you.' Plethora patted the book.
'I'll ring.'
'You do that. Stitt.' Plethora practiced a smile. 'I'd like that.'
He climbed out of the car and began the slow walk to his front door.
'By the way,' Plethora called from the driver's window.
Stitt turned.
'I rather like the jacket.'
'Thanks.'

📖

The front door opened before Crispin reached for it.
'Amanda.'
'Crispin.'
They stared at one another. Amanda stood aside

as Crispin stepped over the threshold.

'I'm so very sorry.'

📖

After five days of Crispin Stitt the public was a bit over it. You can only keep people interested for so long before their eyes glaze over and the paper is used for the bottom of the birdcage.

Stitt, not being the flavour of the month was getting his life back.

He knocked on Jim Broker's door and waited. The door opened and Jim flew into his mate's arms.

'We thought you were dead.' Jim hugged his mate. Big dollop tears rolled down his cheeks. He stood back to take a good look at Stitt. Crispin took a good look at Jim, who was wearing a frilly little number with an off-the-shoulder look, accompanied by a rosette in blush pink all held together with pins.

'Nice.' Crispin mimed to give a twirl. Jim obliged.

'Bloody wedding. Bloody kids. Love 'em to bits.'

'Mate.'

'Mate.'

📖

A few days passed in blissful suburbia. Amanda pencilled in and then made a conciliatory dinner for Crispin's parents. They now sat in the dining room, listening to Crispin tell his story. His mother, Bertha Stitt, wrung her napkin in her hands at every prickle, every snake (now apparently, there was more than one). Mr William Stitt sat stoically and fiddled with his dinner roll.

'Yes, we read about that,' William interjected throughout the telling.

'And that's about it, really,' Crispin reached for his wife's hand.

'We were so worried.' Bertha dabbed her eyes.

'My son's as strong as an ox. He's a Stitt. Don't fuss, Bertha.'

It was a proud moment to be loved by your parents, one Crispin relished. Amanda squeezed his hand. Yes, life was grand.

Now, Stitt was sitting at his desk and chucking out his old life. Whisky bottles, snack wrappers and detritus of a life ill-spent went into the wastepaper basket. His accolades looked at him from the wall. Crispin went over and read them one last time then pulled them from their hanging space and put them in a box. It felt good to compartmentalise his past, box it up and shut the lid.

He went to his wardrobe and looked at what was left. A man really doesn't need twenty-three neck ties or seven white shirts. He bundled them up for the Mission of Light, then added a few pairs of shoes, a jaunty hat he'd bought in Florida, and some Bermuda shorts. He wouldn't be going to Bermuda anytime soon, or would he?

Block 67 was still under Crispin's skin. He looked at the mozzie bites on his arms, the suntan on his legs and thought of his friends. *What would Len be doing now?*, he thought. *What would Avis be up to, and Ted and Norm?*.

'Lunch, darling,' Amanda called.

It was just about the best sound in the world. His wife loved him. She made him salad sandwiches.

'Plethora rang while you were next door,' Amanda pulled at the olive garnish.

'Oh.'

'She said if you'd like to pop down to the office, they have the proof of *Resurrection.*'

'Are you coming?'

'Wouldn't miss it, darling.' Amanda blew a kiss to Crispin over her club sandwich.

Yes, the world was delightful and wonderfully wonderful.

📖

George was sitting in Plethora's office with the proof copy of *Dead Man's Shoes* in his hot little hands. He looked up as Crispin and Amanda walked in.

'Oh hello George.'

George held up his book and broke out a smile from ear to ear.

'It's really rather good, you know.' Plethora pulled a bottle of champagne from an ice bucket. 'Apparently the public are absolutely gagging for western adventure.' She popped the cork and poured four glasses of the best Bollinger champagne.

'This is a little bit of a celebration.' Plethora smiled - it was getting easier by the day, although the first time she did it Angel took fright and ran out of the office.

'Oh?' Amanda took her glass. 'A celebration?'

'Yes. Stitt has taken off in Russia of all places. We've had another print run of *He Lives* and *He is*

Dead. Turns out they love a book full of pain and suffering. Every Russian can identify with a man in existential pain.'

'I'm big in Russia.' Crispin toasted his good fortune.

'We have got that fellow Nib-bobble to do the translation of *Resurrection*. He's a professor of languages. Wasted in journalism, but there you have it.'

'You mean Boris Niblobski?'

'Yes, that's the fellow.'

'Good ol' Boris.' Crispin sipped his champagne.

'Good ol' Boris,' George echoed.

'And here it is,' Plethora held out the proof copy of *Resurrection*. 'This one is good, Stitt.' Crispin gave the book to his wife.

'To a beginning, middle and end.'

'To a beginning, middle and end.'

Twenty-seven

When you've been the darling of the literati-glitterati world, there is a propensity for the critics to be... well, critical.

That they get some sort of satisfaction in pulling an icon off the pedestal is one of those things that probably only a Russian would understand. Sort of, "if I'm suffering, so should you". When a chap wrote that one should suffer for their art, he was probably talking about critics. They suffer more than most with hanging participles, incomprehensible gobbledygook and utter tripe.

Crispin paced as he waited for the first reviews to come through. The advance copies had been in the critic's hands for several days. Several days of agony on Crispin's part.

George was riding high on his horse, as the public like a good shoot 'em up at high noon. Once his superior found out, courtesy of *The Mercury* newspaper, that he wasn't missing, after all, and had been doing his job, they found they quite missed him.

Binks put his superior brain power on the table and negotiated a part-time position. The man now had options and didn't want to keep it under his ten-gallon hat.

He was sitting at his kitchen table diligently

going through his receipts when he found the bill for petrol at Block 67 scribbled on the back of an envelope.

'Avis Varkov,' he read and smiled and then in one of those spur-of-the-moment moments, he rushed downstairs and with some change rang Stitt. George had developed a taste for life experiences.

'Hello?'

'Stitt.'

'George.'

Life experiences are all very well, but they don't prep you for small talk.

'How's things?'

'Good, and you?'

'Good.'

'Look, I was wondering,' George began.

'Yes?'

'Just wondering if you'd sort of like to... well...'

'Yes?'

'It's just that I have a receipt and I can't read it and I need to verify it, and that would necessitate going to Block 67 and,'

'I'd love to.' Crispin grinned.

And in one of life's co-incidences Boris rang Crispin and outlined his brilliant idea.

'We could go back to the scene of the crime, so to speak. Pictures, words, the whole story in five parts. We could recreate your adventure. Step, by painful step.'

'No.'

'Pardon, Stitt?'

'I said no. I don't think Block 67 should be put on the map.'

'Oh.' Boris doodled on his blotter. 'Bit late for

that, I'm afraid.'

'What have you done?'

It was a blistering day as Crispin set off, Amanda at his side, Boris in the back seat smoking like a chimney and George next to him with his U-beaut bush hat plus fly net firmly planted on his head.

'Is it far?' Amanda asked.

How do you explain that Block 67 is a place far removed from the everyday, far from the madding crowd, you might say, if your name was Hardy.

They travelled the dirt road in silence, the Australian bush not able to break the monotony. If you've ever been to the Australian bush, you will know it has a monotony all its own.

'It's left,' George pointed to the junction, and in half an hour they slowed and drove into the Block to be greeted by a woman in the middle of the road with an M1 Garand 30.06.

'Podi Proch',' Avis said, bringing the firearm up to her eye.

Boris translated, 'She said, go away.'

'Ukhodi.'

'She says get out.' Boris went to put his head out of the window and a shot whistled past his ear.

'Darling, back up.' Amanda crouched down in the footwell.

'Steady Avis, steady,' Crispin opened his door and put his hands up. 'It's me, Stinky.'

'Podi Proch'.'

'That means go away.' Boris hid behind the

front seat and smoked a cigarette.

'Avis,' Crispin stepped away from the car, when Doc came out of the Buff bar. 'Doc,' Crispin waved.

'Ernest.'

'Etot chelovek smut'yan, I bol'she nikto.' Avis waved her gun in the air.

'She said, that man is a troublemaker and nothing more,' Boris translated while hiding.

George opened the back door and stood behind it.

'It's me.' He waved a white hanky.

Avis spat in the dirt.

Len appeared from the Institute and rubbed his eyes in the sun.

'Ernest? Is that you?'

'Len.' Crispin shooed a fly and resumed holding his hands in the air.

'Podi proch'.'

'That's go away,' Boris offered.

'Yes, we have that,' Crispin said. 'Boris, you're family. Show yourself.'

'I don't think you know how Russian family connections work.' Boris remained behind the front seat.

Doc moved on Avis, and in a quick snatch disarmed the woman. He threw the rifle into the bush at the side of the road.

'It's Ernest. And George. And Boris.'

Avis spat and stormed back to the Buffalo bar, slamming the screen door.

'All clear,' Doc called and walked to the car. 'Ernest,' he held out his hand.

'And this is my wife,' Crispin pulled Amanda from the footwell of the passenger seat.

'She's a bit feisty.' Amanda put a hat on her

head, straightened her linen blouse, and brushed a fly away.

'Feisty? She's as mad as a cut snake,' Doc said.

'Ernest,' Len finally made the walk over the road. 'I thought I was dreaming.'

'It's me. It's good to see you, Len. This is my wife.' Amanda shook Len's hand. 'I've heard a lot about you, Mr Gillespie.'

Len smiled, 'Gilly to me friends.'

'Boris,' Len said. 'George too. Well, well, well. Home is where the rolling stones gather.' Len patted the men on the back. 'This calls for a bit of a celebration.' He winked at Boris. 'Goes down like a mother's lead balloon, me special does.'

'It's "go down like a lead balloon", Amanda tried to be helpful.

'You said it,' Len gave a toothless grin and snapped his eye patch.

They all trooped across the road to the Institute and Len pulled some bottles from under his bed.

'This'll put hair on ya dog.'

'It's hair on your chest.' Amanda shook her head and frowned. She couldn't quite understand why Crispin wasn't rolling around in agony at the mashing of the English language.

'Why is Avis angry, Len?' Crispin pulled out a chair for Amanda and then put the kettle on, wiped over the bench top and shook out the tea towel.

'We've had all sorts comin' through like ya wouldn't believe.'

Crispin and George looked at Boris.

'I may have mentioned it.' Boris poured a special

and let out a small giggle.

'They been eatin' everything, usin' all the petrol and stuff.'

Crispin poured the tea and sat down.

'I bin doin' some business with me special. One man's trash is worth two in the bush.'

'Treasure?' Amanda offered. 'One man's trash is another man's treasure.'

'You said it.' Len took a long draught of special and sat on his bed.

'I'd like to give you something, Len. For a new roof.' Crispin brought out his cheque book and ripped off the one that had Len's mane on it, plus a few noughts.

'Nah Ernest. Give it to Bruiser Brown. I don't need it. I 'ave everything right here.' Len looked at those sitting at the table. 'Friends.'

'Perhaps we should go over the road. Explain things. Apologise.' Crispin looked at Boris.

'Alright. Alright.'

Ted and Norm looked up as the famous five walked up to the bar. It was a close-run thing whether Norm would try out his one joke on fresh blood. He was urged on by Ted with a jab in the ribs.

'G'day. Did ya hear about the Chinaman and the black fella who walked inta a bar?' He raised an eyebrow in Amanda's direction. 'No?' Norm answered. 'Well they stayed there.' Ted and Norm laughed at the punchline, then Ted said, 'I'm the blackfella.' It was hilarious the first time they said it around the mid-1940s, but the joke had worn so thin it was see-though.

Amanda smiled politely, then turned to Norm, 'And you'd be the Chinaman?'

Norm didn't see it coming. He let out a guffaw and slapped the bar. Ted joined in, and soon the place was a riot of giggles, shrieking laughter and hilarity.

'I don't get it?' Len scratched his head which only heightened the fun.

Avis watched the amusement with a steely glare, but when Boris produced a long sausage made by a man who knew a thing or two about how to make Russian sausage, her visage softened.

If there was any place in the world Crispin, George, Doc, Boris, Amanda, Len, Avis, Ted and Norm might want to be, it would be hard pressed to beat the Buffalo Bar in Block 67, with friends.

📖

The reunion took all day, so, by the time the sun finally dipped, it was too late to drive back to town, and there wasn't a sober person within fifty miles who could drive.

'Where will we stay?' Amanda asked as the generator kicked in with lighting.

The Institute of C.R.A.P accommodated the motley crew with hammocks and a camp bed, Boris electing to sleep in the car. The tin roof ticked and creaked as the heat dissipated. Crispin reached over and held his wife's hand.

Yes, the world was delightful and wonderfully wonderful.

Twenty-eight

Making peace with your past is a cathartic exercise. Crispin had expunged all his bad habits, all his anxieties, and his stubborn fat from his waistline.

There was a party in progress on Everard Drive as the Broker daughter finally tied the knot of matrimony. Cars lined both sides of the road as relatives, friends, and neighbours stood outside under the marquee, drinking the good health of the young couple.

'Isn't it just great?' Jim beamed and slapped Crispin on the back.

'Yes.'

'Just wonderful, really. You watch 'em grow up and now, well...' Jim wiped a tear from his eye. 'She's looking really lovely in the cream tulle with the lace accents.' Jim gazed with adoration at his first born.

'You're looking sharp, Jim.' The Messer's Myer & Goldstein tuxedo had been altered and looked the business. Jim smoothed the lapels. 'Thanks for the bit extra, Stitt.'

'Not a problem, Jim. Any small help I can give you, it's my pleasure.'

'Brenda and Tom will put it as a deposit on a house.'

'That's the way.' Crispin smiled.

'Yep. I reckon life is what you make it.' Jim dabbed his eyes with a hanky.

'Absolutely,' Crispin nodded. 'That and a good think.'

'You got that right, Stitt.' Jim slapped his friend on the back.

Crispin smiled at Amanda who was wending her way through the crowd.

'First reviews darling.' Amanda held *The Mercury* out to Crispin.

'Later.' Crispin shook his head.

'Listen up people. Stitt has his first review. He's an author of those books, you know.' Jim beamed at his neighbour.

The crowd looked at Stitt as if he would do a circus trick or conjure something out of a hat.

'He's written books.' Jim slapped his friend on the back.

'What does it say?' Crispin put the paper back in his wife's hand.

There was a hush.

'It says,' Amanda read, 'Resurrection is a delightful book you can read without feeling like you need a bath afterwards.'

There was a resounding cheer. Jim toasted the good fortune to live next door to Stitt and the crowd moved to the sweating hors d'oeuvres.

'Oh, darling, how wonderful.' Amanda kissed Crispin and smiled. Crispin looked at his wife, 'Flattery is alright, as long as you don't inhale.'

A little bit of history

At university in the UK (1985), I belonged to the sub aqua club and we would go on expeditions to Scotland etc.

So...

One night we were all sitting around at the pub congratulating ourselves on being alive—youth has that advantage – and a Doctor in the group told us a story.

A very old fellow came into his surgery with an earache. Naturally Dr Michael put the thing-a-me-bob in his ear to see what the problem might be.

Low and behold, Dr Michael pulled out a wad of cotton wool.

The fellow admitted he didn't quite know how it got there, then in a moment of recollection he said he put it in to stop the gun noise so he could get some sleep in THE GREAT WAR!

Some stories are too good to pass up!

All my books are available from my blog. https://hettieashwin.blogspot.com/p/published-books-to-buy.html

They can also be seen loitering on-line in the usual places.

Reviews help authors enormously.
If you want to leave a review on-line, it would be most welcome.
Thanks
Hettie

This is book 10 of the 10 terrific laugh out loud series.